Praise for Lawrence Scott

'A really accomplished writer.'
Derek Walcott

'Rare and magical.'
Sam Selvon

'An extremely gifted writer. Moral dilemmas underpin
much of his fiction.'
Bernadine Evaristo (The Guardian)

'Impressively written work, subtle but compelling.'
Wilson Harris (Wasafiri)

'The prose is economical and beautifully veined...
Scott's writing is full of light and promise.'
Robin Blake (The Independent)

'Mighty impressive.'
(The Literary Review)

'An author in control of his form.'
Carl MacDougall (The Scotsman)

DANGEROUS FREEDOM

Elizabeth d'Aviniere's Story

LAWRENCE SCOTT

PAPILLOTE PRESS
London and Trafalgar, Dominica

First published by Papillote Press 2020 in Great Britain

Printed and bound by CPI Group (UK) Ltd, Croydon, CR0 4YY
Book design by Andy Dark

ISBN: 978-1-9997768-6-2

Papillote Press
23 Rozel Road,
London SW4 0EY,
United Kingdom
And Trafalgar, Dominica
www.papillotepress.co.uk

For Jenny

By the same author

"it was not enough to be for abolition
while the spirit of the masters
flickered in the abolitionist's heart

it was not enough to name ourselves anew
while the spirit of the masters
calls the freedwoman to forget the slave..."

'The Spirit of Place',
A Wild Patience Has Taken Me This Far,
Adrienne Rich

1

AT THIS TIME of her life Elizabeth d'Aviniere was living in a modest house on Ranelagh Street. It was the winter of 1802 and the last of autumn lingered in the fallen leaves. Another war was stirring. She felt that she was in a fortunate state, though not with all her freedoms. Many of those had been threatened or never given. But, nevertheless, she was satisfied now with her husband and her sons, and mostly occupied with her memories, which on evenings came gently, as evenings could.

She recalled when she was a small girl swaying in a hammock in a different climate with its brief sunset, her mother telling her the story of her life. *Is four years since you born on your father ship. We up and down the islands. Remember the year, child, 1761. You go have to write it down one day.* The ribbons of light then were mixed with the shadows on the pitch-pine floor of the porch. They swung to and fro in a silence filled with the breaking of the waves on the nearby shore and the scratching sound of palm branches in the breeze; *a long long time ago,* as her mother would say in her singsong voice. That was in Pensacola, the British port in Florida. It was a geography her father had taught Elizabeth with his maps, pointing to where he had bought her mother from the auction block and then put her in his house, which was on the front with the tall ships moored between the shore and Santa Rosa Island.

Light was different here on Ranelagh Street, not far from the banks of the River Thames where the creeks, water meadows and marshes lay just beyond the streets of Pimlico, choked in spring and summer with nettles. It had been her home for these last eight years. What was even more different now was her name, that she was called Elizabeth, or Lizzie, by her husband, John. He would keep to formalities in public, calling her Mrs d'Aviniere. But he called her Lizzie when he greeted her with kisses and cuddles, whispering, *Lizzie, Lizzie, Lizzie darling*, like a young lover. How sweet it was now to have his name in marriage, a proper surname, a real name, a free name, not that silly name, Dido, not that slave name. Her sons called her Mama. She was fortunate, she had to keep telling herself, despite the loss of her mother. Was she like Mr Olaudah Equiano, the African, *a particular favourite of Heaven* as that author's narrative so elegantly described his circumstances? She hoped that her pen would work a similar magic in the telling of her tale.

Her mother's voice was talking of rivers as Elizabeth settled down to write her story: *far over there and so long*. She traced the distances on her father's map, which he had given her during one of his last visits, long ago when she was a child in London. She pressed out the creases where it lay upon the table, travelling with her fingers from the hinterland of the large continent to the coast where they had lived at that time. *Is an eternity they take, oui, girl*. She remembered her mother teaching her to pronounce the name *Mis sis sip pi*.

Elizabeth's tongue had been straightened out to fit into England though she always felt that she had never quite achieved what was expected. People still turned and looked at her, even now, and sometimes asked her origin, though they could always see it plainly, she thought. This left her feeling uneasy.

Some of her more gentle memories and her mother's stories of Pensacola were filled with names, just sounds now, like those of the birds that sang in the trees, Creek and Chickasaw, Choctaw and the name that made them laugh aloud, almost falling out of the hammock, Chief Cowkeeper. Her mother would go on to talk to her of the rivers: Apalachicola, Yazoo, Matanzas forming thoroughfares to reach the north by ship and canoe, paddling on and on. *Far, far away, they say,* her mother said. She had once asked her father if she might ever go there on a canoe. He had smiled as he often did, shaking his head, *No, my pet,* his favourite expression when talking to her then.

Elizabeth listened more intently when her mother started to tell a harder story.

We find them people here when we reach by boat and they drop the anchor in the harbour, we so exhausted, so starved and thirsty and not daring to think that we might step upon land again, them chains such a part of we limbs that not to have them shackled to each other, to our ankles and to the boards, don't seem usual and ordinary at all when we come to stand upon the dry ground and have to walk, stumbling like we accustom on the deck of that terrible ship.

Elizabeth enjoyed making up her mother's voice. She wrote it as she heard her speak. To find her on her tongue was to keep her close, to try it on the page was to keep her even closer and not to lose her, ever.

She had promised to keep on writing and to send for her. She never found out over the years why her mother had stopped writing, after only one letter, despite all the letters she herself had written: *Dearest Mammy...* Had she been recaptured? It remained a mystery, despite the many inquiries Elizabeth had made over the years. When she had asked her father on his infrequent visits he always answered, *Soon, my pet.* Then she had asked her Master the Lord Mansfield, and his wife Lady Betty, and then, above all, Beth, her Master's great-niece, her sometime childhood companion. They had all evaded her questions.

Elizabeth used to wonder if *they* — to whom her father had given her on arriving in England — had ever really understood her and her loss. For while she grew up seeming so obliging and grateful, as they said she was, of such an amiable disposition and so accomplished, as *they* saw it, gaining her Master's highest respect and that of his relations and visitors to the house, they, nevertheless, were always so surprised, eyes growing larger, eyebrows so raised. There was no knowing what they had really expected to see. *She is so black*, they would say in consternation. What had they imagined? What had they been told about her? At the same time, she kept the loss and the sadness hidden. While it had not destroyed her, maybe even made her who she had become, her whole mind and body were still filled with longing, her longing for her mother.

Time will not wait for me now, she said to herself. How much longer did she have? She pondered this question more than ever, her illness being so unpredictable as Dr Featherstone would say. Would her mother ever write after all this time, Elizabeth not writing either? Where was she now? The world was constantly being altered with the changing geography and boundaries of countries belonging to this one here and then to another there, people in their thousands captured and transported each day from one place to another.

Where Elizabeth sat looking through the French windows she was already anticipating the first intimations of the spring with the snowdrops, looking forward to the crocuses and the other bulbs that she had planted with the bluebells. Christmas, a quiet one for her, had come and gone so quickly. Her illness had forced the lack of celebrations at home. Mr d'Aviniere had taken the boys to his twin sister, Martha, at Isledon, where she lived near the wells. She did not have children of her own. Poor Martha, with all she had gone through with her brother, was pleased to have the twins and William Thomas; twins ran in the family, it seemed. With her they had enjoyed the jugglers and other circus acts. Then no sooner was the festive season over than it was January with February approaching. Where was her time disappearing?

She drifted off to the sound of Lydia's sweeping; Lydia who had come with her from Caen Wood, her Master's residence. Elizabeth was imagining the yellow of the increasing sunshine which would get filtered through the willows and eventually light up all the new colours: the fresh green of the weeping silver birch, the patchwork of her different plants so well looked after by Seamus, Lydia's brother and their new lodger.

Lydia now called her Ma'am. That was very different from long ago when she had called her, *Miss Dido*. There she was, a good ten years older than herself, a kind of mother once, a kind of nurse, walking along the garden path after sweeping up the leaves, still with flame in her hair, now tied into a bun and constantly doing everything in the house and looking after the boys. She looked up from her sweeping and waved to Elizabeth, smiling with that broad smile which so often broke into laughter and a story, making the most ordinary things extraordinary.

In warmer weather Elizabeth would sit outside constantly following the sun's journey to find the strategic warm patches around her garden — the rose-covered arbour was her favourite spot outside for writing, once it was not too cold — till eventually the evening brought the shadows to her sequestered spot. She would sit there with her sloping, Japanned writing-box with its lacquered inlays. It had been a gift from her Master when she had begun in earnest to do his secretarial work, reading to him and writing his letters. *You are my amanuensis*, he had said then, such a long time ago.

Elizabeth knew that she had to reconcile herself to the truth that she had not heard her mother's voice for the last twenty-eight years. How old would her mother be now? Fifty-seven? Would that be correct? She counted. She had hardly been a girl of sixteen when she had given birth, she had told her. She must have been fourteen or fifteen when Elizabeth's father bought her off the auction block. They called her Belle and at some point that became her name, Maria Belle. Did she not have another name? *Belle, a pretty name for dirty work*, she had once told her daughter. *Belle of a great house and then of the street*. Elizabeth had listened as a little girl and had hardly understood then what she had meant by that description. Many of those cruel things that had been done to her were done to her as a child and as a young girl, sold and resold, captured, runaway and recaptured. She had had to become a woman long before her proper time.

During these last years, with Elizabeth herself becoming a wife and a mother, she felt the longing for her own mother even more. Her suckling of her own children at her breast, before she was obliged to pass on one of the twins, Johnny, to Mrs Halifax, a wet nurse down the street, gave her a greater sense of loss. She had not made sufficient milk for both her babies. Johnny had been so little, coming after Charles. She could still see John with the baby, a small bundle in his arms, going off to Mrs Halifax. He was so excited by his sons, two of them all at once. Martha had come to help, allowing Lydia more time for the household chores while looking after the twins. Her husband had been so patient with her worry and with Johnny's slower growth, trying always to give both boys equal attention. What if they lost them? It was their constant thought; Charles their black son and Johnny so much fairer. Her mother would say when she saw a black child like him in the street, *That child so fair, and watch them eyes, I sure he mix up with something. He go sell good if they catch hold of him.* She had laughed ironically when she said that, pinching her daughter's chin, and saying, *There's your father in you, sweetheart, but you have plenty of me.* When she said that her mother drifted off into a world of her own.

The very earliest of Elizabeth's own memories were of her father's estate, El Paso de Arroyo Ingles. *Is to the plantation they going,* her mother had told her when she peeped through the jalousies at the coffle passing in the road, shackles round the ankles, chained each to the other, some with iron masks, others with bits weighed upon their tongues to keep them from screaming, and always the sound of the lash of the whip upon their backs. She remembered a young African girl her father had bought to work in the house, such a contrast and contradiction of things. Her mother reminded her of this when she wanted to impress on her daughter that at times she herself had been a kind of mistress of the house and that she had not liked her father making eyes at the young girl. This was when her father yet again would insist that he could not make her mother a lady *at home*. Here she could be his woman, he had said. Nothing more. *Is which one you want? Is me or them, you know?* He had turned his back on her and walked away when she spoke with that tone. But she was not always so brave to say that. She heard her again one day, *the things I have to do to keep myself and my pickney alive.*

Elizabeth could still see her father, her fair captain in his uniform of white and navy blue with gold braid; his blond hair tied at the nape of his neck, his slender face, his raddled cheeks. He looked down at her, smiling and reaching to pull his slender fingers through her hair, while tying her plaits. She came to understand that he remained in her mother's imagination that young man with those hazel eyes who had chosen her off the auction block, a Scotsman who could not resist her nakedness, her fourteen-fifteen-year-old breasts, even in that awful place when he was forced to prod and poke her to please the merchant slaver and assure him that he was inspecting the merchandise properly. That she had been able to fall for his beauty in that moment of her ordeal was to Elizabeth a marvel, a desperate leap for freedom. Anyway, she thought now her mother had not had a choice. She had been bought. *Is fall, fall, fall... child, your mother had to do to save she self.*

Her mother was such a contrast to that Scotsman John Lindsay. Her skin shone with blackness and where it was not injured, broken by beatings, it was fine and smooth. It was bumpy only where the welts had healed on her back and legs. There was the scar upon her brow, another bump, which Elizabeth stroked with her fingers as she looked up into her face while she sucked her thumb and comforted herself, and knew not then what to comfort her mother for or with. Her father described her mother as *pretty*, a slight word for a beauty much more sumptuous. Her black eyes were luminous. Her mother could look so sad at times and so solemn even at such a young age. Her father used to say, *You look as if you are going to cry at any moment.* She smiled at him and came back from some place far away, some journey, which she had survived. That story was hard for Elizabeth to tell. For now, she was trying to keep to fond memories.

She wished that she did not all the time get caught up in the story of their departure from Pensacola in 1765, then later her mother's departure from England in 1774. The dates were indelibly seared on her mind, spoken by her mother. She had never really recovered from those early departures, those comings and goings to and from her mother, those leavings when she had felt abandoned. She kept anticipating departure. To be left only for a short while seemed like forever.

Not to have heard from her all these years; this more than preoccupied her mind, particularly now, when she felt that she did not have much time remaining.

2

'LYDIA! IS THAT you at the door? Billy?' Elizabeth was awakened, having nodded off, dropping her pen and pages onto the floor, coughing herself out of sleep. Was it just tiredness or her tinctures of laudanum? One did not always help the other. She knew this yet she could not resist the comfort of the opiate medication prescribed by Dr Featherstone.

William Thomas, their Billy, Elizabeth's and John's third boy, was shooting up fast, catching up with his older brothers and particularly imitating eight-year-old Charles. Billy was four years old and already he was his own person, a little man his mother called him. He was named William, after her Master, William Murray, and Thomas for her husband's foster father, Thomas d'Aviniere, but he was their Billy. He was a mixture, her child, of course he was. She might never know his entire ancestry. But in this last of her children she saw the evidence of her father. He was a handsome boy with the fairest skin in the household and already he had the silver-tongued eloquence of her Master.

The front door slammed. That would be him, his excitement bursting out to tell her of his afternoon's adventure with Lydia beyond Ranelagh Gardens, and no doubt close to the river bank with its many excitements and dangers.

'Lydia, is that you?'

'Yes, Ma'am. Sorry. We're late.' She was speaking from the hall, telling of Billy's adventures, climbing trees, falling out of them. 'Almost breaking their necks. Don't you worry, Ma'am, don't you worry. It was a grand time.' Lydia was laughing and tearing off her coat, bundling her long red hair to the top of her head.

'I thought you were both lost.'

Billy bounded into the room, 'The fish jumped all over the grass till it was stunned...'

'Stunned, was it? Maybe Papa will take you fishing. Your father loves fishing when he can get a chance. You get your pull-horse to play with now and give Mama a chance to talk to Johnny. Where's Johnny, though...?'

'He's here, Ma'am. Johnny's fine, a little slow, aren't you laddie? He's having a drink. He's a grand boy, no problems with him this morning.'

Elizabeth was concerned about the boys dawdling. 'You know how it was in our day, Lydia, with the leash.'

'Of course, Ma'am, couldn't keep either of them on a leash.' Lydia was helping Johnny out of his coat. She was tired out and hoped that her mistress would manage the boys while she caught her breath and she got some time upstairs in her own room. She knew that she had to wait to see how the boys settled.

'Johnny come. You know I can't be getting up easily. What should we do? A story? The Latin exercise that Charles brought back yesterday?'

Johnny was tired out, but more from having to cope with the boisterous Billy than the actual walk and adventure on the river. He got out his extracts of Virgil.

Mr d'Aviniere had recently decided to keep Johnny away from school after Charles had reported his brother's disappearance on their way home one afternoon. The boys' journey from the new development in Belgravia took them over the marshes, then past Locke's Asylum and Jenny's Whim, a notorious inn known for attracting sinister characters. Charles had arrived home without his brother. Lydia had

had to go looking for the boy because Mr d'Aviniere had not yet returned from Holborn where he was a steward at one of the large houses on Gough Square. It was late that evening when Johnny was found, disorientated, having lost himself on one of the many paths across the water meadows. It was still a mystery. He had dropped behind his brother and had quite suddenly found himself alone. Charles had gone on ahead, not noticing his brother's absence he often wandered off — till it was too late and he had thought it better to get home and report Johnny's disappearance rather than go looking for him and himself get lost.

The incident had become a lesson to all the family. Their father had spoken to the boys, but had got very little from them. The episode encouraged Elizabeth's anxiety that she herself had had since she was a girl; being lost was the worst fear. There had always been talk that she must not get lost. What they had really wanted to say was that she must not get captured. She had been told of the gangs that roamed the city to pick up boys and girls either to sell by advertisement in the shops or by deporting them back to Jamaica or the Carolinas.

'Mama, Mama.'

'Billy, please, please. You're so heavy now.'

'I'll take him, Ma'am.'

'You must get your break, Lydia. Is that Charles by the door? Everyone's back at the same time today. Come, tell me what you did in class.'

Billy, suddenly quiet and pensive, looked up at his mother and asked, 'Have you slept well, Mama, or was it you I heard coughing in the night?'

'Probably, probably. You don't miss a thing, do you?' She marvelled at the composition of his sentences, the directness of his questions. She worried particularly that the twins and Billy might hear her coughing. She knew that it was inevitable because of the nearness of the rooms. She did not want her illness in their minds.

'Johnny coughs at night as well,' Billy piped up.

'I don't...'

'Boys...'

'We lie awake and whisper in the dark, don't we?' Charles spoke up, commanding the attention of his younger brother with a story of a horse galloping by in the night. 'I caught a glimpse of the rider.'

Elizabeth had noticed since Johnny's disappearance that her boys had been talking and playing at getting lost and having to survive on very little food. They had created an adventure about a mysterious man on horseback who went about capturing little black boys and girls, making them vanish.

'I never disappeared. I can't disappear. I'm not going to disappear.' Johnny was not convinced by the game.

Billy was pulling his horse across the room with an awful screeching noise.

Elizabeth did find Lydia was a little vague about this matter of getting lost. She seemed at times not to take her anxiety seriously.

'I parted the curtains when I heard the horse,' Charles continued with his story. 'I peeped through the window. But he was gone in a flash. *Festina*.' Charles was proud of his knowledge of Latin.

'I saw him too,' Billy screamed.

'Billy!' Charles shouted, silencing William Thomas.

'Lydia, can you help? Charles, can you?'

'It's from one thing to another at this time of day,' Lydia complained, as she entered the room, not yet able to take her rest, wiping her hands on her apron. 'Come on boys,' she commanded, 'your mother wants you to play gently. Charles, you can stop Billy pestering to blow bubbles. And let Johnny have your most recent work from school. I'm going upstairs and I don't want to have to come down for at least an hour.' This announcement was as much for Elizabeth who had had most of her day to herself and her writing. The boys knew Lydia did not threaten without consequences. They watched her leave the room and then they looked at their mother, understanding that her illness was something they had to cope with. They found that difficult, a mother with an illness which required quiet. At last, peace reigned.

Charles had always been strong and alert from birth, the first into the world, screaming his head off and startling the midwife Mrs R with his black skin as she passed him over to Lydia to cut his umbilical cord. 'My Lord,' she had cried out, 'another son. Twins! What's this?' She turned to help Johnny, with his sandy, crinkly hair and his bright green eyes. 'My dear, he's your child, no doubt, and some of his father thrown in. What will the parish make of these two coming from the same mother? They're your children, my love, no doubt sweetheart,' the midwife talked all the while to Elizabeth as she cut Johnny's umbilical cord and the babies were bathed and bundled up and placed in her arms where she lay, exhausted. Lydia cleaned up the mess, reaching for damp linen to soothe her brow with lemon balm. Charles was immediately at her breast while Johnny was less eager. Elizabeth and her husband always joked that there was no more milk left for Johnny once Charles was replete.

William Thomas, coming four years later, was an altogether different experience. Her white child, she called him. Elizabeth saw in him the ancestral connection to her Master and her own father's looks, fairer skin and eyes, almost hazel and, above all, he had her Master's adventurous personality.

That very morning she had found one of Billy's small shirts hanging over the back of a chair and it moved her while she handled it and folded it, the small arms and the little collar, so tiny. She remembered that his birth had been so much calmer than that of the twins. Elizabeth had told her husband not to worry when he left for work that morning. 'When you return, my sweet, there'll be a new boy or girl,' she had said to him. 'You must not stay.' The fire had been lit, new kindling and coals brought in by Lydia, delivered the day before by Seamus. She remembered Lydia's gentle hands, so soothing. She had already once examined her, so gently entering to be assured that all was well with the baby's passage. It was Lydia's hands that she trusted most, with Mrs R to supervise.

John d'Aviniere had returned to the sight of his new baby. He held him and cried as he lifted him out in front of him, examining the smallest fingers and the littlest mouth, which he imagined smiled at him with eyes that blinked in the light. 'You look like your mother's Master,' he had said. 'How ironic, my white child, *my* son.'

Elizabeth sat back and enjoyed the brief tranquillity of her boys, thanks to Lydia settling them down before going for her rest. She could now get on with her writing in one of her favourite spots. Her garden was her solace when the weather permitted or when she felt that she could not stroll through Ranelagh Gardens to view the river and the visitors to the Rotunda, which had faded since its great days when the boy Mozart had played there and Canaletto had painted its ornamental lakes. She remembered her Master's oil by the same artist, which had been hung at Caen Wood. Those had been the grand days when the crowds used to come to visit the murals and the Chinese architecture, the illuminations and the fireworks, when the crowds drank syllabubs, ate cakes and listened to Mr Handel's music.

It was still like that when she and her new husband had walked hand in hand in their freedom and passion after they had first moved to Pimlico in 1793. Before the twins were born, they loved to enjoy the delight of the Gardens. They were still like a courting couple. So much had been a secret when they had first begun their romance and her Master was still alive. Marriage became their unfettered freedom from that bondage.

The simplest of his words had excited Elizabeth on that first encounter at the Shoreditch Meeting House. The weight of John d'Aviniere's presence pressed upon her in the narrow passage between the boxed pews. *The meeting start in ten minutes, Miss.* She had felt him overwhelming her with the ordinary words of information, which he spoke in an accent that had her curious as to his origins. It was an inflection she had not heard since her mother's tongue, that French patois, as he spoke his name, d'Aviniere. *I am Mr d'Aviniere the son of the Elder, Thomas d'Aviniere.* There had not been any further declaration of anything deeper, not then, not that first morning. She had kept smiling at the dip and rise of his voice. She had glimpsed him once before, where he sat in front of her, his black hair crinkled into tight curls on the nape of his neck. She found that she looked out for him after that meeting asking herself if she might arrange a rendezvous, a tryst, as Beth would call such a meeting. She found that she was allowing herself these fantasies on the way back in the carriage to Caen Wood.

She had, after that day, planned to arrive earlier than she needed for meetings, to linger in the porch for his arrival with Martha. She was later introduced to the white gentleman, his foster father. She concealed yet garnered the details of the passion that she felt rising in herself in such small, almost indiscernible ways, feelings she had not had for anyone else before. She fed herself in this way, to hold within her the smell of him, which she inhaled as they made room for each other on the tread of the stairs to an upper room after the meeting where the congregation met for refreshments and informal conversation. She once brushed against his sleeve, and on another occasion when he had hung his jacket upon a hook in the porch, she pressed her face into its collar to breathe him in. She allowed herself this passion. It shocked her that she searched for those stolen moments in this vicarious way. She recognised her hunger with wonder and felt a little embarrassed at herself that she should fall beyond herself and not know how she might get back to feel ordinary again. She wondered what prospects there were for the fulfilment of those inner desires.

It surprised Elizabeth that she now conjured her husband in this way, on this strangely warm January day on Ranelagh Street, a storm brewing as black as purple over the pastures of Pimlico behind the house. The river would be turbulent with waves, the barges crashing against each other, churned beyond its level, brimful to overflowing into the water meadows. Her husband would soon be home for tea.

She never forgot that first day in the porch of the Shoreditch Meeting House. It had earlier become the place of her education on abolition, taken there by her mother. She remembered her mother's instructions when she was a girl: *They is your people, child, look out for them*, talking about the black people her mother had met in Shoreditch and Camden who had been enslaved or set free by their masters but still fearful of capture.

She had also noticed the stares when John d'Aviniere first entered the housekeeper's room the day he came calling at Caen Wood. She had heard the whispered words behind raised palms among the girls as he came through the pantry. *Another nigger? Two of them!* That was the new girl from Finsbury. What minute evidence they worked on, skin not as dark as hers, hair not as woolly, as they called it, but his speech, foreign in its accent, lilting a little like hers, all not yet quite straightened out.

As he stood in the doorway that day, she saw how his dark eyes welled up with expectation. Had he known that he had enveloped her with a kind of pity as she noticed the rejection of others in their stares and their cruel whispers? Did she know that that was what it was at first, piercing and opening her heart to his love? She had slept each night with his face close to her own in her mind's eye, so real. Could it become more than a dream? She pretended to touch and trace the contours of his face with her fingers, and draw him towards her, to place her lips upon his. Almost inaudibly, she whispered words to conjure him, words she herself hardly wanted to hear, stifled into her pillow.

There was another day when she had been called to the front door at Caen Wood by the bell, wondering why it was not being answered by one of the maids, its repeated toll clattering throughout the house. It was then that she found him standing at the door, the snow falling, and his hair the texture of her own, sprinkled with white flakes. She stretched out her arms to him. *You must come in from the cold*, she had pleaded. But this encounter got swallowed up in the bustle of the time, the preoccupations of duties, the service of her Master, in those last days at Caen Wood having to minister to the grieving widower. Mr d'Aviniere sat there for her Master's inspection, the most powerful man under the king. Their courtship moments had had to be stolen and kept secret; her Master had insisted on discretion.

Lydia entered the room to announce that supper was ready.

Elizabeth continued to express her anxiety. 'You know we're plagued with the sharpers and the pickpockets in the Five Fields. We still don't have Johnny's full story. Such a mystery, Lydia.'

'You must trust me, Ma'am.' Lydia could get exasperated with her mistress. Their relationship was at times a conundrum to sort out; the little black girl brought into the household, *neither fish or fowl nor good red herring*, they kept saying in the kitchens and then the seeming favourite of the master of the house, which grew into nasty rumours, *his little black girl for his use*. So much had changed.

'I do. But I can't help my anxiety. It's my own terrible memory.'

'It doesn't help to constantly relive it. I do remember the frightening episode when you were a girl.'

'All sorts visit the area. There's the hospital near Pimlico and Locke's Asylum in the marshes, which gives the passersby the jitters. We can hear the cries of the lunatics, poor souls. What did really happen to Johnny?'

'Trust me, Ma'am. I do know how to look after children, as you are well aware. My mother had a multitude.'

'Lydia, of course I know.'

Elizabeth enjoyed her boys' company as Lydia served their supper. Charles and Johnny were still at their books, Charles helping his brother. How would others describe them, the gentlemen who used to visit her Master's drawing room with their strange talk, those odd words to describe the mixture of blood, of breeds, as if they were newly discovered animals: mulatto, quadroon, marabou, sacatra and octoroon and all the rest, weighing on scales that hung in their minds the percentages of black and white. Is this how they would describe her small sandy-haired, green-eyed boy, her hazel-eyed, black-eyed lamb, her *bête noire* as someone had once called her, addressing Lady Betty? *She's your bête noire.* All those fractions of colour! What did it all mean? She had once in a fit of madness thought she should put white powder on Charles' face to make him less conspicuous. What would the world make of them when she had gone and they had to find themselves out there? Where would they find themselves in the world in what her father used to call *our empire*?

After supper, Billy continued to blow his bubbles, translucent orbs that hung momentarily in the air, catching the light, and then dissolving. He was looking more and more like her Master and her own father.

With the children in bed, Elizabeth got out her writing box and laid out her pens. In the quiet, before her husband's return from Gough Square, there would be some time for her story. The very earliest days of her childhood were continuing to come back to her in fragments.

3

WHEN IT WAS daytime back there, it had been a white blinding light, and the heat, 'like a desert,' Dido's father said. He was that hazel-eyed, blond-curls-on-the-nape-of-his-neck gentleman, the captain, up on deck, directing everything. He spoke of the extremes there could be at the different ends of the earth. 'We're almost on the equator,' he said to her mother, explaining the fiery circle that encompassed the earth, as he put it then, his ship just off the coast of Trinidad, travelling towards Cartagena. He talked of rations with alarm. Were there enough rations of water? 'Let me explain the geography.' He laid his maps out on a trestle table, his slender fingers pointing. 'Let me first explain longitude.' Dido was lifted up into his arms so that she could see above the edge of the table. When he talked to her mother of these serious matters he laughed and smiled and called her pretty things, 'My sweet, my darling,' stroking her cheeks, and resting his lips upon hers in the privacy of their cabin, with the maps of their journey, their voyage, all laid out upon the table. He would turn from kissing her mother and wink at the child, Dido.

Her mother would say she did not understand such matters, but then added, 'You must teach the child.'

Dido carried the word, *longitude*, spoken by her father. It stuck in her mind. Its sound, if not its meaning, always meant that she thought of her father up on the deck, spying, pointing, gesticulating and talking of what he had discovered on his voyages and travels. And, of course, he tried to explain the magical clock that had been on his ship *Tartar* on the trip to Barbados with Mr Harrison in 1764. He returned home in Pensacola from that voyage in time for her third birthday. 'You is three, child. And is you father ship I see in the harbour.' If the Harrison clock worked, he explained to her mother and herself, the trade would be safe. No more would His Majesty's ships founder on the hidden shoals and rocks. All the wealth of those precious cargoes from Guinea to the Americas and the islands spreading like an arc between north and south upon which an empire depended would be saved, no longer lost or wasted. Such wasted cargo, such wasted fortunes and investments, such wasted property and returns when the longitude was not known. Since a boy of twelve or thirteen, he had been at sea serving His Majesty. There were other ships that he had captained and spoke of, often with pride: *Trent*, *Cambridge*, *Temple* and *Devonshire*.

Dido's mother doted on this talk, of her Scotsman who would not make her a lady. For Dido it was a language that she kept and she made of it what she wanted to imagine. She learned of *doldrums* and *trade winds*.

◁ THE FOLLOWING EVENING Lydia and Billy had gone out with Charles to play in the Gardens before dark. Johnny had stayed behind with Elizabeth. He was the one whom she talked to most intimately. He liked to get down her chestnut box and open it up for her to tell him the stories attached to its contents. Charles had inherited her proficiency with the Latin and Greek she had learned from her Master.

It was Johnny who had her feelings for the stories of the past. 'Sweetheart, do you want your tea now? You've done a lot today. You're ready for bed. The others are still out and will be back soon. Bread and butter? What's Lydia got here, something in pastry? There you go.'

She sat at the table with him after his supper where he preferred to arrange and rearrange the mementoes from her chestnut box, her mother's blue kerchief folded over and over, and to hear his mother talk of his grandmother as she told of her dancing on the deck of the ship. She told him of the wide ocean and all the voices which came up from the sea. Johnny held the kerchief to his face to inhale the past his mother talked about, to smell his grandmother, to imagine her dancing. 'Can I do that?' He looked up at his mother and smiled. He knew it was a fancy and that he was being silly. She pulled her fingers through his hair as he played with the gold earrings, holding them against his skin, hearing how his grandmother had pierced his mother's ears with African gold she had sewn into the hem of her cloth for the journey across the ocean.

'You're not feeling well, are you? Not quite right?'

'I'm not hungry.'

'You go on up. Let's put Mama's things away. I'll be up later to tuck you in.'

Elizabeth had to guard against these moments with her small children, that she did not indulge her own anxieties at the expense of any morbidity in their young lives. Johnny's attentions always affected her with greater intensity because of his soft intimacies, which appealed to her secret longing for a daughter, though she knew that a girl child might not survive as well as the boys with their father when she had gone. It had been the wet nurse that had saved Johnny, trying him slowly with arrowroot, which thankfully he managed to consume. But he had never been strong. It was a wonder that he was alive at birth.

Charles and Billy, ravenously hungry, were consuming their supper while listening to their mother and their nurse. The pairs of eyes moving between the two women, back and forth, ears as alert as foxes.

Charles was particularly attentive. 'I think I saw that gentleman that Johnny talked about when he got lost.'

'You've never said that before.'

'I wasn't sure.'

'What was he like?'

'Who are you talking about?' Billy asked, with bread and butter still stuffed in his mouth and holding one of Lydia's small pies.

'Charles, that's enough. I'll talk to you later. But...'

'Just an ordinary gentleman, you know...'

'Charles, I said, that's enough.' When Billy was not paying attention, she whispered, 'Why do you think he was the same man?'

'Johnny told me later that he had a scar on his cheek.'

'Why haven't you boys told us this before? Why didn't you tell your father when he spoke to you?'

'Johnny was scared. Anyway what can the man do? What are you afraid of him doing?'

Elizabeth looked at Lydia, her eyes questioning and askng, should we talk about this now, just before bedtime, with Billy all ears? 'It's time for bed. We'll talk to your father about this tomorrow.'

The boys went upstairs to their room. Elizabeth waited for her husband. Lydia cleared up and went off to her room in the loft.

Elizabeth's mother had been insistent in reminding her daughter of where she had come from, no matter her very young age. Moments alone with her mother accounted for her memories of that beginning time. There were the smells of her mother, tastes, snatches of her words, the music of her voice. She wanted to capture this in the pages of her story. She still felt the touch of her hand as she stroked her on her arm or when she kissed her cheek. She wanted her back. What she remembered were her stories of caution, her constant reminders to take care of gentlemen talking to her in the street. Her mother told her what she herself was in England, a black and a slave. *That is you too my child, black and a slave, no matter John Lindsay blood running in your veins.*

THE FIRST TIME Dido heard her father's name called was by his lieutenant, second in command upon the ship, in a relaxed moment at the door of the cabin in which she and her mother were sequestered. 'Lindsay.' In another moment of intimacy she heard his other name, 'John.'

Her mother told her, 'He's your father.'

Dido absorbed these facts: John Lindsay is your father. Maria Belle is your mother. Belle, what a funny name. She remembered her mother telling her it was a name for *dirty work*.

Dido knew she was everything to her young mother, and she thought it was the same to him, her father.

'You must not go further than,' then he pointed, 'my pet,' he said, resting his hand upon her head in a kind of blessing, or at least an affection. He pointed hardly yards from the cabin door to the deck above, where she must not go without supervision; that square of light, that glimpse of sky, that noisy thoroughfare above deck. When she climbed out of the cabin she was stunned by the expanse of the sea.

Her mother told her that she cried out, 'Look!' pointing to the sea. 'The sea, the sea. Water, water.' She learned the word *ocean*. At three going on four it was immeasurable to her. She was that young when she first beheld that wonder from the deck of her father's ship. She stared and stared and pointed, 'Look.'

Up on deck, her mother strolled arm in arm with her father flagrantly. The sailors stared, their captain and the black woman. He and her mother at sea were different to being *at home*.

'I cannot be seen with you at home,' he told Dido's mother. She would not, could not be taken for a *lady, ever*. 'No matter our love,' he said to her mother.

Dido lay awake listening to their romance and their kisses in the dark, the silences that followed, their sighs drowned by the wind which drove the ship, the wind and the sea all around them, travelling up and down the islands, then the long crossing of the ocean, the Atlantic ocean, which was another geography lesson from her father as they spotted the Azores in the distance. They stopped there to increase their rations of water. She remembered the islands as blue and purple. Her mother once told her it was because of the flowers. She later learned their name, *hydrangeas*, a purple and blue haze over the hills as they departed in the evening, staring from the stern of the ship till the islands were black dots and then no more.

Then it was the worry of her mother still being ill upon the bunk, forever coughing, not ever coming up on to the deck for the sea air. 'You must come up for the air, my darling.' Dido's father spoke to her in that way, *darling*. It was reassuring to hear him speak to her like that. They had travelled over many days and nights, weeks, her father said, to get this far. Dido did not like to think how long and how far, for would that not be the great expanse which would lie between herself and her mother, between Pensacola and England, which her father called *home*? She had heard them talking of the voyage back her mother would have to make. 'You go send me back?' her mother asked. 'And what about the child?'

When she looked at the sea it seemed very lonely — the Atlantic ocean — a faint blue on her father's map. She was allowed to look over the railings from the deck, holding tight, a black sea below. The ocean moaned. Her mother said it wailed and called to her with voices. She learned later why her mother turned away from the deep swells which were hollowed out in that wide expanse of water, swelling and crashing against the sides of the ship as it ploughed with its sharp prow.

'It swallowed them so quick,' her mother described. 'One moment they on the deck, screaming and fighting, the next that glimpse when them was forced to jump over the side of the ship. They was gone.' She told Dido that there was one, just one, she saw struggling, calling out, a small voice, waving her arm. 'She get smaller and smaller as the ship speed on with the sails like big bellies. We stand and look and look. I knew her. I uses to talk to her.'

Her mother and the rest were then taken back down into the holds, shackled to the floor and to each other so that the women turned away as they were put in their quarters from where they saw men reach for each other and comfort themselves with each other in the darkness, grasping for forgetfulness; up on deck, just lonely on their own, gazing at the open breasts and legs of women, daughters with their mothers and sisters in that naked state. She told Dido: 'So many dead on the passage almost each day a burying as they call it, pitching the body into the sea. Worse when they alive, pushed over or jumping themselves to the comfort of the ocean rather than stay on that terrible ship.'

Her mother talked as if to herself, staring into the sea, Dido listening without understanding.

⚡ THE FOLLOWING DAY Elizabeth was in the house on her own. 'Is someone at the door?' she called but there was no answer. She caught herself looking up from her writing out into the garden from the upstairs back window. She had forgotten for a moment that she had come upstairs to the box room. Was it the laudanum playing tricks with her mind?

'We're back!' It was Charles shouting in the hall. Billy was running after him and Lydia came in last with Johnny closing the front door behind him.

'He gave me a fright,' Lydia said to Elizabeth quietly, not wanting to alarm the boys.

'Who did?'

Lydia explained that the boys had been dawdling behind and she was pressing ahead because they were late.

'Dawdling! How many times, Lydia...'

"Ma'am...' She began to explain in whispers that he was a very respectable-looking gentleman. He was dressed unusually for the district, respectable, but sort of roguish. His coat had a reddish colour. His hat was pulled over his eyes. He had stopped them politely and pointed to the children.

'Who, Lydia?'

'He appeared suddenly. I did not see where he had come from. He asked... I cannot say it, Ma'am. He had such a unique way of talking.'

'What, Lydia?'

'He said...'

'What, Lydia, spit it out...'

'I don't think the children heard...'

'What?'

'They're a fine pair. I expect they might fetch you quite a good price if you knew the right people to do business with.' He rested his hand on Johnny's head saying. 'This one...'

Lydia looked terrified. Elizabeth felt sick.

'I did tell you...'

'I thought you were fussing unnecessarily, Ma'am...'

'You do remember what happened to me when I was a girl...'

'Of course, I remember.' Elizabeth and Lydia recalled her distraught face, a girl, shaking, banging on the front door of the Mansfield house in Bloomsbury Square. She had been uncontrollable, screaming, convulsed. Lydia had taken her straight into Lady Betty in the drawing room. 'You threw yourself on the floor, breathless. Lady Betty administered a tincture of laudanum to still your spirits, Ma'am.'

Charles, despite the whispers, was alert to the conversation between his mother and Lydia.

'It may've been the same man that made Johnny get lost in the marshes.'

'Well, it's a good lesson. Two scares.'

'He didn't look like a catcher, Ma'am, but he might employ one.'

'Quite so, they're not isolated individuals, but organised. Let's have tea and then bed. Charles you've homework, haven't you? I'll talk with you and Johnny tomorrow. I don't want you to frighten Billy with your talk. Straight off to sleep tonight when you're in bed.'

'Can't I wait up for Papa?'

'Not tonight.'

Mr d'Aviniere was late that evening. Elizabeth told Lydia to have an early night. She then pulled herself up the stairs to supervise bedtime. She read one of Aesop's fables: *The Fox and the Cat*. Without saying anything directly about the afternoon's events, she repeated the moral of Aesop's tale as she turned down the lamp: 'Good to have one sure way to deal with difficulty. I think coming straight home is the best way to avoid any dangers. Sleep well, my pets.'

They lay on their backs, their large eyes turning from the ceiling to their mother at the door.

'Mama...'

'William Thomas, not another word.'

Elizabeth had never told her boys about slavery. Her sons were free. She did not have any proof. It certainly was not in the colour of their skin. It was not written down anywhere. She had no papers to show if they were ever apprehended or carted off. Whenever she had got close to the story of the trade with Johnny, playing with the bits and pieces of her mother's life kept in the chestnut box, she had closed the lid on that past.

When that evening they sat over their supper of cold meats that Lydia had laid out, Elizabeth retold Lydia's tale. John listened carefully and became visibly moved by this threat to his boys. That his small boys could provoke this scandalous offer of a so-called gentleman both weakened him as a father and then emboldened him as he began to feel a rage within himself. Could he apprehend such a man? How endangered was he if he drew attention to himself with the law? He leaned over to hold the hands of his wife to share their common distress. He was trembling as he explained himself to Elizabeth.

'We'll tell them what they are threatened by and why. We must give them an honest explanation…'

'How to find the appropriate words, though…'

'The right moment…'

'I've told Charles that I want to talk to Johnny and himself tomorrow, then…'

'Maybe Charles should stay off school…'

'Yes, we need time.'

Elizabeth felt better having spoken to her husband. She could see that he was shocked and angry. They went up to bed together, falling asleep in each other's arms, each worried about the safety of the boys and nervous because of the stories they would have to tell.

Lydia went out early with Billy the following morning, leaving Johnny and Charles to speak to their parents. Mr d'Aviniere sent Seamus with a message both to Gough Square and to the school in Belgravia, one to give his own excuses and the other to excuse his son from school.

'Johnny, you remember the man with the scar?' his father began by asking.

'Sort of…'

'Do you know what he wanted, Johnny?'

His son did not answer.

'Do you, Charles?'

'I'm not sure. Lydia said that the man said Johnny and Billy could… I can't remember the actual words…'

'Fetch a good price. Do you know what that means?'

'No…Maybe…' Johnny had his head bowed, refusing to look at his parents.

Then Charles spoke up. 'I've seen a sign in a shop saying, BLACK BOY WANTED – GOOD PRICES GIVEN. Is that what the man was saying, like that sign?'

'Yes, something like that.'

Elizabeth felt herself becoming emotional when what she wanted to be was as calm as possible and as factual as possible in order not to alarm her children.

'Why?' Johnny asked, still with his head bowed and not looking at his parents and fidgeting with a marble in his pocket.

'Is it because Johnny has black skin?' Charles asked.

'He's darker than I am,' Johnny said to his mother and father.

'Son,' his father drew his chair closer to him.

'Boys have said things about us at school because we're black.' Charles was becoming excited as he spoke and he was looking at Johnny for confirmation of what he was describing.

'Not to me,' Johnny snapped.

'Well they do. You're not there now to know. And I heard a boy call you *nigger* one day. You must remember because you wanted to fight him and Mr Butler stopped you. They called us *niggers.*'

'You're lying,' Johnny snapped again. 'Why're you lying?'

'I don't think Charles would lie about something as serious as this, would he, sweetheart? Come look at me. Your father and I want to explain and we want to help you. I'm glad to hear that you fought back, because it shows you know it was wrong and hurtful what that boy called you.'

'But why?' Johnny was now angry and hurt. 'I'm not black like Charles.'

'We're brothers.' Charles leaned over and cuffed Johnny on the shoulder. 'You're my twin...'

'Boys, come on. Don't fight between yourselves. It's complicated...' Charles and Johnny stared at their parents.

Johnny was now more composed and had stopped fidgeting. He snuggled up to his mother, while Charles was waiting for his father to speak.

Their father took hold of them both. 'Come here...' He looked at his wife and smiled encouragingly.

'When I first came to this country, I had to be very careful. I was living in Hampstead Village at the time. My foster father spoke to me as I'm speaking to you now...'

'Why did you have a foster father?' Charles asked, drawing closer to his father.

'That's a longer story for another day. He told me that in this country I had to be careful because of the colour of my skin. Your mother had a similar experience.'

'Why should that matter?' Charles was persistent.

Johnny had started fidgeting again. Elizabeth had to stop him rolling a marble across the table.

'You're both going to have learn many things as you grow up.'

Elizabeth could see that her husband had that longer story going on in his head as he chose words carefully to instruct his two young sons, words that he felt were hopelessly inadequate for what he really wanted to say. She knew the memories that had scorched his mind. There was the journey from Martinique, trying to keep himself and his sister safe. This was a story he shied away from. There was life on the plantation at Coulibri in Martinique. His white father had told him that his birth had come about because of a moment of weakness though he had come to learn differently when he saw babies born to be bred and sold. He had not been intended, his father had told him, to be a son. His mother remained on the plantation. His father had a proper wife, a white woman. He and Martha had been taken to work in the house but not to take their father's name. They were paraded to be sold when other white gentlemen visited the house. He had never been sure which of the women down in the huts had been their mother.

Then when Martha began to grow up she became the object of her father's attention in a way that John could see was not what should be between a father and a daughter. She would be dressed up to look pretty when the other gentlemen visited, make her a *belle* for their pleasure. Then Martha told John what she was expected to do when she was left alone with them, what would happen when she refused.

He had to nurse her wounds, comfort her in the night, plan an escape.

When John told Elizabeth this story it brought back fears she had had at Caen Wood. He could never tell the whole story and left her to guess what Martha had suffered. Elizabeth had to imagine the horror of what the brother saw and how he had challenged his father. It was then that he was very badly beaten, the scars still on his back. It was then that his father had them sold to a slaver that transported them to France. There was that passage, the arrival in Bordeaux, their journey to Paris. It was then that Thomas d'Aviniere, the Quaker, offered them their freedom, buying them and then giving them their manumission, and a better life after crossing to England. He gave them his name. Their life had been a list of places. John revealed very little about what had happened on that Atlantic voyage. Elizabeth felt that she could not ask Martha to tell her.

She also remembered John standing out on the terrace at Caen Wood when he had first come to the house. He was lost in his own mind, his brow furrowed like a sugarcane field. She noticed his calloused hands, the fingers rough with cuts and bruises. He had been better at listening to her story than telling her his own. She knew now those times when he would seem to go away from her in his mind, like her mother used to when she told of the terrible ship.

Elizabeth leaned over to encourage him, as the boys were getting fidgety and wanting to get off their chairs. She leaned over and stroked the scar on his cheek. 'Sweetheart, the boys…'

'I know.' John d'Aviniere smiled at his wife and then concentrated on the boys. 'There are men like that gentleman with the scar and the one who spoke to Lydia who will want to capture you and sell you because you are black, or because you're of mixed race. They're not allowed by law now to do this but it happens. You've got to be careful without being always terrified.' He made them promise to tell their mother and himself about any danger that they noticed. 'You must also tell us of any insults you get. We need to talk to your teachers.'

'What's a slave, Mama?' Charles was ever alert.

Elizabeth and her husband looked at their sons and then at each other, fearful of shocking and hurting their children, but determined to answer this question that Charles had put to them this morning as they drank tea and ate the last slices of Lydia's cake, which was being nibbled at by Johnny, bowing his head.

'A slave, darling, is a person who has been captured and made to work for nothing. Slaves are their captor's property.'

The boys nodded, but she was not sure what they had grasped.

'Do you understand what I'm saying, boys?'

'It's a bad thing…'

'Yes, Charles, it's a very bad thing, but not all people think so.'

John was all the time looking at his wife and then at his sons to see what they were making of their mother's words. He rested his hand on Elizabeth's. She had started coughing uncontrollably and had to leave the table. The boys had had enough and needed to go out to play, or go for a walk with their father.

When Elizabeth came back into the room. Johnny stood up and spoke to his parents and to Charles.

'I didn't tell anyone because I was scared. The man with a scar on his face tried to bundle me into a sack. He persuaded me to come and see a fox that he had shot. He had not shot a fox. It was a way to get me to come with him. He took out a sack with a chain. He was going to tie me up and put me into the sack. I fought against him. He had a bad leg. I pushed him over the bank into the marsh and ran away. I was too scared to tell you. I ran away. He shouted that he would come and catch me again. He said he would wait for another day. He called me that word, *nigger.*'

'Johnny, you're being very brave now. You've done the right thing to tell us.'

That afternoon John d'Aviniere took his sons out to Ranelagh Gardens for a treat and to buy each one a toy. Charles suggested they might meet Lydia and Billy coming back from their outing. Watching him leave the house, Elizabeth imagined where he and his sister Martha had come from. What a long journey to the comfort of his own sons, to the comparative safety of where they were now.

Elizabeth was exhausted. The full horror of her own danger of capture long ago came back to fill the parlour where she and her husband had been in a huddle with their sons, in a communion of whispers trying to protect them from the fear that had taken hold of their parents when they were children. That night she broke the sequence of her childhood to describe that moment of danger.

❦ DIDO HAD LEFT the house to run a quick errand around the corner just near St George's church where she had been baptised in 1766, and which she loved to visit. After coming out of the small shop that sold the ribbons that Lady Betty said she and Beth could have, Dido strolled slowly back with the intention of popping into the church just to sit a short while — for there it was she remembered her mother in the back pew, while she sat among all the white people at the front next to her father, her new family, they told her, and the priest ready to baptise her, Elizabeth — and then to run home as fast as she could, always turning away from the shop windows which exhibited their sales of collars and padlocks, and the signs in the window of some negro or negress for sale, or a notice of a runaway.

She had heard the gentleman as she came out of the shop, 'Little girl with the pretty ribbons, how many more of those would you like?' Her presence of mind told her not to talk to a stranger. Lady Betty's caution was constantly remembered. But then she kept with her plan to visit the church, thinking she would above all be safe there in that sanctuary where her mother, or the spirit of her mother, lived. She had noticed that the church was empty. She sat in a pew near the entrance. The organist was practising and she allowed the music to calm the alarm she felt at hearing the voice of the gentleman outside the shop. She wished now that she had gone straight home.

The dramatic organ recital descended into the quiet notes of a repeated fugue, and it was then, as if part of this music, that a gentle voice just behind her spoke into her ear the repeated question, 'Little girl with the pretty ribbons, how many more of those would you like?' She was shaken out of her reverie and felt stuck to where she sat when suddenly the innocence of the question about pretty ribbons changed to the snarl of a harsh voice, whispered and rasping, telling her to move to the side door of the church and to obey what he was telling her, not to struggle or to make a scene or he would kill her. She heard a scraping along the floor and saw the man pulling a rough sack with a chain. She understood at once his intention. She felt a heavy hand clamped on her shoulder and then the voice returned to its soft allure, talking about ribbons and other attractions. She did not turn around to identify the voice, but could feel the bulk of the man, could smell his stinking breath. He forced her to the side entrance. At the crescendo that sounded from the organ recital, he stumbled between the pews where he was pushing her. She made use of this advantage to break from his clutches, and took her chance to run as fast as she could out of the church and down the street to her Master's house. Lydia came to her rescue as she banged and screamed at the front door, rather than at the entry to the kitchen below the street.

❧ THESE WERE STORIES Elizabeth wanted to tell her children. But, how should she tell them? How to explain it all? She had had to learn that the word *home* changed its meaning many times, and depended on who spoke it and with what meaning they gave to it. She wanted her children to feel at home in this country.

'I better go up now, Ma'am. Mr d'Aviniere seems very late.'

'Yes, Lydia. It's unusual. Thank you for everything.'

Elizabeth was anxious about Johnny's condition. He had given them so many frights in his short life. She felt sure he had a fever developing. She went back to her writing as she waited up for her husband. She returned to the sequence of her story as the fragments of memory arose.

4

BRIGHT-BRIGHT LIGHT. Green-green trees. Scarlet flowers. There were such blue skies that could turn black. There were vast clouds seeming like caravans travelling across the skies. There was sudden rain. The music was played with castanets, those maracas, which accompanied her mother's flamenco which she had learned from the Spanish, dancing for John Lindsay upon the deck.

Captain John Lindsay's eyes were constantly searching through the sailors for any untoward and riotous movement because of the dance and Maria Belle's beauty. No man would dare touch her. She belonged to him. He had bought her upon the auction block.

Dido saw what he, John Lindsay, her father, for so he was, her mother told her, saw and spoke of in the intimacy of that cabin where she had been conceived, maybe, and born, maybe, in the snugness of his bunk. 'They bring a woman from the lower deck who was a midwife for your birth. We was lucky. I could've lose you,' her mother told her.

Dido still felt his gestures, his finger on her cheekbone tracing there as he spoke. 'There's an olive ripple in your skin,' he said, 'that enhances, what's there, the black colour.' He said that it heightened the ebony of her African black. 'It's a combination most extraordinary. You're my girl. It's my blood that flows in your veins. You're indeed a *belle* like your mother.'

'Don't call her that,' her mother said, angrily. 'Is a dirty word.'

Her father laughed and tickled her so that she too laughed.

Her mother scowled. 'She not to become no *belle*.'

There was so much travel. It was after, or during a battle, after leaving Jamaica, and crossing the channel to Cuba and then along the north coast to Havana. She thought it was then. It was after seeing the burning warships of the Spanish and the castle taken, and her father besmirched by his captaincy upon the deck with the smoke of guns and the burning ships. He descended to the cabin to the safety of herself and her mother. He was swearing that he should never have brought them into this present danger. He swore that it was his love for her, and his inability to leave her, to ever have her out of his touch.

Now they were on their voyage to England. Dido climbed the ladder on her mother's legs with her eyes, knowing and never daring to ask her the origin of those stripes indelibly seared into her flesh since she was a child, the sutures on her ankles. She fingered the lattice traced upon her back, which, with time and a sort of healing, had become a filigreed pattern that she had heard John Lindsay describing in a whisper the other side of the partition on the ship. 'Adds to your beauty, my darling', much like the crinkled scar upon her brow, which she had seen him more than once kiss and stroke. Had it been his whip that bruised her brow or the cruelty of some other in her past? He would try to assuage those wounds long after the wounding.

Two Africans were drumming. They had allowed them to keep their drums. Dido's father said, 'It's not usual.'

His second in command advised against the custom, saying, 'It's savagery,' himself finding it difficult to resist the rhythm or the sight of the beautiful dancing Maria Belle. He had had to bite his lips and swallow his words fast because he had spoken of her in that way, which, even if his captain suspected savagery in her, would not have another talk of her like that.

'She dances like an angel,' he said. Sometimes he described her as a fiery bird, when she was in a trance with castanets and stamping her heels upon the deck, and when she lifted her swishing skirts about her legs and her ankles, barefooted, standing on the tips of her toes, as if she might leap into flight.

'I fly back to Africa, come and catch me,' she said to him.

In the night, on the other side of the partition, it sounded very different to her *savagery*, which all the others seemed to enjoy in the circle upon the deck. She glowed then, all of a sweat in the end and used a blue kerchief to wipe her brow, which she tied around her neck. But still it trickled, that stream of salty sweat into the gully of her bosom, where her young daughter so often laid her head for her comfort, all eyes for her upon the deck, the fiery bird, leaping. A sailor once caught her at the railings, and her father ran towards them and took her into his arms, knocking the sailor to the floor.

That may well have been upon the ship to *home*, or on another ship sailing up the islands. Or, may it have been in their house behind the white picket fence in Pensacola at the corner of the street? Her mother was telling her father that he had to learn to play with her.

'Take the child and play with she.'

He did. The captain of the *Devonshire* obeyed.

Dido cried, 'Mammy, Mammy.'

Her father despaired, calling out to Maria Belle, 'The child does not trust me. You must carry her.'

She laughed, enjoying his hopelessness. 'In time,' she said. 'In time you will be romancing her as you do me.'

He laughed and picked up the child again to carry her.

'Mammy, mammy,' Dido cried once more.

'You want Mammy?' He answered, 'while here is your Dada, Captain of the *Devonshire*.'

As Dido and her mother descended to the lower deck, she told her daughter not to look, not to listen to the sound of the chains in the coffle dragged along the boards, iron on wood, constantly tugged and rattled, cries of pain, cries for help. They were carrying prisoners, maybe even slaves, to be illegally sold in England.

Is it night?' Dido asked her father.

'No, my pet,' he answered. 'It's the middle of the day.' He laughed, taking a pleasure in her innocence. She had learned to know his teasing was affection. Then she knew they were in another country. Her first glimpse of it was while standing on deck with him and seeing the neat fields with hedges and stonewalls defined and etched white against a pewter sky. Then they entered a large river, overhung with shrieking gulls and sails that hung limp in the early morning quiet, reflected in the river's mirror. 'This is England, pet.' She heard his voice distinctly, another voice altogether different from her mother's. He focused on his geography lessons, his fingers pointing. Dido then realised that this new place was altogether distant from where they had come from, the place they had left behind with its blue-green sea, palm trees and chattel houses down by the harbour where the clamour and the cries arose. Santa Rosa Island lay across the bay from Pensacola. Would her mother return there without her? She did not ask. They were always so caught up in each other's arms, with her looking on, peeping in on them, separate from them.

She had slept by and by, in fits and starts, while they were upon the sea, and that was why she had thought it must still be night, so dark it was. It was quite still, the ship gently moving on the river's tide, moored, and its rigging creaking; the jangling halyards, resonant bells that she never learned to rid her head of whenever this beginning time came back to her.

Dido's mother whispered in her ear, 'Is the Thames.' She did not at first know what she meant. When she looked out of the porthole, she explained that it was the name of the river and that they were in London. Everything was new and different. The deck was so finely sprinkled all white with the morning light illumining the fall that dawn of their arrival. 'Snow,' she whispered again in her child's ear, her cheek upon hers, pulling her shawl about her child's shoulders. Her mother had never seen snow but she told her how her English mistress in Pensacola had once told her how to recognise the white drifts which were building in the wind, whipping up over the river and covering the roofs of the houses and the boards on the docks at Deptford.

Dido's father took her hand tightly as they prepared to leave the deck and descend from the ship to the dock; words she learned upon the voyage, words and sounds deep below deck on a bunk next to his cabin. Her mother travelled separately. 'The child will travel with me,' her father ordered.

Dido cried out for her, not understanding. She kept crying, her mother taken off in a carriage, her father lifting her away. She was so small in such a big, busy world. She remembered her father explaining as her mother was escorted off by two of the crew, whom her father trusted. She had seen them often in his company while they were at sea. He insisted on having her near to him. He could be gentle and kind, but she had seen and heard him speak harshly to the sailors. 'You must not let her wander over the ship and be lost,' he commanded. It was something distinct, that note of authority in his voice. 'I'll not have your life endangered, abandoned, and a fire and brimstone will fall upon the man who is ever responsible for your disappearance.' He added, 'That man who is responsible for your capture must fear for his own life.'

Dido looked up at him, not understanding fully what he meant, but she remembered the word *capture*. Capture did occur from time to time, it seemed: capture and selling, put upon the auction block. It was this that he explained to her mother as if she would ever need such explanation. Had it escaped his memory how he had bought her mother? 'She must not be captured, I will not have her sold on. I will not see a daughter of mine standing on an auction block in the market place, having her teeth examined as if she's a horse, her breasts fondled and her arse slapped by some brigand.'

Those words *capture, selling, auction block* were like a threat, a fear laid upon Dido for her survival. She grew up quickly in this regard, constantly fearful and suspicious.

ɕ ELIZABETH WENT OVER the facts again and again. She wrote them out. She and her mother had both been his slaves. Her mother had been paid for, and Elizabeth was, by law, a slave's daughter. Her father was their master. They were his property. She learned all of this in England. There had been so much to learn, day after day, for years.

Was it then, with the ships burning like a pyre on a far shore that he was inspired to name her what he always called her after that time, Dido? It sounded to her mother and to herself, Elizabeth supposed, like the playful, affectionate diminutive for a child. She became his Dido. *You are my Dido.*

Of course, it was her mother who was his true queen of Carthage, neither she nor Dido knowing the terrible story at that time and of that lady and her love for someone called Aeneas. But, with her education, from the books in her Master's library at Bloomsbury at first and then at Caen Wood, she learned also that it was the cruel custom of slave owners to give their slaves what they called classical names, adding insult to injury.

It was difficult to stay away from the story and difficult to know how to tell it: the black queen who climbed upon the pyre, her self-immolation when deserted by her true love. And Dido, that silly name. What a silly name for a girl like her, Elizabeth thought. That it was used for so long shocked her. She felt freed of that name now.

Her father had been a romantic. He was always that little boy who had joined the navy looking for adventure at the age of twelve.

Imagine! He give you the name of a queen. This was one of the last words her mother spoke to her about her father as she boarded the ship to leave London. Then she added: *You will never be no queen, girl. Watch yourself. I go send for you.*

⟨ DIDO'S FATHER POINTED out of the carriage window through the darkness to a glow that came nearer each time Dido looked at it, a distant fire that threw shimmers of shadows upon the expanse of snow, a vast waste that compared only to the ever-expanding sea that she had grown to stare at on his ship. Distance terrified her. What frightened her more now was immediately churned to mush beneath the horses' hooves and the wheels of the swiftly travelling carriage as they journeyed through the narrow streets, with the overhanging buildings, out to beyond the city. *Slush*. He leaned closer to her cheek and whispered in her ear, 'London. It is all London, pet,' as if she would now be able to fit it altogether, the puzzle, with what she knew of things before and what was to lie ahead, all expectation eluding her. They had left her mother in a small room in Deptford.

'Is my mother gone?' She asked him.

'No,' he said. 'You will see her soon. She will not leave you.'

Dido and her father had left Deptford and gone far out of the city, climbing through orchards covered in snow and along a river he called the Fleet. 'It rises in the hills above,' he said. It flowed so swiftly just there at the side of the road, their carriage managing the rough contours of the banks as they climbed among the snow-covered hills of Highgate and Hampstead, then down among pastures, and up again through farms, the river a stream at times, then a torrent, to the house at Caen Wood on its snowy terrace looking out at the darkness and into the hollows of the immediate environs, the lamps of tinkers among the far woods, and in the further distance the amber glow of the oil lamps in the city of London, which they had left behind.

'The river's power comes from its two sources, from two different springs,' her father instructed her in an effort to entertain her thoughts and distract her from the departure from her mother.

'You will be meeting here with your great-uncle and aunt,' her father said to Dido as they alighted from the carriage, 'He's the most powerful man in all of England under the King.' He carried her in his arms across the snow to the entrance, and then into the room all warm and aglow with a huge fire of logs. The great-uncle and aunt were indeed great, very tall and dressed extravagantly, and staring down at her.

The great-uncle, with a glint in his eye and a chuckle on his lips, said, 'So this is the little girl you have brought us.' He spoke and looked like a figure in a portrait. The great-aunt looked anxious, wringing her hands and then stooping to get hold of Dido's hand and leading her, crushed against her skirts, lost among brocades, closer to the fire which felt to her like the heat in Pensacola.

'What have you got there?' the great-uncle pointed to her bag.

'My belongings.'

'Your belongings?'

'Yes.'

She noticed the great-uncle's cold reserve, despite his chuckle, a certain sharpness in his speech, an ironic humour she came to understand many years later in her Master.

The great-aunt was distressed. Dido learned this from snatches of talk between her and her father. They were broken sentences, disconnected, left to her to make sense of alone in her room that night. 'You have surely seen our streets... Greenwich, Deptford... when those ships from the West Indies are in port, the stench is unbearable. What is her mother's name?'

'Her name's Maria Belle.'

'A family name, Belle?'

'Her mother... I've found her a house. She's got her wits about her. But she won't be able to protect her child.'

'You need a home for her, John,' his aunt said with concern.

'I must marry and then I'm to go to India. I'm to serve between the East India Company and the Nawabs.'

Dido tried to thread these snatches of her father's and the great-aunt's words together into some kind of pattern. But then there was more to sort out.

'Your uncle will do anything for the family. You're his sister's son. He'll be on the bench all day. But I'll have to become a kind of mother to the girl. I won't know how...'

'You can't be her mother. She's got a mother. You'll be her guardian. I know you'll be kind. You know the streets of this city are treacherous with catchers, only too eager to slap irons on her, throw her onto a ship bound for Kingston, Bridgetown or elsewhere. My daughter, just a mite, will be snatched. The mixed ones are the most desired.'

John Lindsay floundered under interrogation, trying to explain the impossible to his aunt and uncle.

'And this woman?'

'You know I can't make her my wife. I cannot make her a lady. My knighthood, besides. It's impossible. Their skin speaks volumes before they even enter a room or dare to speak in their lilting sentences. It is unfortunate. I do confess to have been smitten for the first time by the beauty of a woman.'

Dido saw her father stumble further with his explanations and requests. She could see that the great-uncle and the great-aunt did not approve.

It was freezing in the room now for her small, unaccustomed body, even with the great singing fire in the grate. There was this chill in everything, her father squeezing her hand on his departure, offering her up and taking her back all at the same time. 'I'll return to take you to your mother. She will not leave you. You will see her.'

He had delivered her mother from hell he had once told her.

When Dido visited her mother at Deptford, she argued with her small child when she could not be comforted at the idea of parting from her, could not believe that she was leaving her, giving her over to those other people. 'He rescuing you from that hell, my child. You is his flesh. Blood. Don't be stubborn, girl.'

And still Dido asked herself why, a child who knew that without questions she was lost.

'For there's no liberty for you where I've got to eventually go child, where I can't give you liberty, where I can't be sure that I can keep you safe. You must accustom yourself to your father people.' Dido's mother was adamant that she might not be able to defend her daughter against capture. She asked her to remember their life in Pensacola, how outside the stockade of her father's house, outside the picket fence, not far from the fort, treachery laid snares no matter manumissions and talk of freedom.

'Catchers? They prowl this city too.' She told her mother, repeating her father. 'They're the agents of powerful men.'

'We can't change the colour of we skin, maybe you survive better with that *blanche* that is his.'

'He says they like that the best.'

'You listening to big people too much.'

She would be prized upon the auction block for her youth, her strength, her ability to breed, and most dangerously, for her beauty, a mother's prejudice, and that *blanche*. She called her yellow. 'They would make you a *belle*, my darling, and that's a cruel thing, a terrible bondage, double bound, black and a girl child.'

Belle was a name Dido kept or did they keep it for her, keep telling her that was her name, her mother's name, Maria Belle, a slave name. Two names, one real, one their dressed up whore. She bequeathed it to her. It was her mother's name that she carried, not her father's. Dido Belle. He did not bestow his name upon her. She was never to be a Lindsay.

When did Dido first hear the name that she learned meant Tuesday? It was part of a story she half remembered. On the shore there was a big white castle in the story. *Elmina...they call it.* It was her mother's voice. *Abenaa, it means Tuesday. Elmina, that is the castle.*

And all along the rocky shores below the castle walls and in the inlets canoes were putting out to sea. On the sands, white merchants exchanged gold with Africans for Africans. In the outer harbour the slaver ship with a belly full of sails waited for its cargo. While one departed another arrived. It was an endless fleet that came from Bristol, Liverpool and London, crossing back and forth across the ocean, drawing a triangle.

Dido looked out for her father's intermittent visits in the dark of night to Bloomsbury Square, or his carriage wheels announcing his arrival on the gravel of the drive through the trees of Fir Hill, then coming to rest before the entrance of the villa at Caen Wood, that white-columned Palladian retreat among the Highgate and Hampstead Hills above Kentish Town and the city far off in the valley upon the banks of the thronged Thames.

Beyond was Deptford where her mother was. She would not leave her. That was the promise.

Who was she to believe?

5

ELIZABETH'S FATHER HAD brought her mother and herself to another climate and geography. She eventually fell in love with London but she continued to dream if she might ever return to where she had come from, ever see her mother again. Some people asked her why she had fallen in love with this place. She had no simple answer. Here she was Elizabeth d'Aviniere, Lizzie. She relished her names. She was no longer Dido.

She had to be careful to clear up the evidence of the night: the basin at her bedside, a spittoon, sodden linen rags, those stained with blood. She washed them out herself instead of leaving them for Lydia. She did not want Lydia to notice anything and suspect the worse and tell the news more urgently than she would wish her family to know. Coughing up blood was not altogether a new development, and it had been less until just recently. That gave her a little hope. Her remedies were kept in vials, others as powders in boxes. She returned them to the drawer of her medicine chest; a veritable apothecary.

Her husband, but not the children, was aware of the truth. They had to be protected, particularly now with this clear danger of getting lost and the fear of capture. Her possibly imminent death was not something that should be put upon them. What they surmised of their mother's changed situation was not discussed openly with them. Yes, the coughing could not be disguised. They would look at her asking questions without words. Charles particularly was alert to his mother's weakness. Johnny's sympathy was given quietly during their intimate moments. William Thomas noticed more than she realised. He had his questions. After one of Dr Featherstone's visits she had overheard Charles telling Lydia he thought that his mother was dying. It made her pause on the stairs to hear Lydia's reply and his comment.

'Don't talk nonsense, child, your mother is as fit as a fiddle. She just gets tired sometimes.'

But he insisted. 'The doctor was here for a long time. I'm sure that Mama is dying.'

Elizabeth sat with a cup of tea and watched the early morning sun travel over the brick wall at the end of the garden. The wet, grey slates on the roofs sweated the colour of mercury. There had been some rain in the early hours.

What a mystery it all was: her children, her husband, her garden and the weather, and then all that lay beyond, the tall ships on the river, the wars in Europe, Napoleon, the trade, and so much more that needed adjusting in this world that came to disturb her and threaten the lives of her boys. The war invaded her mind if she read the newspapers. The noise across the countries of Europe was the sound of soldiers marching and pillaging. What would be the future of her boys? *Is cargo, we is cargo*, her mother's words kept on interrupting. Trade was everything, they said. And, indeed, it was everything to them, building the cities of Bristol, Liverpool and London. They told her they were thriving. The cotton came, ready picked, from America for the first mills in the north.

Elizabeth had once heard of a woman who had called out for her mother as she was nearing her end. *Come and get me*, she had cried. She felt that she was both here and over there, always in that place of hurricanes and heat. Everything was so vivid in her memory, the terror and the joy. It was how she kept her mother alive in her mind.

She watched the light congregate more intensely upon the ochre brick before it then vanished under the veil of a cloud pulled over the sun. The morning mist was still rising from the nearby river. The cry of a gull brought the river closer to her garden.

She looked up from her writing. She wanted to try and live each of these days with passion. She hoped she was going to be allowed to leave with some grace.

'Sorry to interrupt you, Ma'am. You left this for me to wash?' Lydia stood there with linens folded over her arm. Elizabeth was embarrassed.

She thought she had cleaned up all the evidence from the night before. 'Where did you find that, Lydia? I'm sorry.'

'Don't be Ma'am. On the scullery floor, Ma'am.'

'What is it? Let me see.' She stretched out her arm, pretending to avoid the evidence of the blood stains.'

'Your bed linen, Ma'am?'

Lydia was no fool. Elizabeth knew that she was aware that her girlhood condition had worsened. Lydia had cleared up and cleaned up all her life since she was a little girl in her own mother's house, looking after smaller brothers and sisters back in Dublin. Mess was not something to disturb her. They had both grown to see more of themselves in each other; Lydia having to leave her mother in Dublin to come to London for work. But this morning, Lydia seemed to play the game of pretending as if she had not taken in the evidence. Elizabeth knew that Lydia could not bear to think of her leaving her small children and was worrying herself about what would become of them, imagining the boys left motherless with their father.

'Lydia, you know all there is to know about me. You must remember the expenditure for the course of asses's milk, which was prescribed by the doctor who travelled up from Kentish Town to examine me.'

'Of course, Ma'am. What brings back that memory?'

'You must remember your walks to the apothecary in Highgate Village for the powders and tinctures. I remember it myself vividly, all being noted in Miss Anne's ledger: £3 4s 1d.'

'Miss Anne, she was a one, wasn't she? She and her sister Miss Marjory, his Lordship's nieces...'

'We were a house of serving women, Lydia.'

'Scuttling around...'

'Yes, fussing over the ageing and increasingly demented Lord.'

'You were the one, then, Ma'am, picking up soiled linen in those days, running up and down the backstairs at his beck and call. You, caught between, as always. What days they were.'

'Yes, I was fond of Miss Marjory. She looked out for me. Miss Anne? No. She had a sharp tongue and an ungrateful manner.'

'Those two...'

'But I was thinking of your fears over your settlement. Those women in the papers who were like characters in a novel...'

'Tabitha Reynolds and Hannah Wright, those poor servants, their stories in *The Advertiser*...'

'Hannah Phillips from Shropshire, and yes, Hannah Wright from Derbyshire.'

From right across the country the cases had constantly come up in her Master's court. He would not reform the unjust legislation within the Poor Laws though he hated to pronounce on them when they came before him on appeal.

Elizabeth and Lydia got caught up in the terrifying stories of the serving women captured in the thicket of the law, cases unattended, thrown out, livelihoods threatened forever through losing their relief from the parish because they had not fulfilled the requirements of their settlement in relation to the terms of their employment.

'And what of Charlotte Howe?' Elizabeth remembered her particularly. The story of the woman who had been bought in America as a *negro slave*, coming to England as part of the chattels of her Master; the woman's predicament in neither being hired because a slave and then losing her service, and that this meant that she had no legal position. She walked out of her position as a way to free herself.

But to what, what was her freedom? 'She was accused of being drunk on freedom. Imagine.'

'We were all Mansfield's women, weren't we Ma'am?'

'We were, Lydia.' They both laughed. 'We were. But you must know now, Lydia, that when I'm gone Mr d'Aviniere will look out for you. Your position here is secure. You will not lose your employment, so your settlement, your relief, will be secured. The boys will need you more than ever then, as you well know. My husband will not be able to do without you.'

'I don't want any of this talk about you going. You're not going anywhere just yet. Your boys, your husband, as strong as he looks, will be lost without you. You're not going anywhere...'

'Lydia...'

'You just get on with your writing and leave the chores to me. Let me get this laundry all washed, dried and folded away before Mr d'Aviniere and the boys get back.'

Elizabeth settled down to some sewing and knitting, her writing would have to wait that morning. There were garments to be left for each of her boys. She had not managed many woollens in the long winter the year before. Only one each, matching, had been completed for Charles and John. Her writing competed for her time. She took a peep at her last entry. Another woollen must be knitted for William Thomas. He was quickly out-growing his. Then the cottons, they had to have fresh shirts. It felt as if she wanted to have a hold on their future, clothes that would last, that the boys would grow into. It would have to be Lydia to fold and unfold them and lay them down in drawers, help arms into sleeves, button up buttons, carry on as she already was doing.

Mrs Halifax and Mrs R came in that afternoon to help with knitting and sewing. 'You must not worry, dear. Rest assured, we'll be here, won't we Mrs R?'

She did not care to look at herself in the glass now. But she had to continue to make an effort for her husband and the children. Lydia was right, 'For yourself Ma'am, your pretty self.' Lydia had reminded her that they had thought her pretty back at Caen Wood. Though they had not said so. It was always *woolly hair, tawny* and *nigger*. Those were the words of some below stairs. This thought took her right back to her arrival at Caen Wood and Bloomsbury Square.

⟨ 'LET US SEE how she behaves and how Lady Betty manages her,' her father had said to his uncle.

He was about to depart for India, as he had told Dido earlier. As he prepared to leave, she lay down on the floor and screamed louder and louder. She would not be comforted by either Lady Betty or Lydia.

They had spent his last days at Caen Wood and then he left from Bloomsbury on the Monday. Dido felt so tiny, while her father and his uncle and aunt were tall and stood over her. They were walking out to the carriage together and waiting in the Square outside the front door for it to take her father away. He got in and it pulled away with the neighing horses, and she stood and stared till it disappeared down the street towards St George's church where she had been baptised. She did not think she would see her mother or her father again.

Dido did not stop her sobbing.

It was dark and she was taken downstairs where there was a table with a place set for her to sit and have her supper. Her father's aunt left her there with several young women who fussed around doing jobs, preparing a meal. This meal was taken away on trays. They left her to cry. She sat and watched and slowly she stopped crying.

'You cry all your tears? Eat something now. For sure you'll starve if you don't. I'm Lydia.'

Dido stared at the red hair falling over her face. She learned the word *auburn*. 'Such lovely auburn hair,' one of the other girls called it.

She rested her head on the table and fell asleep. Then she was being lifted and taken up flights of stairs.

'You must go and say good night to the master and mistress in the drawing room before we put you to bed,' Lydia told her.

'So there you are, Dido.'

This was the same man, her father's uncle, the most powerful under the king.

'Come, sit here.'

He pointed to a stool near him. Dido had seen him resting his feet on that stool when she first entered the room. She sat and stared at him and then lowered her eyes and then she looked around the room again, at the mirrors and the paintings and at the high windows and the curtains. She felt so little and everything else in the room seemed so large and tall. The fire burned as she looked into it. She felt that it held a mystery that she thought she must find out about. Then one of the logs collapsed. It fell further into the fire and flared up, scaring her and banishing any thoughts of a mystery she had to discover.

The tall people talked and she did not understand what they were saying. She kept staring into the fire, which had settled and there was a sense of that mystery again, as it sang, hissed and crackled.

'My dear, you know it's only recently I alerted you to the entry, either in *The Daily Advertiser* or was it *The Public Advertiser* listing there among the items of a carriage, a gelding and a mare, a black boy of eleven for sale or auction.' Lady Betty smiled nervously. 'You must be tired after your journey, Dido. Lydia will take you up to bed.'

She was falling asleep on the way. It was a small room at the top of the house. It was a tall tall house with so many stairs, so many landings, right to the last floor with the tops of the trees just outside the window and the sky so close when it was clear and there was a certain slant of light. There had been sun, but it was now cold cold.

'Molly, look. She is so black all over,' the girl called Lydia was saying to another girl as they undressed her and tucked her hands into the long sleeves of a nightdress. 'She's like a floppy doll, a little black doll. All that frizzy hair.'

In the morning, Dido came down and down the stairs to the pantry at the very bottom of the house. She had her breakfast alone. She looked up to the street level through the railings. She sat and watched the horses' legs and the carriage wheels passing in Bloomsbury Square.

'You're in a world of your own child. Cat bite your tongue?' Lydia said and continued sweeping around her ankles. 'You better eat your bread and butter. For sure, there's no more food till later.'

She looked up at Lydia and then she looked up to the horses' legs and the carriage wheels and the leaves falling in the wind. It was only half a world. She could not see the tops of the trees. She could not see the sky. The passersby were only legs, people with chopped off bodies and heads.

'Where are you, child? You need some work to do. Stop your day dreaming.' That was Lydia again.

❧ 'OH, MY GOD, Lydia, you've given me such a fright. Where was I? You were there at Bloomsbury just now. I was a little girl. Do you remember? The wheels of the carriages spinning and spinning seen from below, looking up from the kitchens, the horses' hooves, the leaves in the wind?' Elizabeth remembered when she was so little. 'You were a girl of fourteen. Do you remember how you undressed me for bed and found me *so black all over*? You thought I was dirty.'

'Ma'am? That's impossible I couldn't be so stupid. Ma'am I must tell you...'

Lydia was not listening to Elizabeth's story of the past, the pages stacked on her writing box.

'Yes, what?'

'It's Johnny, Ma'am...'

'What? Where's he?'

'Down the street...'

'What do you mean?'

Elizabeth felt that her worse fears were to be realised.

'At Mrs Halifax.'

'We can't leave him there.'

Billy was hiding behind Lydia's skirts.

'What's going on? Where's your brother?'

'With Mrs Halifax, Mama.'

'Tell me. What's happened at Mrs Halifax? Do you remember when he was a baby, Lydia? In the end she had no milk left. He nearly died then. What's happened now?'

'He collapsed, Ma'am.'

'Collapsed! What've you been doing that he's collapsed?'

Lydia told of how she had taken the boys off Mr d'Aviniere and had gone for a walk to the Gardens, the usual, down to the river. It had happened so suddenly. Johnny had a cold and had been complaining of a sore throat. He had been weak of late generally and not keeping up with her, dawdling behind on their walks.

'I know about his cold and sore throat. I'm not blaming you Lydia.'

Elizabeth felt guilty herself for not having noticed how suddenly he had worsened.

'Mama, Mama, he was breathless. He was red in the face, all red. Then pale, so pale...'

'Sweetheart, don't you worry. We'll go and see what's happened.'

'Come, Lydia, fetch my coat. I'll have to walk slowly.'

Elizabeth and Lydia got Johnny home. A message was sent to Mr d'Aviniere to bring the doctor with him. Johnny's glands were swollen. He lay on the sofa in the drawing room at first, and then with the help of Seamus, he was moved to the box room.

Elizabeth worried about her ability to care for her son, given her failing strength. She forced herself to sit at his bedside while they waited for the doctor. She made sure that he drank enough water. Lydia brought him his special jelly. His breathing was becoming more and more difficult.

'Stay calm. Try this, sweetheart. Your favourite, raspberry.'

Lydia looked in. 'Is there anything else, Ma'am...?'

'No. Yes, please, fill the glass with water.' She went to the door to speak with Lydia. She needed the doctor to prescribe some remedy. She could not understand how Johnny had got so weak, so quickly. She had not noticed such a drastic change in his condition. It had all come on so suddenly. It must have been one of those chills. The weather had been so changeable, a cold wind and then warm and wet.

'I'll just bring that water, Ma'am...'

'Yes, and keep the boys quiet with reading downstairs.'

'Yes, Ma'am, and I'll listen out for the doctor and Mr d'Aviniere, Ma'am.'

'Your boy needs the comfort of his mother. You must sit with him.' Dr Featherstone explained what might have to be done if the breathing became impossible. He might have to make an incision in Johnny's trachea to improve his breathing. He looked gravely at John and Elizabeth d'Aviniere, and then at their son on the bed.

Elizabeth and her husband were stunned. They asked if the doctor would operate soon.

'We've not got to that stage as yet,' Dr Featherstone explained. 'You may have heard that we call the illness the strangling angel, this disease, diphtheria,' he added, packing up his bag of remedies. He explained that the medication would soothe for a while, but do little to help the restriction to Johnny's breathing in the long run. 'We have to trust to him regaining his strength and natural health. He was the weaker of the twins, yes?'

John and Elizabeth both nodded, turning to look at their son.

Charles and Billy were peeping in at the door but not allowed into the room. Elizabeth did not want the boys to hear what the doctor was saying. It sounded like murder, yet it was meant to keep Johnny alive. Dr Featherstone took his leave, but promised to return later. He said that he had to be called if the breathing got worse.

John and Elizabeth took it in turns to sit with Johnny. Lydia brought up hot and cold drinks and more jelly. 'Easy to slip down,' she said to Elizabeth.

Mr d'Aviniere had to get back to work. With Seamus in the house, Elizabeth had sufficient support for lifting Johnny if needed. That afternoon Mrs Halifax visited with an egg custard. 'I told Mrs R I've got to make sure that baby we delivered gets strong again.' Johnny had to listen, not for the first time, to the story of his birth. 'What a surprise you and your brother were, twins, yes, but so different. Weren't they Mrs d'Aviniere?'

'I think we should let him rest now, Mrs Halifax. It's kind of you to come and egg custard is one of your favourites. Isn't it, darling?'

Mrs Halifax, for all her kindness and understanding, could persist, at times, with a patronising attitude that Elizabeth was not keen to hear that afternoon. She preferred to encourage her neighbour's more tolerant characteristics.

Aesop's Fables were Johnny's chosen stories. He smiled and even laughed at the tales with his own interpretations. Today it was the tale of The Crow and the Pitcher.

'Little by little does the trick,' Johnny said with a weak, disturbing wheeze. Charles stood in the doorway and talked to his brother about what was happening at school, trying to amuse him. 'You'll soon be up, Johnny.'

'That's enough, Charles. Johnny can't do much more talking.'

It was sad to see the twins separated .

Dr Featherstone visited again that afternoon. After checking on Johnny, he expressed alarm over Elizabeth's coughing. 'Your lungs must be in a state.' He then returned to his concern for his patient.

The doctor explained how easy it was for children to just slip away. 'You're lucky to have had safe births and your other boys so healthy.'

He smiled encouragingly at Johnny before he took his leave. 'Keep him warm and calm.' Johnny looked more diminished than ever, as if he was shrinking. His two small eyes were peering over his sheets pulled up to his chin.

Elizabeth was pleased that the doctor had not mentioned again the incision in the throat.

As she said goodbye at the front door, Dr Featherstone turned and said. 'I'm very happy to come to visit your son at any time. Reassure your husband. I could see that he was a little worried when I first came into your house, wondering, I expect, what I would make of things. You understand, don't you?'

'I'm very grateful for your visit doctor. I suppose I do expect the best from a doctor. I do appreciate your visits. My husband has had to be very careful. He may seem suspicious at times. Our boys are our treasures.'

Spring was a wonderful solace. Elizabeth felt invigorated. It brought a respite. She postponed her writing for the moment. She and Johnny sat by the window in the box room and identified the different plants that were coming up in her garden below. He learned their names. They made lists. She propped him up with pillows in an armchair so that he could lie back and look into the well of the garden. He sat in the best way to breathe more easily. As they talked, he wrote down his lists: box, holly, laurel, yew and privet.

'The box and the privet are for making Mama's hedges. See the patterns.' Elizabeth hinted and pointed at what was to come, where they would climb on the fences and the trellis against the brick wall. 'Let us list the shrubs and climbers: honeysuckle, lavender, lilac, viburnum, Virginia creeper and the passion flower.'

'What about the roses?' Johnny asked.

'Yes, let's write down the different names. You'll have to look for these as they begin to come out in June. All these new importations.'

She looked at her boy and wondered if he would last till the summer.

'We're going to get you better.'

'I will Mama.'

'There is the Apothecary's rose, yes? They're many stories of its origin with its blood red colour.'

Elizabeth explained how they made beads from its petals. 'That one will be flowering at the bottom of the garden. Nearer, just under the window is the *Rosa Mundi*. There is the *Rosa Gallica*.' Last of all, she pointed out the common moss rose and the *Rose de Meaux*. 'They will bloom on the arbour where I like to sit with my writing box.'

Johnny was trying to pay attention as she pointed out the plants. Elizabeth could see he had a slight fever and asked Lydia to go with a message to Dr Featherstone.

'Be patient, darling, look at Mama and how she copes, breathe slowly, try not to gasp. Try and rest a little. We'll leave the writing down of the herbs and bulbs for later.'

They both rested. They both read, Elizabeth reading to her son his favourite fables.

From the window she saw a blackbird flying in and out of the laurel bush. She knew that it was building a nest. She wondered how safe it was there from the fox or the neighbour's cat.

Johnny was coughing again, becoming breathless. She fixed his pillow to allow him to breathe more easily. He was then quiet and fell asleep.

Elizabeth had brought her writing box up to Johnny's room to grab moments for her memories and stories. She was taken back to her childhood, drawn to it by Johnny's condition.

〈 'YOUR HAIR IS a tangle, Dido,' Lydia said, 'so difficult to brush, keep it tidy, in plaits.'

Her coughing started and frightened her. She was alone at the top of the house and she thought she would stop breathing, altogether. Lydia was calling for help. 'It's Dido, she can't breathe.'

Lady Betty called up to say that she was coming with the medication. This was when Dido missed her mother the most. She cried out for her. 'Now, Dido, you know that's not possible. Your mother cannot come. Here, drink this. The air in Caen Wood is so much better for you.'

She felt guilty because Lady Betty was trying to be kind. She thought she wanted to be her mother. But she wasn't her mother. Dido was adamant about that. She told Lydia, 'She's not my mother.'

'Dido. You must quiet yourself.'

This was when she felt so very different. She was not like them even if her father was one of them. She did not even talk like them, though her Master commended her for her grammar, but still bemoaned her accent. 'You must try, Dido, to eliminate all that music from your voice and keep your hands to your sides, dear girl. It can be charming to gesticulate but it's more refined to be less mobile.'

Between crying, coughing and not being able to breathe easily, she was in a state, such that she could not be comforted. She heard Lady Betty's footsteps on the stairs. She counted each tread and then she could not hear them anymore. Lydia too had gone back down to the kitchen. She lay alone and felt homesick for her mother. She imagined her living in her small house in Deptford. She would have preferred to be living there with her.

'That would not be proper,' Lady Betty told her, 'for your father's daughter,' she added.

'Why? Is my mother not proper?'

Lady Betty did not answer.

'Because she's a nigger?'

'Dido, we say negro.'

'And me?'
'Mulatto.'
'Mule?'
Lady Betty did not answer.

ᘒ Elizabeth looked in on Johnny. He was sleeping peacefully. She tried to imagine what Dr Featherstone said he would do and what help an incision would make. She tried to understand his medical language. *Trachea* and *tracheotomy*. It was a hole made in the windpipe. She could not imagine how Johnny would survive that kind of operation. She sat and watched. She held his hand. She left him to sleep. Then she thought she had to get him to sit up when he awoke, ease his breathing. They could list the herbs in the garden. He was safe from strange gentlemen on the marshes. But she would not be able to keep him safe if he began to slip away. A *strangling angel* was a frightening image. She sat near to him sharpening her quills.

ᘒ 'Tucked away, my darling. This is better,' John Lindsay said to Maria Belle describing the new house which he had arranged for her in Greenwich on his return from India. 'There should be little danger here rather than on the docks at Deptford, little less bother from the catchers. You and the child must not go out. I've arranged a Mrs Phillips to deliver food and fuel. She can be trusted.'

Dido had spent the week listening to the church bells tolling the time of the services and the clocks the time of the day. The halyards jangled at the end of the street where the wind whipped up the river, through the forest of moored ships with their tall masts like trees at Pensacola. Her mother pointed across the river and said it reminded her of Santa Rosa Island in Pensacola harbour, the view across the water from their house. 'The Isle of Dogs, they call it here,' she said.

Her father had been a reassurance to her mother and herself at that time. 'You see the kind of kind man he is, your father.'

That was her mother comforting Dido as she peeped out of the window at his departure in the carriage carefully curtained from public view, a gentleman in this part of town, leaving from that house, 'where two niggers live,' her mother said, now cross, so she put it that way. 'He is to take a wife,' she told Dido.

There had been the old argument. Her mother could never be his wife. 'What is to become of me?' She asked, as if her daughter knew.

Her parents had been laughing all the night before. She was happy to hear them. It was different the next day just before her father left. Sometimes her mother would laugh at his jokes. She would quote him: 'Queen Charlotte! You should see her face and you will know what I mean. Watch her lips, the flare of the nostrils, the size of the bosom and the roundness of those hips and you'll not be mistaken, that there's Africa in her. There's no mistaking Charlotte of Mecklenburg Strelitz.' She had told him he must not laugh at his queen so, laughing mockingly. The jokes hid her sadness.

Before Dido and her father left her mother's house in Greenwich to return to Bloomsbury, her father said to her mother, 'My uncle and aunt are taking in another child into their home. She's the daughter of my uncle's other nephew and his heir. We're hoping that Dido will be a companion for her.'

Dido overheard them as she played with a doll her father had bought for her.

'A servant, you mean. A slave, perhaps. How could she be a companion?'

'Well, she's my daughter. They do respect that. The girl, Elizabeth, whom they call Beth, has recently lost her mother, Henrietta Frederica. She was Polish. My uncle is doing my cousin a favour as he's engaged in diplomatic work on the continent. He's a favourite of my aunt's.'

'What a lot of names for important people. You'll be far away, with your wife. And your daughter, a servant. I'll have to fare on my own.

This uncle of yours collecting a lot of children which are not his.'

'They're kind people both he and his wife.'

'Yes, but she's also my daughter and the colour of her skin won't change. In this country I'm your slave and you know that that little girl is your slave too. How long this go remain?'

'This is the arrangement of things in the world, woman. You must see your good fortune. You need to be patient.'

'To lose my daughter?'

'To save your daughter.'

'And myself?'

He did not answer.

Dido then returned on the river with her father by ferry from Greenwich to the dock at Blackfriars. She and her father had watched the boats upon the Thames on their way to Blackfriars. 'Learn the names of places,' her father instructed her.

He clutched her hand tightly.

'Fine little negress there, Sir.' Her father shooed the man away, brandishing his cane. Dido clung to her father, hidden beneath his cloak. He kept his arm around her.

All this was in Dido's mind when she got back to Bloomsbury and Lydia came to fetch her and make sure she was dressed appropriately. 'You must make a good impression.'

She was then taken down to Lady Betty's dressing room where they were to have tea. A little girl sat on a stool at the foot of Lady Betty's chair. Lady Betty's sister, Mary, was also there. They both remained sitting when Dido entered the room with Lydia. Lydia presented her. 'The child, Dido, Ma'am,' Lydia giggled.

Lady Betty continued speaking to her sister. 'If only I'd been blessed with my own children. We couldn't refuse our nephew. The child will be like our own daughter.' Dido could imagine her as such.

'The other?' Her sister asked.

Lady Betty did not answer. They then both looked at Dido standing by the door with Lydia.

'Yes, Lydia.'

'Here's the girl, Dido, Ma'am.'

'Very well, Lydia, you can leave now.'

Dido stared at the girl who was sitting on the stool. She looked very sad. She wore a beautiful blue dress.

'Come and sit here, Dido,' Lady Betty invited her with an extended arm. She did not take her hand. She was embarrassed. Dido did not like the dress that she wore. It had an apron that was a drab colour and it had a stain at the waist. Lady Betty directed Dido to the stool on her other side.

She had noticed the little girl raise her eyes at her name when Lydia introduced her and she did so again. This time she noticed a movement on her lips as if to smile and then she looked sad again, lowering her eyes.

'Dido this is Beth who is coming to live with us. Beth this is Dido who lives here. She'll be your companion. I want us to have tea together and then I want you to play. It's fine in the garden at the back of the house. I don't want you playing in the Square.'

'Yes, Lady Betty,' Dido said.

Beth did not say anything.

'Beth?'

'Yes, Lady Betty.'

Dido noticed that her accent was different to Lady Betty's. She remembered her father saying her mother was Polish and that she had died.

Molly entered with a tray, carrying a kettle, teapot and cups and saucers.

'There you are Molly. Is that tea brewed?' Lady Betty was trying to keep everything in order.

'In a moment, Ma'am.' Molly looked bored as she stood there waiting for the tea to brew.

Lady Betty and her sister continued to talk of many matters that Dido did not understand at the time. Beth's father, her Master's nephew, was mentioned. They spoke of the American colonies, something about riots, a tax that was not popular, stamp duty, the loss of a colony. She heard words without meaning. They discussed the dairy and the poultry. They also talked about the house at Caen Wood that had to be decorated and refurbished.

'These activities keep me sane,' Lady Betty argued.

Mary listened sympathetically.

'The thought of having to look after these very different children is already too much for me,' Lady Betty said.

ELIZABETH KNEW NOW how Lady Betty had felt. She herself could not do without her sons. She had been a kind lady. She had been a good woman.

With Johnny's condition worsening, Beth and her plans to visit had gone right out of Elizabeth's mind. She needed to write to her. Beth had written that she wanted to come to London. Then Elizabeth had not heard anymore. They had hardly seen each other since Beth's marriage to Mr Finch-Hatton. They had met at her Master's funeral. Of course they also saw each other at the reading of his will. She visited soon after the birth of William Thomas. That was five years ago. They had not had any contact since then. Why was Beth wishing to visit now? Elizabeth did not know whether she could cope with seeing Beth. Her husband would not be able to bear it.

As the seasons changed, days sped into weeks and Johnny seemed to be rallying. Dr Featherstone said he was surprised how well the boy was doing. But then he said, 'There's always the possibility of a relapse.' To Elizabeth's relief, he did not again mention the incision in Johnny's windpipe.

She saw the doctor out and returned to the box room to be with her son who was now sitting up more than ever before. He was breathing easily.

Family life was restored in the following weeks with much less worry. Martha visited. The boys enjoyed their aunt. It always pleased Elizabeth to see the brother and sister together. Sadly Mr Thomas d'Aviniere was ailing and his death was expected sooner rather than later.

With Johnny so much better, Elizabeth had more time for her writing.

⚜ 'AT THE BULL and Gate Inn in Holborn. Sale and Auction,' Lady Betty read out of the paper.

This was near to where they lived. Dido was not allowed to go into Bloomsbury Square. 'They will catch you, take you to Kingston Town.' Lydia said.

'This terrible story of a girl, sixteen, a negress, a maid, also with smallpox, her left ear bitten off by a dog.' Lady Betty looked at Dido and then put down the paper she was reading from. Her Master looked over his spectacles at her to see what her reaction was to Lady Betty's remarks. Dido had kept her head lowered, but puzzling over these facts read out from the newspaper. *Sale* and *auction* always alarmed her. They were words from Pensacola. These facts persuaded her that Bloomsbury Square was indeed dangerous. Lydia was correct on that point.

After tea that afternoon, Beth and Dido went to visit the Foundling Hospital at Coram Fields with Lady Betty. It was a short walk from Bloomsbury Square.

The foundlings distressed Dido. She feared that she might be put there with them. But who would adopt her? She asked herself this as she looked upon the beseeching faces of mothers with their infants and toddlers at the entrance, hoping some kind woman would take their child, handing them out beseechingly. She was already adopted. But then, why was she thinking of adoption? She had a mother in Greenwich.

Beth and Dido sat next to Lady Betty, the other philanthropic ladies staring at her, wondering, she supposed, at the little *negress* from the Lord Chief Justice, her Master's home.

'They say...' She heard them, hiding their insults in their whispers, in the creak of the chairs, muffled by bonnets and wigs turning here and there for gossip. But still she could hear the horrible words people called her as she passed in the street, trying to hide close to Lady Betty's skirts.

'She's a half-breed, bred in the West Indies. The Chief Justice keeps her in his house, they say...for what?...for what? Well we know...'

Back at Bloomsbury Square, she heard the same insults and suspicions whispered on the stairs. The echoing rooms of the house behind her were full of the noises of busy footsteps, doors that banged between the kitchen and the pantry and echoed in the cellar.

Molly came and swept around Dido's feet. She felt so alone. She went and hid in the library among the stacks of her Master's books.

'Dido, Dido, Dido, where are you?'

It was Beth who became her friend, her first real friend. She remained her friend off and on. She was meant to be a kind of cousin, then she was called a companion, whatever that was, to one who had her meals alone, or with the servants in the pantry. She knew one thing that separated them. It was the colour of her skin and that was connected to her mother being a slave and she also a slave. She heard her mother tell her father that.

᠔ ELIZABETH WENT IN to look in on Johnny. He was sleeping too much. His breathing was laboured. What was in that medication from Dr Featherstone? She wondered whether he should have another dose.

It was not clear whether the medication should be repeated. She sat by her son's bed for the long hours, Lydia looking after Charles and Billy. With her writing box on her lap, she continued to distract herself from her present anxiety with her story.

6

DIDO PEEPED THROUGH the crack in the door of the drawing room in the Bloomsbury house. In her agitated state she stumbled, pushing on the door inadvertently, not as quietly as the kitten they had for mice. She stood transfixed to the spot at the open door and began to sob, more out of fear than any particular sadness, a mixture of nervousness and many emotions she hardly understood or knew how to control; those tantrums when she lay on the floor and screamed; *a little savage* as she had been called by one of the girls in the kitchen.

Lady Betty took her by the hand after her initial shock and glances back and forth between her husband and herself. Dido's Master smiled, she thought, so that she would not be afraid. But, then, she cried more and more deep sobs.

'Have you escaped from Lydia?' This was Lady Betty's playful way of describing what had happened. 'Your great-uncle must leave for Lincoln's Inn Fields and we must read a story,' Lady Betty said to her.

Dido never called him uncle, always, Master.

'You'll be a good girl for Lady Betty this morning, yes?' Her Master chuckled and pulled a flower from his nosegay and handed it to her. She noticed his growing affection, as he smiled. 'Come now, come now, Dido, dear.'

Lady Betty led her into the drawing room where she had not been before. She felt so little, despite shooting up in height as her mother had said the last time she visited her. There she was among such grand furniture and glass, porcelain and paintings of horses, and a larger one of birds in flight; the bigger bird was tearing at the flesh of a smaller bird. It might have been what they called a falcon. There was a portrait of two small girls, like herself and Beth, but not, because they were *both* little white girls playing with kittens. The painting of the birds reminded her in a flash what those in Pensacola called a *gabilan*, a hawk, which soared and dived and captured small prey running along the ground, like they said an eagle pursued a running hare.

Lady Betty's voice was soft and what she said came from what she read in the little book, *The Children in the Wood.*

This tender tale must surely please,
If told with sympathetic ease;
Read the Children in the Wood,
And you'll be virtuous, and be good.

Dido was still swallowing her sobs, but intrigued by the magic, as it were, of Lady Betty's voice, the voice she used as she read, and what she pointed to in the little book upon her lap, Dido sitting close to her on the sofa.

'See, see, look, look,' Lady Betty kept saying, her finger moving across the page with the writing, pointing. Then she turned back to the beginning and showed a picture of a boy and girl entering the wood. 'These are the children in the wood.' She then made a suggestion, 'If we like, and if the sun comes out, we can walk a little in the walled garden at the back of the house. This can be our little wood and we can be the children in the wood.' What she read and said became one in Dido's imagination.

Lady Betty pulled her up even further on to the sofa with her, their dresses ballooning about them so that they were a great flower together. She approved of nurse dressing Dido in her bodice, which she had fastened from behind, and looked fine with her petticoats new and laundered. Dido did feel comfortable as she spread her hands out on her embroidered apron that was pretty; forget-me-nots in patterns that were knots of blue thread and trimmed with ribbon. Lady Betty said that her father would find her delightful; that she looked so pretty. She was not sure that she thought that she herself was pretty, but that her apron and her bodice were, though she found the stays uncomfortable and her leash restrictive.

She had called Beth pretty one day. 'But you, Dido, must do something with your hair, my dear. It will not do.'

Dido did not know what Lady Betty thought she could do with her hair. The girls in the kitchen had also been intrigued by her hair and were always touching it and giggling with each other.

She had ceased sobbing and was absorbed by the little book and Lady Betty's large hands.

'This is for you,' Lady Betty said, handing her the book so that she held it open in her hands and turned the pages and repeated after her, 'This tender tale must surely please.' She did remember and learned more from repetition than understanding how the letters corresponded to the sound and the meaning. She repeated almost immediately the second line of the story, struggling with *sympathetic*, not understanding entirely what it meant but that it meant something kind by the tone of Lady Betty's voice.

'You can play with Beth after she has completed her schoolwork,' Lady Betty said, after concluding the reading of the story.

'Will I get to do schoolwork?' She was not sure what it might mean. But she was curious and wondered why she was not doing schoolwork.

Lady Betty paused in what she was going to say, and then she said, 'We'll have to see.'

Dido was kept at Bloomsbury for a long time without being taken to visit her mother. When her father eventually visited she had the opportunity to go to Greenwich.

'What a lovely dress, my pet. Yours is so pretty now that you're growing up so quickly.'

Lady Betty let her father know that she was pleased with Dido's behaviour. Then her Master arrived later from Lincoln's Inn Fields. They sat after supper to chat in the drawing room and she was brought in to sit at her father's knee on a small stool. She had the book Lady Betty had given her.

That evening she pretended to be reading, repeating the beginning of *The Children in the Wood*, looking at its pictures and listening to the talk of her father, her Master and Lady Betty because she knew it was about her though they spoke in a way as to avoid making that plain. But she did understand that the matter was *settled*. Then it was debated whether it was prudent to return her to her mother for a farewell, or whether to depend on her present good behaviour, and the distractions, which were offered her in the large Bloomsbury house. It would be altogether upsetting to stop her going to Greenwich. But going back and forth was also upsetting if she was to settle down. That was Lady Betty's argument, agreed with by her Master. She could see there was alarm on both sides and her father saying, 'I have promised her mother she will see her daughter.' Dido could see her father losing his patience, as they seemed to barter for where she was to live.

Then another story started with her father announcing, 'My marriage is now fixed with Mary Milner, and then I'm leaving again for India.'

She had heard her mother's fear on this matter of her father's marriage. He was to marry someone he could make *a lady*. He could not make her mother *a lady*. Dido remembered that talk from a long time ago.

'Father, you're going to India, again?' She asked him in astonishment afterwards when they were alone. It was as she used to talk to him on the ship when she was little. He had his map as he usually did when he wanted to capture her imagination in crossing seas and continents. They were in her Master's library, where they stood at the globe that he spun to show her the extent of the world and his travels around it.

'It's our empire, my pet.' He enunciated each and every word, spinning the globe to entertain her with history and geography, of conquest and rule, 'and your father is going here,' he said, as he placed his finger over India.

Over the years Dido saw her father less and less. He came and went. He paid little attention to her, as he swept by. He arrived at midnight and left at dawn. She used to be brought down, almost still asleep, from the attic to wish him welcome and farewell. She flattened herself against the walls of the corridor and watched him as he passed her by as if he had just stepped down from one of his portraits, a knight of the realm. He was more concerned to talk with her Master and Lady Betty of the American colonies, the ever consuming interest of stamp duty that had made people there angry with the King. These conversations made Lady Betty tense and they irritated her Master; the possessions of the King and the maintenance of the commerce of the realm his main concern. Dido was lost in this talk. She was brought in to see him in the drawing room when they were staying at Caen Wood. She asked about her mother. He would produce a gift of silk cloth and some bauble that glittered.

Why was he not taking his wife to India? Was she to have a baby sister or brother? Dido plagued him with her questions, but she did not get any answers.

When Dido visited Greenwich, her mother said, 'I hear he has a wife, some woman, Mary Milner, from Yorkshire. I sure is to do with money and position. Is always them things that marriage and a wife is made of with those kind of people,' her mother said scornfully. She was well accustomed to the fact that she could not be his wife, though when he stopped at night in Greenwich he shared her bed as if she were. They were in love, she maintained to Dido. Maybe that's why she was not his wife. That is what she thought. 'Never a lady at home.' She laughed and laughed. 'I will never be dressed in those elaborate dresses and tall wigs.' Maria Belle still wore the dresses she wore in Pensacola. They drew attention to her when she walked the streets of Greenwich.

That was a danger, John Lindsay had told her. 'You'll be put in irons and taken to some ship on the river bound for the West Indies.'

'Then what?' She had challenged him. She did not heed his warnings and wore her head cloth and her petticoats dragging in the street, getting dirty in the drains when she shopped to buy fish by the side of the river. She even wore the gold he had given her, pierced through her ears, where she banked her life savings. If not there, they were hidden in the folds of her head cloth with an accumulation of other savings. Dido learned to keep her own secrets there when her mother bound her head. There was a white pebble found upon the shore, a gull's feather, a tiny gold ring her father had once given her, and a coin she found between the floorboards.

Dido's father worked hard to persuade her that she would be happy with his uncle and aunt. She would be safe there when her mother returned to Pensacola. 'He's my uncle, Dido. He can keep you safe. You mother has only this small cottage in Greenwich. I cannot secure you from the catchers there. You mother does not want to understand this.'

She was still seduced as her mother had been. Her mother knew that for her, as she told Dido, she had little choice but to acquiesce. 'He never propose,' she laughed. Amidst all of that, her mother laughed.

A Highland boy, he called himself, from Aberdeen and Montrose, names her mother had distractedly related once. He was a tender child when he put to sea on the *Pluto*, a boy among men, first of all bound for the Seven Years War with France. He loved to tell his tale in the night at the house by the sea. He told it upon the ocean itself on their journey. He filled the time he was not on deck with these tales. This was when he captained the frigate *Trent* with 28 guns. It was the time of the capture of the *Bien Amie* off Jamaica. It was impossible to keep up with his voyages. He was always away on the business of the realm. Dido and her mother were hungry for his stories, anxious for his protection. Their own safety depended on it.

'So this is the girl?' Mary Milner, her father's new wife, looked Dido up and down. Her father had brought her to Bloomsbury on a visit before his departure to India. That was all she said. Dido had heard it said that she was a charitable woman. The poor in Yorkshire benefited from her dispensation. Her father could be seen with her. She was a lady. But then, a month later, he was off to India and not taking her with him. Would she bear him children? Dido wondered whether he wanted Mary Milner to be her mother. She guessed Mary Milner would not have her in the house because she was part of that *nigger* woman. How could she ever be presented anywhere? How could she be really a part of the family?

Dido did not know her mother's family. 'Do not look', she used to say when they went to the market place in Pensacola and a slaver had arrived. She never found anyone who might have come from her village. 'Come, child, we must look for people, someone I must know.' She often went to look down on the docks among those not bought upon the auction block, but still yearning for some place to rest, pleading to be bought and branded rather than be corralled and have to wait for another market day. There could be some shame in not being bought. There was danger either way. Maria Belle never knew her mother or her father since she was a small child. She had been sold and passed on and grew to love many women as mothers, all left behind. There had not been any fathers. All those men wrenched away from any family to breed far and wide.

❧ ELIZABETH TURNED FROM her writing to Johnny, to read to him from *The Children in the Wood*, the book that she had kept since Lady Betty read it to her on the sofa at the house in Bloomsbury Square. He seemed very peaceful.

It was Billy who alerted the household to the crisis. He had been standing at the door to Johnny's room, curious more than anything else. He ran down the stairs. 'He's dying, Mama. Johnny's dying.' The words of the doctor, *the strangling angel*, came to Elizabeth's mind. 'Johnny's choking.'

Elizabeth called Lydia to go to Dr Featherstone. 'Take a carriage. There's enough money in the jar by the door. Get Seamus to go to my husband.'

She told William Thomas to stay downstairs and play quietly.

She was breathless herself with the stairs. Johnny's breathing was so laboured, just as if he was choking. She sat and held his hand to reassure him. 'Mama's here, sweetheart.' She tried to make him more comfortable. She sat him up and propped his pillows behind his back so he could breathe more easily. She administered arnica and aconite. 'Just a small tincture, a couple of drops of each, sweetheart.' He was agitated. Elizabeth had to keep calm. 'Keep as still as you can, my pet.' She was speaking to herself as well. 'Till the doctor comes and advises us.'

Elizabeth needed to say something to distract her son. How long would it be before the doctor arrived? 'Let me get my book of herbs, darling.' The recitation was as much for her as it was for him. 'If you could be at the window you would see where exactly they are going to come up. Imagine the box hedges. The beds among the hedges. There is mint, sage.' She stumbled over her list: 'lovage, yarrow, lamb's ears…'

'That's a funny name.' Johnny smiled.

'Sweetheart, you're so brave. Let me tell you about the herbs. There's a story for each. Yarrow, now, that's a new one. It stops hair falling out.' They laughed together.

'Mrs Halifax, her hair is falling out,' Johnny whispered between short breaths and smiled.

'Yes, maybe Mrs Halifax should prescribe yarrow for herself.'

Lydia had not yet returned with the doctor.

'Johnny, I'm just going downstairs to see what Billy is up to.'

'You'll come back?'

'Of course I will, won't be a minute. But Mama can't rush.'

No sooner was Elizabeth down the stairs than there was a knock at the door and the doctor entered with Lydia who then took hold of Billy.

'Doctor, how good of you to come so quickly. He's calmer but he gave us a fright. The strangling angel returned.'

Dr Featherstone smiled ironically at her mention of the visiting angel.

'Let me have a look at him.'

They found Johnny again quite convulsed. Dr Featherstone put his head against his chest and then against his back, listening intently. Looking up to Elizabeth, his face was grave. He said little and patted Johnny on the head and shoulders and told Elizabeth to give him a tincture of the aconite he had left last time.

'It'll soothe and should quiet him but he's getting worse.' He lowered his voice at the end turning away from Johnny.

Elizabeth saw the doctor to the door. He said, 'I must talk to your husband.'

'He's not been able to get here in time to see you. He's kept so busy at his work. I will talk with him when he gets here. Then we'll talk together again, doctor. You're so kind.'

'I must talk to your husband. I'll be back this evening. Call me immediately the moment that angel returns,' he smiled reassuringly. 'And, you must take care of yourself with your rattling lungs.'

Later, the next day, as Elizabeth sat by her son, Johnny made several gasps for breath, struggling terribly. Then, it was suddenly over. She sat and waited for Lydia to return with William Thomas before she could send a message to her husband. She sat by his beside and watched and watched. He seemed less and less to be Johnny, his sunken face became crumpled and grey. She took his hand. She lifted him and embraced his small body, his small shoulders. She let herself cry quietly as she held his hand and waited for her husband to arrive.

John d'Aviniere returned home immediately on hearing the news. 'We've lost him,' Elizabeth said. He took her hand and they sat together for a while before Billy and Lydia returned. They held on to each other, each suffering the loss in the depths of their own pasts. 'I must protect my boys, I must.' John laid his head in Elizabeth's lap and sobbed.

'My darling, you do, you protect all of us. I could not cope without you. Johnny's passing will make us closer to each other, to Charles and Billy.'

They decided to keep the body at home till Charles returned from school. They thought that Charles should see his brother's body and that they should be present together as a family before he was prepared for burial. News was sent to Martha. Later, Lydia and Mrs Halifax helped with the washing and dressing of the body. Mrs R said she also wanted to help. The women dressed him in a new shirt, which swallowed him up.

His father came in when the women had completed their preparations and stood beside them with Charles and William Thomas, whom he held close to himself. Billy stared and asked awkward questions. 'When he's better, will he wake up?'

John and Elizabeth now had to think of the welfare of their two remaining sons. 'To lose one to death is not extraordinary in our times. How would we've coped if he'd been captured and taken away?'

'Lizzie, you've got to be strong about this, both for ourselves and the boys. But they do need to be kept aware of what dangers lurk in the district.'

In the days that followed Lydia played with Charles and Billy distracting them with games and going out for walks, leaving John and Elizabeth to be together with their grief.

7

THE D'AVINIERE family buried Johnny at Tyburn on the first day of May, a week before his and Charles' tenth birthday.

Mr d'Aviniere was allowed some leave from his stewardship. He was spending a lot more of his time with his sons. Billy's birthday was also that month. Lydia made a cake for the birthday and the boys had one or two of their friends from the Belgravia House School.

Charles had to be kept back from school. He was the one most affected by his twin's death. Billy had been quite matter of fact about it, interested in all the details and asking questions. It had made Charles ill.

The weeks passed, measured by *since Johnny's death*. The spring was opposite to the family's melancholy, then gradually encouraging them into life and stories by which they remembered Johnny.

Billy continued to ask when his brother would return. He was persistent with his question. 'Will he come back when he's well?' He asked his question with logic. Johnny had to die because he was unwell but he might get better and then return.

'Don't be silly, he's dead,' Charles said as he left the room.

'Will you answer my questions when I'm at your school?' Billy shouted after him. 'At least he can't be captured. He won't get lost on the marshes anymore.'

Elizabeth and John looked at one another. That threat was still alive.

Charles listening at the door came back into the room. 'But you and I, Billy, can be captured if we aren't careful. You better keep close to me on the road when you begin to come to school with me.'

One of her mother's stories came back to Elizabeth, the one about the woman who had preferred to lose her child to death than have her taken into slavery. She had killed her own child rather than have her captured.

'I think we're all aware that there are some dangerous people in the district. We need to keep our eyes and ears open and not wander off the main road when returning from school. Charles is quite right. Just remember what your father and I've told you. Charles will keep you on the straight and narrow, William Thomas.'

'Your mother is absolutely right. Enough talk of capture, now. Who is for an afternoon walk to the river?'

'I am,' Charles and Billy shouted together.

Elizabeth had postponed Beth's visit. She had sent her the account of Johnny's death and a report on her own diminishing health. Beth promised to find another date and deliver what she had been promising. Elizabeth wondered what on earth Beth could have to deliver. She was even less prepared than ever to have Beth visit.

Elizabeth returned to that world that they had shared as both friends and rivals. She wondered what that would now mean to them both. She could not see what they might share now. They had lived in a bubble and that was now burst. Her thoughts took her back to her writing after a period of mourning Johnny's death.

❧ THE-TUG-OF-WAR had started. Dido moved constantly between the small house with the lace curtains at the window, which she parted for a view of the river, on the narrow lane at Greenwich, and the house of her Master, the Lord Chief Justice of England, as her father had explained to her again and again. She was never allowed to forget how powerful her Master was esteemed.

Beth and Dido were caught up in the fantasy of their guardians. They learned that two girls growing up so quickly were certainly not something that had been part of Lady Betty's original idea for herself and her busy husband when they thought it would be charming to refurbish Caen Wood as somewhere to escape to from the stench of town and the traffic of Holborn.

It was the way that Lady Betty spoke. Her words stayed with Dido. Dido loved the escape to better air and the fragrance of the countryside in the hills above London. There was more space for her to wander than at the house in town. There were far less restrictions and she was given her role to play in the household, working on the farm and in the poultry. There was also, and not least, less danger of catchers. Or, so everyone thought.

The girls lived in their own fantasies as Lady Betty and her husband had their own dream and told their story to the girls. Dido felt that she was being invented anew as part of what her Master and Lady Betty were planning. She could feel herself changing. It was not just her clothes that were being kept under control. 'That hair of yours.' Was Lady Betty complaining again when she had not plaited it and tucked it away, but had it, as she put it, in an unruly state.

'We seized the opportunity, *absolument*!' Often a French flourish embroidered her remarks. '*Nous sommes absolument enchantés par ces formidable nouvelles*, I had told Monsieur Bute when we heard that the sale was settled.'

They hoped their villa might grow to become even more beautiful and spacious under the careful and artful supervision of Mr Robert Adam with his brother James in attendance in transforming the Jacobean brick into something which they could only call Adam so unique were his ideas.

Dido listened attentively to every word, following Lady Betty around, standing and noticing everything. There was such urgency with the way Lady Betty spoke and Dido's Master acquiesced in these affairs and became her accomplice in their common venture. 'We could not resist the view, already so wonderful.' They looked at the way the lawns sloped to the ponds where the swans paddled in their own shadows, coupled there, as it were, each in their own reflection.

Dido's Master and Lady Betty saw immediately that Caen Wood Park was open to improvement and landscaping, as her Master elaborated. They saw the possibilities if they planted cedars and created openings for vistas and perspectives, having some rows of trees pleached, other designs with careful pruning and pollarding carried out among the tall beeches.

Dido's Master was overwhelmed by his excitement for the idea. 'This should create more than a glimpse of St Paul's with Mr Wren's genius of a dome, Greenwich beyond, and the Thames in the foreground.'

Her Master's voice raced ahead, tumbling forth with his inimitable eloquence. He had once told Dido the story of how he had had elocution lessons, the teacher getting him to look into a mirror so that he could see how he was to form his words by the shape of his lips, rounding his vowels, making emphasis of the syllables in the correct place, keeping the stresses so different to his native Perthshire. He continued to encourage her to check the pronunciation of her vowels.

Dido and Beth were dragged along over the park, made to stand in awe, as their guardians talked, one answering to the enthusiasm of the other. The girls followed their stories and gesticulations as they pointed to the fields beneath, sloping like lawns down towards Kentish Town into the valley of the Fleet River, past Fitzroy Farm and the marshes of Brookfield.

'Isn't it an idyll?' Dido's Master asked his wife.

'But it can be improved,' Lady Betty quickly added.

'Yes, it can.'

Beth and Dido followed and got to know each other, never fully understanding at first what was their actual relationship; but as they got older they grew fond of each other in their play.

'How are we connected?' Beth questioned.

'Connected?'

'Related. Aren't we blood relatives?'

'Our fathers are first cousins.'

'That's close.'

'Yes, but...'

'But there's the problem of your mother...'

'My mother? What about my mother? What about your mother?'

'She was Polish.'

'My mother was from Africa.'

'That's the problem, not the geography, but...'

'But, what?'

Beth could be so final. She looked at Dido not knowing how to describe.

Dido was almost in tears, but refused to cry because she knew the answer.

'Her skin, her hair...what she is, where she's from...' Beth ran away with her list. 'Come and find me. I'm going to hide in the wood.'

Dido stood and stared as Beth ran down towards the Thousand Pound Pond and the woods beyond.

'Dido, Dido, Dido, come and find me,' she shrieked.

Dido turned back to the house. The day was spoilt. She's never even seen my mother, Dido thought angrily.

When she complained to her father on one of his infrequent visits, he would repeat the facts about her Master to impress upon her the safe place in which she now lived with 'the most powerful man in the realm, my pet.'

While visiting her mother she explained her father's intentions. 'They're noble. He wants me to be free. He's arranging all that is necessary to give me my freedom. He promised me...'

'He promised you?'

'Yes. He's not all bad...'

'Child…'

'You must listen to me some of the time…'

'Eh eh! You have spirit in you. Good.'

'You must believe him. I have to believe him.'

Dido's mother looked at her daughter and drew her close. 'You're right. You will need him, and that master you talk about.'

Dido felt that her mother was preparing her for that departure to Pensacola which she had always known about but did not ever want to think was going to happen. But she knew in her heart the day would certainly come. She dreamt of that ship and the ocean it would cross.

❖ 'MY BOY! BREAD and butter! Has Lydia given you those slices? Yes, you eat them up. Have you been running over the meadow with Lydia?' Billy's eyes grew larger, engrossed in his eating.

Charles was late back from school. 'You'll get him tea, won't you, Lydia? He'll be starving. I wish he would not be late. He knows that it worries me.'

'Come and sit by me, pet.' Elizabeth was giving all her attention to Billy.

The presence of her two remaining sons gave her joy, but they also brought back the loss of Johnny. Billy climbed onto her lap. 'You're far too big for this…'

'Let me, Ma'am…'

'No, you have a rest. I'll call when he becomes impossible.'

'My treasure. Give Mama a big hug and a kiss. Your cheeks are so red. Have you been running all the way back from the river? I mustn't lose another, must I Lydia?'

'Ma'am? He's such a healthy boy. You've nothing to fear.'

'Do you really think that?'

'He looks the picture of health.'

'You know what I mean. Run along now. Too heavy for Mama.'

'Come along Billy, see what we can find as a treat.'

Lydia left Elizabeth to her worry.

'Charles's very late back?'

It was still all over the papers, the children for sale, the padlocks and the manacles you could buy for a good price. There were still the criers along the pavements: *Black Boy for sale!* What a world? Years on from Jonathan Strong and James Sommersett. So many continued to be deported after her Master's so-called narrow judgment. What had it changed?

Elizabeth was more nervous now on her own. It was that question of her mother's. *You hear of the woman who would rather have her child dead than delivered into the bondage of slavery?* It was part of her mother's logic to leave her where she thought she would be safer, rather than living in some frontier town in the Americas. *I will send for you in time.* Since she had left, Elizabeth had repeated that promise to herself almost every day.

Where was her mother? She would have to recreate her.

◂ 'DIDO, CHILD, YES, he make you a Christian. Right there in that beautiful church in St George's, Bloomsbury, so I know the house they take you to that morning on the square afterwards, that bleak late November day, 20th 1766. Is so it state on the certificate. How I go forget? All the family, and you my black pickney lost among them in that paid for pew, and me not at the front with his family. You father allow me to be there, to stand at the back and witness your forehead poured with water at the font. And my name upon the document: *Maria Belle, Mother.*

'He think that go save you? Baptism doth not bestow freedom. You hear what I say? That's their law. Don't let him fool you. Like that other lie that because we breathing English air we go be free. And you breathe sufficient? You free?

'And look where we is in this secret place that your father must come at dark of night, don't dare bring the carriage down this lane, but walk furtively looking behind him to visit his two niggers. He bring me so far for this? And you, a prisoner in some big house? He show you any papers? Any deed? Manumission, they call it. You well know that. You must put your hands on that piece of paper. Is not dressing up in these pretty clothes that will make you free. You must be your own self, free. Dress up in pretty clothes is easy, easy that way to be a *belle*.'

Her mother's tongue was running all that day with rage. Yes, there were rages, her father's too. She let that secret out. When he seemed not himself, he used her as his property and not his darling. Smitten by her beauty was how he spoke to his uncle and his aunt. But he might smite her, blow on blow, as was his right, he said. She was his property.

Dido thought of her mother as a soft person. But she could be so angry sometimes. She had not known all the promises her father had made to her mother, though she knew that he had said that he could not make her *a lady*, and yet she was his *darling*. The two did not seem to fit together. Or, did they? She heard him call her that again and again, *darling*. So where did that leave her? But once her mother had started with her rage it was hard for her to stop, as she continued that afternoon when her father had taken Dido from the house at Bloomsbury and brought her down river to Greenwich.

There was the heaving water with the tide coming in and the tall forest of ships at Deptford rocked by the waves and her father's arms tight around her shoulders. He embraced her and protected her from the world. 'Don't look there,' he said, as they came down from the ship onto the dock at Greenwich. But she did look where there were three young black men in chains, like in a coffle in Pensacola. She had seen young men like that as a small child from the window, passing on their way to the plantation. She had glimpsed them in a hold on her father's ship.

'Is only last year, *oui*.' Her mother had a way with French intonations because she had had a French mistress once in Martinique, before she arrived on the block on Pensacola's harbour.

'It was the year before your own baptism. Is a story people tell me since I living here. It concern a man called Jonathan Strong. A young fella, eighteen years old. He baptise. Let me see if I remember exactly, yes, on 22 July at St Leonard, Shoreditch. The lady at the bottom of the street, self, that tell me the story, call him a blackamoor.' She laughed. It was not for joy. Her mother laughed a lot with her tongue in her cheek. It was when she had a knowledge to impart. 'He come from Barbados to London. He baptise in order to escape from his master a Mister Lisle. Make himself free with the holy water. I remember the whole story because it frighten me. I not going to tell you that story now. He get beat with a pistol across his head, the same swollen, nearly blinded, young Jonathan Strong. Unable to walk, abandon in the street, by his master Mr Lisle. His name was Strong, but all the strength leave him on that lane in Shoreditch where they find him.'

CHARLES HAD GOT back safely, but had missed his father before bed. John and Elizabeth were alone together after supper. Lydia was off earlier than usual.

'Lizzie, darling? You look tired and sad.'

'I've had a day with my mother and stories of Jonathan Strong. Earlier it was Beth. I've written to her about Johnny. She's in my mind a lot, what with her impending visit. But I do enjoy making up my mother's voice as I remember it.'

'Let me distract you over supper with stories I've heard...'

'What stories are those?' She flung her arms around his neck. 'Tell me.' She kissed him on both cheeks and on his mouth.

'Is this what laudanum does?' He teased.

She continued kissing him. 'Don't tease me about that. I do try to measure it exactly.'

'Well. Listen to this...'

'Charles is still coming back from school late...'

'I'll talk to him.'

'Promise? You know time is running out.'

'Sweetheart. Lizzie. Stop. I don't want to spend our time just looking forward to your death. We've got to live now.'

'We need to offer Charles and...'

'I'll have a little more claret. It's doing me good.' John needed to relax. He could do without Elizabeth's anxieties at times.

'Beth has not given me a date... her visit...'

'Oh, not Lady Beth Finch-Hatton...'

'John...'

'Can't we just have ourselves back, like it used to be.'

Elizabeth knew what John meant. Her illness could at times alter their intimacy. 'Yes, we can, I'm sorry. What was that story? Remember our hands entangled, standing among the pews in the Meeting House in Shoreditch. Do you remember that day when a quiet rage had burst from me? I would have been heard from one side of the park to the next. All of London would've heard me. But you saved me from my rage. Do you remember? You kissed me.'

'Of course I remember. Better to rage than give in to obsessions. Better to kiss.' John leant over and took his wife by the hand. 'Let's to bed.'

Elizabeth woke early, having dreamt of her mother as she used to be, her voice in her head with the story of Jonathan Strong running wild.

◈ 'YOU KNOW, BECAUSE I tell you enough, Dido, since that time on the ship when we leave Pensacola to come to this place, that he will send me back and that you must stay here. Is not you, child. Is not you. Is not he. Is not me. Is the time we living in that make things so. Yes, he have some power, but the man that have the real power is the man who you call your Master. The same blood that flowing in your father veins is the same blood in his and in yours. You right to call him Master. One day I trust he will leave to you papers that have it mark that you is free. You must wait for that and when you get that, maybe then you will choose and come to me. Choose to leave that master. Is the same piece of paper I must get from your father. For I am his slave in law. He can't send me back without it.

'The story I didn't tell you. That boy Strong find his way to Mincing Lane. There was a surgeon there, William Sharp, a good man who served the poor of the city. Sharp had a brother. You tell me you hear his name mentioned in Bloomsbury? Granville is his brother.'

'My Master don't like the sound of his name.'

'I sure he don't. But let me tell you how it go for that young man. Strong get admit to St Bartholomew's. He get fix up and Mr Sharp so kind he get him a job in Fenchurch Street with a Mr Brown who was lucky to be an apothecary.'

'Master call Mr Sharp a confounded man. Always complaining.'

'You listen to what I say. I telling you this story so you go understand. You hearing too much talk from one side only. Two years later, that same Lisle, the scoundrel, see Strong in the street. He follow him to his house and then employ catchers to capture him and sell him for £30. They keep him in Poultry Compter, the prison in the City till they hear of a ship to the West Indies.'

'Master says I might get captured if I walk in the street.'

'He better protect you.'

'I mustn't walk in the Square or to Holborn.'

'Listen what I tell you. These people think they have the run of the world and that there is no law or law that people must obey. Strong get a letter to Granville Sharp and he bring the case to court.'

'That is what Master complains about. Mr Sharp always bringing things before him in the court.'

'You sounding just like them. Listen how you speaking. You listen to your mother. That man so great. Is in Mansion House that Strong get discharge. They say Strong not guilty of anything, no offence, and therefore he at liberty to go. They have bad men about these streets, but there is some good men too, that judge and Mr Granville Sharp. They say that even in the court the captain of the ship try to seize Strong. But there is a bad end to this tale. The Jamaican planter who buy Strong sue the Sharps and they lose because the judge say that Strong did not become free because he come to England.'

Dido listened with open mouth. She kept thinking of her own fate.

'Hear what I tell you. He not free because he breathing English air. I tell you so before. He not free because he baptise. Is the same thing I tell you before. He quote some judgment by other judges from long time. They say Sharp not leaving it so. He go follow it up. He go appeal. We have to listen out.'

Dido began to lose her mother's speech with all the details. She listened at times to her mother and she also listened to her father. She needed her mother to bring things down to earth for her. When she told her what her father had said, her mother replied, 'You think he tell you everything? You mustn't believe every sweet thing that sweet man pour into your ear.'

⯃ THE FAMILY VISITED Johnny's grave at Tyburn that afternoon. It was not too long a journey to the Bayswater District. Elizabeth was rested, having had, unusually, a whole night of sleep.

They stood at the side of the small grave and watched the stonemason fix the headstone with an angel in relief. Billy was fascinated by the mason's tools, his use of the chisel, hammer and trowel. He knelt to inspect and then to play with the spirit level, balancing it on his knees trying to find the equilibrium; the mason, a young man from the district, smiled and humoured Billy. Charles stood without moving, staring as if into nothing. He might have been reading the inscription on the stone, Johnny's name and the dates of his birth and death and the sentiments: *A Beloved Son and Brother*. Lydia put her arms around Charles's shoulders, but he flinched and moved away. Elizabeth stood holding her husband's hand letting her thoughts wander, as they were all absorbed in the stonemason's work until the angel in relief upon the stone was a resplendent presence hovering over the grave.

Elizabeth saw Seamus offering to help with cleaning up afterwards. Billy joined in. Mr d'Aviniere settled the payment with the mason. Everyone seemed to be content that the practicalities were carried out. They were a distraction from their individual sorrows. Mrs Halifax wiped a tear away with her kerchief. Lydia took her arm in hers as they both began to walk away with Mrs R through the yew trees.

Elizabeth whispered to her husband, 'We must not lose another child...'

'No, we mustn't.'

They gathered up their two boys for their journey back home.

8

ELIZABETH DID NOT want the doctor called and she did want to bother her husband. Instead, she called on Lydia. 'I want you to go to the apothecary, the one beyond Jenny's Whim. Be careful with the money, Lydia.'

Lydia left the house with the prescription, which she knew would not cure, but she had learned that it would make Elizabeth more comfortable. This had been going on for a long time.

'No, don't take Billy. Hurry. I won't be able to go after him if he runs off to the bottom of the garden. I'll trust to luck. I need the opium, Lydia. I must have it. I can't stand the pain.'

Her child was staring and wondering at what he saw in his mother's face.

'Don't be alarmed, my darling. Lydia, hurry.'

The front door banged. 'Stay away from the front door sweetheart. I don't want you out there on your own. She'll be back soon. Don't cry. I must keep calm. Come, sit by me and look at how I knit. See, stitch and purl.'

Billy ran off to the door. 'Lydia will be back soon. No, you must not go out on the street. Mama will get cross. You know that. I cannot come to fetch you. Look, a pretty thing I've got for you to wear and keep you warm, and something else, a surprise.'

He was seduced by the enticement, by a windmill on a stick to be blown, a trifle from the entertainments in the Gardens. She did not have the breath to blow. It seemed ages ago when she was stronger and would go out walking with all the family. Billy was then a babe in her arms.

'Come and blow. It's fun, isn't it? I've no breath to stir it, to make a breeze for the windmill to sing. Lydia will be back soon.'

Lydia returned with the apothecary's medications. Elizabeth was frantic with the pain but could not show it with Billy there. Lydia placed the *materia medica* on the table next to her chair. Her mistress was at the end of her tether. The slightest disturbance made her agitated. William Thomas luckily had settled down and was playing quietly at her feet.

Billy followed Lydia out of the room. He helped her with her chores in the scullery. She returned with a small glass of cherry brandy to aid Elizabeth in taking the tincture of opium. 'The smallest drop, Lydia. I do not want to be out of this world, not just yet. Some relief. Is Charles back as yet?'

'No, Ma'am.' Lydia smiled. She understood. Then she returned to the scullery and left Billy with his mother. He was curious about her health. Might a daughter have been more of a comfort? Elizabeth often wondered about that. She could not possibly have another child. Her boys would be safe with their father and they would have their own achievements to take them into the world. A daughter would find it so much more difficult. She could see history repeating itself. She was talking to herself as she drifted off with the pain leaving her. Then her mind began going somewhere else entirely as she woke with a start. 'Mammy...' She was a daughter, but where was her mother?

'Is there anything else I can do for you, Ma'am?'

'Thank you, Lydia. Sit with us. We've been reading a book that Lady Betty gave me when I was a very little girl, haven't we?'

She gazed into the eyes of her son who was sitting at her feet looking at the pictures in the storybook. She could barely control her tears. It had to be the medication. She could usually control herself.

'We'd just come to live in the house in Bloomsbury. You remember? It was long before the fire in 1780.'

'Yes Ma'am. I can see Lady Betty reading to you. You were crying for your mother. I had recently entered service, and was overjoyed at getting a job with the Mansfields of Bloomsbury Square'

'Yes, our very different lives as girls.'

'So different, Ma'am.'

Billy turned the pages. 'He loves the story. I have had to explain. A little beyond him, I think.'

'*This tender tale must surely please…*' she read from her childhood book.

'And he's been attentive. Haven't you? I've not had to run to the bottom of the garden for the ball or lift him from the garden bed collecting pigeons' feathers beneath the dahlias. Yes, he's been absolutely perfect.'

'And you, Ma'am? Are you feeling better?'

'Much relieved. A little miracle, this opiate.'

'Excellent, for sure, Ma'am.'

There was a knock at the front door.

'Who's that…?'

'It's the post, Ma'am.'

Beth had sent a letter saying that she was coming up to London from Kent. She now wanted to make the visit she had postponed. Last time, she was ecstatic about William Thomas, then a baby, and with the twins. She wrote now with sympathy about the death of Johnny. Last time, the boys enjoyed the arrival of her carriage. Charles had cared for the horses, bringing hay and water onto the street from the small nearby farm. Beth wrote that she would bring her children. The parlour was going to be full for tea.

'Lydia, will we cope? She's bringing all her children.'

'We'll cope.'

'You'll enjoy seeing Lady Elizabeth, Mrs Finch-Hatton, won't you?'

'Of course, Ma'am. And you too, I'm sure.'

The two women looked at each other and laughed, remembering Beth and her foibles.

Beth had ended her letter by saying again that she had something to tell Elizabeth and to show her, in fact, to give her. She had said that the last time she wrote.

'Something about a parcel,' Elizabeth said to her husband at supper.

'I'll have to find a way to excuse myself...'

'Can't you try for my sake, John? She'll drive me mad...'

'Lizzie, think, Beth, Lady Beth. You were Miss Dido, she Lady Beth...'

'Yes, how things have changed...'

'She's not changed. She could be really haughty with the servants...'

'And with me. Let's see nearer the time how you feel. It's not that I don't understand.'

'Don't insist that I have to see her, Lizzie...'

'I may need you there.'

Upstairs in bed, John and Elizabeth lay on their backs up against the propped up pillows and whispered so as not to wake the boys.

'See how you feel on the day she comes.'

'Hmm.'

'I wonder what she has for me?'

'Knowing Beth it will be something to do with her...'

'She could be kind...'

'Hmm.'

The last of the embers crumbled in the grate.

They embraced and left their differences to be argued on later.

That night Elizabeth dreamed about Beth. She woke thinking how early on in their relationship their difference had been established. There had been such a lot of pretending. They pretended that she was one of the family, and yet it was very plain that she was not. She had to be grateful, and yet she resented so much of how she had to be. Those scenes returned vividly to her when she came back to her writing.

❧ BETH AND DIDO had known each other since Beth was six and Dido was five.

'I am from Poland,' Beth had announced, that first time she spoke to Dido, speaking not quite like her Master and Lady Betty, so another one with a funny accent. So much was made about the sound of her own speech. Beth pronounced each word with precision as if she had learned it as a foreign language. The household did not comment on her accent as they had commented on Dido's when she first arrived. Beth's mother was Henrietta von Bünau; as Dido's father would have said, *another geography lesson for you*, sending her off to investigate the globe in order to discover Poland.

Beth and Dido were forced to remain within the confines of the attic that day until the afternoon when they were then let out.

'You be good girls, now, and you must be on your leash, Dido,' Lady Betty said, speaking to Molly because she thought she would try to run away and she knew that Beth and Dido were not as yet happy to be together.

Beth called Dido names about her hair. She would pull her plaits. When she did that Dido hit her, pulled her hair, which was like lengths of flax, she said. Beth cried and ran off down the stairs to Lady Betty's dressing room.

That morning the works were going on with Master's great plan for the house at Caen Wood. Lady Betty said, 'The Adam brothers are here today. You must not get under their feet.'

Dido was put to face the wall as punishment. Beth had to return and they were obliged to make up.

In the afternoon they played along the lane to the farm and poultry.

When they came down the back stairs, Lady Betty said, 'It's the wettest winter in memory,' her French phrase thrown in, '*Mais oui...*' She insisted that the children must not venture below the south terrace, or, to the pastures sloping down to the ponds. 'Not beyond the ha ha, *mes enfants.*'

They wanted to run up the hill where the icehouse was situated. The icehouse intrigued Dido. She stood and stared and watched the blocks cut and wrapped in straw and stored. It was the ice upon the pond that restricted their play and accounted for their confinement on winter afternoons.

'Don't go near the pond or walk on the ice. Keep her on the leash, Molly.'

When they got to the top of the hill they pointed towards Kentish Town and St Paul's in the further distance. There was a fine covering of snow and they sat on the hilltop and slid down to the bottom.

Molly called out, 'Your dresses will be soaked,' and they climbed back to the top of the hill slipping and laughing, being children lost in their play, and not calling each other names.

'You're brown as a berry against that snow, Miss Dido,' Molly said.

'It's her natural colour,' Beth explained. 'She could be darker but she's a mulatto.'

'Indeed.' Molly pretended to be impressed by Beth's reference.

The fun did not last. Back at the house, Dido's imprisonment was re-established.

'Mulatto, mulatto,' Molly sauntered off, laughing.

Beth was always up to something, always some secret. 'I know something, you don't know,' she used to tease. It could be sinister at times, particularly as Dido felt there used to be plans, always plans, being made for her that she did not know about. Things could appear quite normal, as arranged by others, but then there was some exclusion, some exception made which reminded her that she was not quite like Beth. It might be to do with something as ordinary as a dress, a fabric that she could not have but that was suitable for Beth. Beth might go for an outing to Hertfordshire and Dido would have to stay to work on the poultry or the dairy. But most sinister were the looks and tones of voices as they spoke, or the raised eyebrow, or just that glance which was difficult to interpret, but the effect was of exclusion, real or imagined. There was something she should not have or some place she must not go. She longed for her mother then. She was both in and out, neither one thing nor another. She never did understand some aspects of this; she could sit and listen to chat in the drawing room but she was not allowed to eat with the family. When she was little she could hardly chew her food because of her loneliness and wanting to get back to her mother in Greenwich.

'Child, you need some feeding up,' her mother would say as soon as she arrived. 'I going cook you some salt fish like we used to in Pensacola.'

Dido was alerted as she passed Lady Betty's dressing room.

'But surely, you must not keep her as anything but a half-breed. She cannot be expected to be treated the same. Her father cannot expect you to pretend that she's really like a proper cousin to Beth.'

'No, quite. But...'

'But what, my dear? What can possibly arise to alter our opinion that half-breed or not there is more in her of the savage than her father's blood.'

'Hopefully, we can do something about that.'

That was Lady Betty and her sister Mistress Mary, so loud in Dido's ears, voices so distinct, gestures of astonishment so visible, eyebrows so raised up, glimpsed through a crack in the door.

She came to know herself as different, so different from Beth. She was Elizabeth too, a name which was given at her baptism, but never used. Why did she have to have that silly name, Dido? It was a trail that led so far back into what they called ancestry and inheritance into what was called slavery.

Beth, losing her mother at such a young age to illness and death, was nevertheless what is called legitimate. She would have a place upon the tree, the family tree. Names mattered: Stormont, Murray. Belle? Now that was a funny name. Was it real? Was there a tree of Belles? Lady Betty had asked. And, how funny was the name, Dido Belle? Really, what were they thinking?

Later, out on the terrace, Beth let her play with one of her dolls, Little Dorothy. Then, she said she might come inside and play with her baby-house, as she called it, the doll's house in her bedroom in which there was everything that was needed for a miniature life.

The girls' mornings then were taken up with the anteroom outside the library and with the work, which had started in the housekeeper's room. The work on the anteroom was most important as it was where guests would wait to see Dido's Master. She was fond of standing at the French windows cast in a Venetian frame. Lady Betty's commentary gave her names for each detail.

At times Lady Betty thought it was best to stay away from the works, but she was curious to see what was taking place. Beth and Dido followed her around the house.

'Now, you must not touch, girls.'

Dido stared at the application of the waterleaf on the capitals of the pillars, the bead ogees above the doorways, the friezes and the decoration of the cornices with flowers and leaves. All blended so well with the theme which was begun with the wrought-iron honeysuckle on the main stairs, twenty-four flowers, each one two and half inches, so delicate and precise.

'Now you must count them and check Mr Adam has not left any out.'

Beth and Dido ran up the stairs counting as they went.

'The whole creation has been living inside Mr Adam's head and is now right here,' explained Lady Betty. She then told them how the clever Mr Robert Adam had employed Mr Zucchi to carry through the theme of food and beverages for the dining room. Dido stared up at Ceres looking after the harvest and Bacchus the wine.

'Beth, you must concentrate,' Lady Betty kept saying. While Dido followed Lady Betty, Beth was distracted by what was going on outside along the terrace where Mr James Adam was directing stonemasons and gardeners to build the new parterre.

Dido prided herself in learning everything. Beth seemed so uninterested as if it was a matter of take it or leave it. Dido felt she might go mad with the language that she learned, and then her mother's voice was constantly pulling her back to her. *What it is they making of you child? Think of me, remember what I say, I go send for you. Now is for your safety to stay with your father people.*

Along the way Dido felt she was receiving her education in classical architecture. It was all so different from the world she remembered in Pensacola, the chattel houses on the waterfront to where her mother would return. She remembered the white picket fence around the house, the *ajoupa* at El Paso de Arroyo Ingles. She had to be a good girl. Beth wandered away and seemed bored with what was perhaps ordinary for her, coming from large houses in Krakow and Vienna. She did not talk about them. She was always anxious to get back to Bloomsbury Square. Dido preferred the country, but would often ask herself what she was doing there, a fish out of water

'What a splendid place it's all going to be when it's completed. Where has Beth got to?' Lady Betty was so excited by the house.

Dido was lying on the floor looking up to the ceiling of the library.

'We must bring all our books from Bloomsbury Square,' Lady Betty mused, passing her hands over the newly fitted shelves.

Dido continued to be entranced by the story that was unfolding on the ceiling. The carvers were working away on the delicate work of the bead ogee in the library, the fluting on the pilasters, waterleaf and bead on the spar of the mahogany door. Dido chewed on every word as Lady Betty described the work and chatted with the craftsmen. She lost herself in allegories told with lions and deer and it was from these myths that she made up stories for the servants downstairs.

They looked at her so oddly. 'She thinks she's a lady,' they said to each other and turned away from her stories.

'Look at the black stains on her fingers and her face.' That was Matty who used to work at The Spaniards. She should have known better than to say such foolish things.

While these decorations continued apace, the furnishings arrived. Beth returned from her wanderings and the girls were allowed to unpack some of the delicate glass and porcelain.

Dido marvelled that she could entertain herself when she missed her mother so much. There was something entrancing about the world of the Mansfields. Then the picture of her mother sitting in her little house in Greenwich saddened her and she wanted to be there with her very different stories.

The packers had arrived that morning to attend to the freight from Calais with Madame Florel's plate and glasses. The upholsterer had been there that week to repair the gilding on the Pembroke chair.

'Don't sit on the new silk.' Lady Betty was more anxious than ever.

Dido watched while he stitched the crimson Indian silk used for the sofa and the framed window seats. The girls had to be kept from under the workers' feet as much as they seemed to be entertained by them. Dido knew as usual she was very much an object of curiosity, her name, especially, causing many questions to be asked and suggesting playful, teasing corruptions like *Dodo* which Lady Betty thought too much a risk, though she herself had entered into some of the banter.

'What a bright thing she is, though at times sullen, moody, cautious. Not a bad thing the last.' Dido heard Lady Betty report to her Master in the evening.

'That's a good girl, Dido,' her Master's voice proclaimed. 'Keep to your reading, Dido, and pay attention to your speech, vowels and syllables with correct emphasis.'

Sometimes, she felt that they thought of her as a performing monkey.

Dido was so intent on being well behaved, that it hurt. She wanted to rage, to rebel. At times she planned to run away. How would she find her way to Greenwich? It had felt at times like she was a mute, stunned by the separation from her mother. She would refuse to speak or take part in play. But she noticed everything.

Dido was ten, going on eleven. Beth was just ahead of her.

It was autumn, October of the year 1771. She remembered the year well because when she returned to Greenwich to see her mother they travelled through the park and could see the river below. Her mother told her on that visit that she must not fear that she would leave her in England and return to Pensacola. She collected dates then. She felt that her mother's departure was always imminent. She scribbled that date and her words in her diary, which lived under her pillow. 'I will not leave you, my darling,' her mother told her. Dido was always thinking that her mother was leaving.

When she returned to Caen Wood there was still colour in the trees. She looked out at the dying sun over the Spaniards Inn where there was a riot of orange and red. These moments helped her with missing her mother. It was always a joy being there in the country, high above London. She had made herself a companion of the weather. When the company of the house, family and servants made her lonely she would walk round and round the park.

She had lain that last summer in the grass, hidden by the blackthorn hedges at Caen Wood, and let the light falling through the trees dapple her belly. That was the first time that she spied the boy Hal peeping from the hedgerow. Later, he wanted to touch her skin.

'Is it real?' he asked. He wished to see the colour that streamed along her legs.

She brushed his hand away.

He smiled and turned to go. It did not end there.

'When I touch, you'll know!'

His threat scared her, like a sharp cut with a knife.

That time was not one of unfettered freedom. It was a kind of bondage and for a long while she had no idea how she might escape from its hold. No one had taught her the route, the way out of that thicket. The words did not come easily, to properly represent to herself what had taken place that day and following.

It surprised Dido at the time how Hal had changed from the kind boy that she had met the first morning on the farm when Lady Betty had detailed her to work in the poultry. Unlike the girls in the kitchen, he seemed not at all surprised about how different she seemed, her hair, or the colour of her skin, or the sound of her voice. He was shy and he was helpful with tasks that she did not know how to do like keeping the straw clean for the hens, or how to prepare their feed in the winter so that they might get more than they were accustomed from pecking in the yard. Though a boy, she took him to be a friend. He seemed simpler to deal with. He told her that his father had been a blacksmith and had had an accident in his forge burning his arm so severely that he could not work again at being a smithy. Since he had worked for Caen Wood he asked for Hal to be given work. Mr Way, her Master's steward, had employed him to help out his father. The story moved Dido.

It was a different Hal who had been peeping from the blackthorn hedges. Once when she talked to Beth about boys, she told her that they did change and that she had to watch them or she might become a wayward girl and then there would be no knowing what might happen to her. This was when she first told her about clouts and having to deal with herself bleeding every month. Beth thought it best to tell her as she was not sure she would hear about this kind of thing from her mother. Lady Betty had instructed Beth. The monthly or thereabouts cleaning and what wayward thing might happen to her became linked in her mind. She was grateful to Beth. She was also convinced that this bleeding had something to do with her mother's impending departure. She was too terrified to talk about it and it must have been at this time that Beth came to the rescue. So she had to look out for Hal. He was no longer that thoughtful friend, a lively boy on the farm, but a young man with other intentions.

Dido resorted to nature to comfort herself and as young as she was she found the moods so changeable, so subtle. She would have liked for them to stay longer at Caen Wood but they were obliged to return on Mondays to Bloomsbury Square because of her Master's work.

While the air of England had not bequeathed her freedom, neither had baptism, as her mother would repeat, the beauty she saw at Caen Wood saved her. Because she also learned how to speak of it and that language made her see and feel. She listened carefully. She listened to her Master, to Lady Betty, to Lydia and Molly, and even to Hal and the milkmaids from Kentish Town. They all remarked about the weather and nature's way in their different accents. She watched the trees being cut down and perspectives and prospects created. She watched the park coppiced and pollarded. She watched an invention take place before her eyes. She had been a part of their design.

'Look at how she speaks now,' she heard her Master say to Lady Betty one afternoon after engaging her in conversation as he alighted from his carriage when she was returning to the house from the poultry with a basket of eggs.

With the dying sun, melancholia grew inside of her, of which Lady Betty told her she must not indulge, and in to which she must not seek to escape. 'That will not bring you and your mother together, Dido,' she said.

But it was the very beauty, which the weather sculpted, that was a solace to her. The lit up *magnolia grandiflora*, it grew beneath her window, her greatest friend in the spring. How she loved the sound of those words when spoken by Mr French, the gardener. He walked around the garden naming plants and trees the way Master walked around his library reading the titles on the spines and pulling them out to open on pages from which he would read to her. All the long summer and in to autumn, the vast purple, brown, red, ever-changing prisms of the copper beeches transported her and translated her feelings beyond her state of mind. She took volumes with her from the Bloomsbury library to Caen Wood: Ovid, Cicero, Horace and histories which her Master said she should school herself in. 'In time, Herodotus, Dido, the father of history. He was a great geographer too, which I know will interest you.'

It puzzled her at times how he offered her so much freedom in this way and yet she always knew she was not her own person. She was his. She belonged to him. Yet many of his books spoke of liberty.

Her mother had told her enough times of the peculiar arrangement concerning the *property* that she was but it was much more her own realisation of that fact that puzzled and disturbed her.

9

IT WAS PART of a story Master told Lady Betty and the company in the drawing room that evening. Dido had just come in having changed her apron and was drying her hands from her chores in the pantry. Beth paid no attention. Her eyes were lowered and concentrating upon her sewing. She laid it out on her stool and then went to the spinet to play a tune, which she knew would please her great-uncle. She had chosen a Scottish ballad. It was that which reminded Dido's Master of the story he had first heard from a friend in Scotland, the story of the escape of an American gentleman's slave who had come with him from Norfolk in Virginia.

The gentleman had bought the man in that town at an auction. Stewart Esquire was the man's owner. He was also associated with that town they heard a lot of at that time, Boston, in Massachusetts. Dido could not hold all the information, which her Master gave to the company. She heard the words *cashier* and *paymaster of customs* at the port of that same town.

This gentleman's man was now a runaway in London and Dido was imagining him at large, along the lanes, in hovels, in alleyways and under hedgerows. She imagined him by the river, hunkered down in a boat moored on the mud flats, waiting for the tide. How would she have survived?

It was like an adventure as she retold it to herself later in bed or sitting on the windowsill, listening to the wind in the trees. Could this happen to her? She had noted his name in her diary, *Sommersett*. Little did she know then that his name would come to inhabit the house at Bloomsbury Square and dominate their lives for a whole year and change their lives beyond anything, echoing through the King's realm in all the newspapers and as far his colonies in America and the West Indies and accompanying her to the dairy and to the poultry, or just while she was stood at the window and watched Master and Beth go out for their afternoon ride as far as Lord Southampton's park. It affected the mood of Christmas that year. Little did she know that she would become so familiar with the life of this man, James Sommersett.

And all the while Beth paid attention to her sewing during her Master's first telling of that story. It was how they, Beth and Dido, were different. On the stairs Beth said to Dido as they went up to bed, 'Aren't you really a slave, Dido? Might it not happen to you, be captured and sent back to wherever, a plantation in Jamaica? Sent back in irons? Do you not fear that?'

So she had been listening, Dido thought, and she had not even pricked her finger with her sewing needle. Dido did not answer her question. Beth had not even dropped her pattern on the floor, she thought, all seeming seamless, not shocking, with her own life and the music she played.

Mr James Sommersett's search had been a yearning for liberty. He was running away from his master, running into the fields of England, through every hedgerow, down every alley and lane for his freedom. His plight was always on her mind.

The legalities were beyond Dido then. *Habeas corpus?* That man Sommersett had good friends who had brought a charge of *habeas corpus* against Mr John Knowles who held Sommersett in the ship *Ann & Mary* on the Thames on the instruction of Mr Stewart with the intention of taking him to Jamaica. He was ordered to bring Sommersett before her Master on the King's bench. In Dido's mind it was the story that traversed such a large number of places: the Guinea coast to Virginia, crossing oceans and continents and coming to rest here in her Master's house.

Servants whispered it along the corridors, stopping conversation when doors were opened or passing Lady Betty on the stairs. The story surprised Dido in the creak of the floorboards, the rattle of the window at night, and in particular when she peeped at the newspapers. Visitors in carriages arrived at the house with questions for her Master about the story. They told it in the bustle of Bloomsbury Square. She overheard Lady Betty's sister Mary saying, 'This reading of newspapers is quite precocious in someone of her kind.' And so it was, Dido supposed, getting her story from the columns of print.

She heard the same story again when Mr French was providing her Master with his nosegay from the very finest flowers as he was leaving the house after his cup of coffee. Then she remembered her Master saying, 'You, young girl, must remember that you must not venture beyond the Square. There'll be much more space for you to play at Caen Wood with your cousin.'

Dido hazarded a question: 'Will I be captured and put in irons and sent back, like James Sommersett?'

'What are you talking about, young lady? Your imagination, Dido, is growing faster than your sentences, or the questions that you frame for me. In fact, your imagination is growing as fast as your body, child.' The blood rose in her cheeks at the mention of her body.

Then Dido thought what next she might ask which was the point of her first question. It was about James. That was his name, Sommersett's name. He had been baptised in the hope of freedom. Her mother had taught her that. 'They say baptism bring freedom, but is a lie.' She had smiled at her blunt assertions.

So then, before her Master entered his carriage, she asked again, 'What about James?' She made bold to call him by his first name, so familiar had she become with his story. She almost knew him and wondered if his plight might be her own.

'And what James is it that you mean, Dido, my dear?' Her Master asked. Sometimes she was a *young girl* and at other times a *young lady* to her Master and *Dido, my dear*, at other times. She thought she was a young lady when she was getting above herself, sounding like she knew more than she did. But then she did know, quite a lot, about this horrifying story. But at this moment she did not venture any further and her Master was already into his carriage which took him to the Great Hall at Westminster or to the King's bench in the Middle Temple where he became like one of his portraits dressed in scarlet with hood and sleeves of snowy ermine.

'You do not know what you speak of,' her Master answered from the window of his carriage.

She stood and stared. Then she turned and went back into the house determined to know everything.

If she had been James Sommersett standing in the dock she would have been terrified of her Master on his bench.

He had sauntered off with his nosegay to sit on the King's bench and pronounce judgment. It got postponed and postponed again. The world hung in the balance on that judgment. The newspapers waited, ready to imagine an outcome if not given a verdict and the facts concerning the horrifying story of a man in irons.

This story took the place of all the stories Dido was reading at the time, even Daniel Defoe's *Robinson Crusoe*, another beleaguered man.

'You see what happen to that one that get capture?'

Her mother had been warning her. She followed all in *The Advertiser*. Her ability to read had started with her English mistress in Pensacola, the mistress who had told her the story of snow. Her words frightened Dido. 'Will I get captured and put in irons?' Dido asked her mother.

The shiver she felt might have been the damp of the season as the evening declined. She had a cough then that persisted.

'Them can't give you no medicine for that?' Her mother knew that they could and that they did. But she wanted to find fault. Dido told her that it would not make her love her less that they were kind to her. Her eyes were distrustful of her words. Her mother could be jealous of Lady Betty. 'Is steal she steal you? She can't bear children of she own?'

She was left to answer and had no other words but 'I love you', kissing her on the cheek.

'Come child, now, none of that when we have things to do.' Her mother could be brusque. Dido knew she loved her affection.

'He come from Africa, taken. Captured is the word I want,' her mother continued. 'They bought and sold him again and again off the auction block. People said he came from Kingston, Jamaica. You don't remember that place? You too small when you father ship pass that island coming from Havana, them Spanish warships burning in the harbour, and you the smallest pickney I have lying between my legs. So, I ask myself where this Scotsman, your father, have me on his ship at war; so much he want to be near to me, he can't put me in a house to breed and feed my little one? Is true what they say, I is his slave.'

As she listened to her mother's words it felt as if the cotton fields had come right up to the windows. There was field upon field as Dido looked out over London from Mary Hill in Greenwich, swaying cane fields and the knocking thud of the mills moved by the tread of men and women in irons. Then she saw the harbour of Pensacola. She saw James Sommersett on a ship in the port. Her mother had told her not to look. *Come inside, child, don't look at them kind of thing*. She saw him standing in her Master's court before the King's bench in the Great Hall at Westminster.

She became him. She was a slave, a slave like James Sommersett.

'He belong to Charles Stewart Esquire who bring him from Virginia. Is he Sommersett run from into the streets of London.' She heard her mother telling the story she had heard her Master tell. 'That ship *Ann & Mary* right there in the docks.' Her mother pointed out of the window in the direction of the river looping round the Isle of Dogs. 'Is here they want to bring him and cart him right back to sell him again. He's Mr Charles Stewart Esquire investment in property. Them people up and down the country here in this England have investments all the way from Virginia, the Carolinas, right past Florida to the islands where you travel with your father when you young. Them never reach these places themselves, know nothing of what there, but they have a plantation or only two or three slaves as present and future profit. They maybe only have one poor girl or boy weeding in a yard who worth some pounds in Antigua, some pennies in Lancashire. You not remember that small island, Antigua?' She pinched Dido's chin and gave her a kiss on her forehead.

When Dido returned from Greenwich after seeing her mother, she went to look for the map in the library to find the whereabouts of that place, Virginia. She kept remembering her father's stories about longitude. He had spoken of Galileo. But it still looked as if it was the edge of the world and that the ship was falling off. What did Columbus think, she had asked her father when she was little, because she had heard him speak of the sailor from Genoa who had discovered the shape of this world they lived in. He said it was round. The map looked flat and the globe looked round.

There was this world and there was *home*. They had left Pensacola and come to England and had not fallen off the edge. Always a horizon ahead till it was just there, a stonewall, a green hedge and fields: England.

When Beth entered the schoolroom Dido did not pay attention to her.

'Dido, you're not paying attention to the lesson. I'll tell Lady Betty it's a waste of time for you to be here. Why did you ask to be here if you're not going to use it sensibly?'

'Why would you do that, Beth? What are you saying? You know how much lessons mean to me, more than to you.'

Affidavit was another word Dido did not understand. Those good people, Thomas Walklin, Elizabeth Cade and John Marlow, witnesses for the defence of James Sommersett, were characters in her story now, jumping out of the newspapers, living in her mind, as they said the characters came alive in Laurence Sterne's *Tristram Shandy*. There were still volumes to follow apparently in Mr Sterne's very long story, Mr Sterne, that friend of Ignatius Sancho who once came to tea with Dido's Master at Caen Wood and had once been a slave. A black man at Caen Wood! They said he had a shop in Mayfair. They said he was even cultured; he had been the slave of Lord Montagu, a friend of Mr Sterne.

'Them good people get an affidavit to bring the case of James Sommersett before your Master. His name is everywhere, everywhere.'

Dido's mother fed her morsels on her visits to Greenwich. 'Food to survive child, stories, seeds we sew into the hem of we dress and the cloth we wear upon we head. Grow them, tell them, where we reach.'

It distressed Lady Betty that her husband's name was mentioned in the papers. It reminded her of the Wilkes' case. Dido did not know of that, about the journalist who attacked her Master over the rights of Catholics and other matters. She was still to learn the details. She heard Lady Betty complain about the slander. 'My husband is maligned,' she said.

'Who are these people you are talking about?' Beth asked when she overheard Dido. That was why she did not talk to her or tell her those stories for, like Lady Betty, she became distressed. There was alarm in her voice.

Dido took Sommersett's friends to be good people acting well, to get this affidavit as she understood the meaning. Two of them were his godparents.

Baptism was not going to get them anything her mother kept telling her.

She asked her Master about the exact meaning. She got no answer on the meaning of affidavit.

She saw him riding with Beth and they were laughing and she wondered what they talked about. Did he question her questions? Beth did not have Dido's kind of questions to alarm her Master. Dido was sure of that. She asked equestrian questions. She wanted a new horse to ride, a new dress or shawl. She was elegant. She rode side-saddle. Couldn't Dido ride side-saddle?

'Read here,' Dido's mother instructed. 'Yesterday, in the *London Chronicle*.' The Sommersett story was all there. 'Under our nose this thing going on, child. You too young for all of this. How I go leave you with them?'

'You go carry me. You not go leave me.'

'Ask your father. You are the business of your father. I is the business of your father. Is so the world turning. Trade, the trade is everything.'

'I will get capture like James Sommersett.'

'The Lord Chief Justice is your Master, child. Let we see how his judgment fall.'

Dido was torn between Greenwich and Bloomsbury. She was torn between her mother and her Master's household. She was black and white, she thought to herself, I am sort of this and sort of that.

'You're a mule,' Hal told her one morning in the cold barn where she was sheltering from the rain and his fingers were undoing the buttons of her bodice.

She had to fight him off. 'Hal, what's the matter with you. Have you forgotten you were my friend, helping me, teaching me? You must still be that boy. You must not force yourself on me.'

The girls in the kitchen were giggling when Dido went to get some lunch. Surely they did not know about what Hal was doing. She heard Matty from Kentish Town saying, 'For sure, she must get a good sponge, soak it in vinegar and stuff it you know where or there'll be a little nigger crawling around this floor. Where will she be then? A half-breed like herself.'

The others in the kitchen stopped what they were doing and stared at Dido. Lydia came to her defence. 'You, Matty, shut that gob of yours.' Dido did not know what to do at first. She was stuck to the ground where she stood and was reluctant to stay in order to have her lunch that morning. She wished then at those moments she could have her meals with Beth and the family.

Lydia led her out to the kitchen garden. 'Don't listen to them,' she told her.

'My one aim is to have you free,' Dido's mother put her arm around her shoulder. 'You see that blackbird there, free. And you see them blackbirds there, what they call us, they not free. They can't fly and if they try they catch them, put them in a cage and take them back from where they come no matter anything your Master say about nobody have the right to catch anybody and send them back. They keep doing it all about this country. But you, my sweet, must stay as free as you can be by staying near his power.'

Her mother's eyes were full. She held them back. She did not want her daughter to see her crying.

'Chin up, as them say.'

Dido realised that she was being prepared for her mother's departure.

It was a cold day. Dido stood with her father on Greenwich dock as her mother walked away and then turned back towards her and came and knelt beside her. 'I promise. I will write. I will send for you. Your father know this. Keep her safe,' she said, as she looked up to John Lindsay. She straightened Dido's new dress which she had made for her. 'Keep it good. Behave yourself with your Master and his wife. Give your mother a kiss.' Dido kissed her on the cheek. She rose and walked away towards the gangway, climbing slowly to the deck with her holdall on her arm. John Lindsay had had her trunk delivered and had made arrangements for her to be made comfortable on board under the protection of the captain. He did not want to prolong the farewell, but Dido refused to leave. Maria Belle waved from the deck and then disappeared. Dido and her father stood together all the time it took for the ship to begin its voyage down the river, till it was a blur out of sight beyond the Isle of Dogs.

Dido found that here in England it was the blackbird that had the most beautiful song. She stood in the wood over by Sherrick Hole and listened to its freedom; but like in a poem by Mr Blake she had another thought about her Master and herself:

> He loves to sit and hear me sing,
> Then, laughing, sports and plays with me;
> Then stretches out my golden wing,
> And mocks my loss of liberty.

It was the song of the blackbird that made her think how much she valued the woods and the ponds, the wood pigeons murmuring in the distance with their plaintive moans. She liked to lose herself there, escape from the bustle of the dairy and the routines of the poultry farm, escape from Hal.

'Dido, where's Dido?' She heard Beth calling from the house.

She remained hidden, listening to the hammering of the woodpecker at the door of heaven, her fancy, so high in the wood, almost in the sky. The bird was at the blue door between the branches and the clouds, with the red flash of her head, nodding, pecking for food and making a nest, a home for her young.

10

IT WAS FINALLY decided that Mr d'Aviniere would be absent during Beth's visit. Beth had been quite demanding, especially at the time of her courting and wedding. Elizabeth and John never forgot that. They had had to steal their moments. Beth could parade her suitors, strolling in the park arm in arm, a public freedom. And then, of course, they were not now acquainted in the same way as they were at Caen Wood when all was topsy-turvy. The Right Honourable George Finch-Hatton, Beth's husband, was not part of their company now, not a natural acquaintance for Mr d'Aviniere.

'You understand Beth. You've known each other for so long,' John continued to argue. 'She's not changed that much as to be able to have a steward at table for tea. Don't force me.'

'Sweetheart… A parcel? Beth's presents, what on earth is she talking about?'

'I leave her to you. Lydia will be at hand to attend and hopefully lighten the meeting. I might not be discreet.'

Beth's presents had not always been a joy. Lady Betty would provide something suitable, which Dido had to give her. Presents from Beth were quite different. *You may like this dress Dido, I don't wear it anymore. You can have it. Let me see you wear it. It will be an improvement to your wardrobe.*

Elizabeth was not sure she would be able to reminisce with Beth.

What would be the point? Anyway, she was surely visiting out of kindness because she had heard that Elizabeth was out of sorts and Johnny's death, of course. Talk of a parcel. What parcel? Always talk of parcels, Beth's secrets. *There was a parcel come for you this morning, a letter brought to the door. Who can be sending you anything?* She could still hear that snigger.

Could they laugh now about the asses' milk when everyone made such a fuss about £3 4s and 1d and that sort of thing spent on Dido; her tooth extracted for 5s and her Master's Christmas presents? Strange, that history in a bookkeeper's ledger, stories about Dido told in the family. Mrs Burns, with the bustle of her housekeeping, used to insist that Dido *had the best*, those new hangings in her room, as she would put it. Elizabeth did not understand why at times that was the case. Lady Betty was kind and had been overwhelmed in supervising her care. She could always see that.

Charles was going to be kept from school for Beth's visit. Elizabeth had explained to her boys that Beth's children were, in a way, cousins. Charles was already talking about the carriage and the horses outside the house, remembering Beth's previous visit. Lydia had been scrubbing and cleaning and tidying.

Seamus had been working in the garden. 'I'll fix everything Mrs d'Aviniere, weeding, digging,' he said.

'Thank you, Seamus, and for laying the fire so well in my room last evening.'

Elizabeth was trying to keep Billy calm. She was conscious of how she wanted to appear to Beth. She wanted to seem in control, independent now, in her own home with her own husband and children, with her freedom, though she knew that Beth would be putting out her hand to detain her in some task, to speak for her, *Let me Dido*, in her usual imperial manner. Will she still call me, Dido? Elizabeth asked herself. As young girls they had once vowed friendship, pricking their fingers with their sewing needles and mixing their blood, vowing against all the odds to be blood sisters, before they knew how soon time would change all of that. Mixing blood, she was mixed blood. *You are already mixed blood.* She remembered Beth looking at her and smiling wickedly and then laughing as she ran off down the corridor. She had looked at the prick at the tip of her finger with a drop of blood as red as a ruby.

Elizabeth remembered wanting time to stand still when Beth and herself played as if there was no other time. Then, at another moment, she wanted it to race ahead so she could change her circumstances and return to her mother at her house in Greenwich before she went away.

She carried so many feelings of betrayal, her mother's and her own.

Elizabeth was overwhelmed. She had quite forgotten what was happening this afternoon in her own home, where Lydia was, what Billy was up to, and who was preparing tea for Beth's visit. Oh, where was John? Elizabeth thought.

The boys were scrubbed and dressed in their finest suits. Lydia had fetched the best plate and cutlery and laid the damask cloth upon a table in the parlour.

'I'll help the boys this afternoon with the horses,' Seamus volunteered.

'You watch them. They are not accustomed to horses.'

Elizabeth could see that it was better now that John was absent for the visit. She herself had never eaten at their table with their guests — how odd that was, a daily reminder that she was and was not a member of their family. That went on for twenty-eight years. There were other kinds of intimacy, but not table; so curious, the conceptions of people, she thought.

She was jumping through the years from when she and Beth were little girls to when they were lasses, as her Master would call them in his Perthshire tongue, and then as grown young women. Her mind had been made almost mad with the memories.

She must get dressed. She would wear one of her best dresses but something plain, not too decorative. She kept being distracted. She relented and had just a tincture of her laudanum, which afforded her some respite. It reduced her anxiety.

Beth was arriving at any moment. How do I look? Elizabeth asked herself. No sooner had she said so than Beth's presence was announced by Lydia shouting up from the front door, 'Ma'am, Ma'am, it's Lady Beth.'

There was such a commotion on the street. Charles and Billy were tearing down the stairs and through the hall. The door was flung open. The enormous carriage obscured the view across to the other side of the street. The horses were stamping and snorting with the disturbance and bustle. Beth's footman was accommodating her safely as she stepped down from her carriage. She alighted in a froth of pink skirts, a confection of summer flowers for a bonnet, like a profusion of roses, followed by her three children George, Daniel and Louise, all flowering, as it were, and fashionably dressed for the summer.

Elizabeth stood at the front door. She squeezed Lydia's hand.

'Dido, so good to see you.' Beth cried out.

'Beth.'

Elizabeth noticed that Charles was curious about Beth calling her Dido. He was mouthing, Di-do? He did not question it openly, but he looked back at his mother before he then distracted himself with the horses and seeing his cousins.

'Come here. Your loss, your terrible loss. Little Johnny.' Beth continued embracing Elizabeth extravagantly. She had not remembered Beth being so loquacious.

Lydia led off the younger children, Daniel and Louise with William Thomas into the garden, while George, Beth's older boy, went off with Charles to help take care of the horses with Seamus.

'Come back here, all of you. Children, say hello to Aunt Dido.'

The children trooped back and looked at her curiously. 'Hello, Aunt Dido.'

Charles looked even more puzzled.

Elizabeth could not believe that Beth was still calling her Dido.

'Aunt Dido,' little Louise piped up.

'Just look at the cousins.' Beth pointed at the children trooping off.

They were cousins, at least some percentage of them was related. Of course, that bit which did not have a touch of the tar brush, Elizabeth imagined Beth might be thinking.

'Should we leave them to play, yes?' Beth now looked a little doubtful. Was it that touch of the tar brush she was thinking of? Elizabeth looked at her curiously. She knew she was going to find it so difficult to hit the right note. It was why Mr d'Aviniere had stayed away. He would have found it impossible.

They entered the house through the narrow hall now seeming crushed with skirts and the taking off of bonnets.

'Lydia has laid up for tea in the parlour. Let's sit here by the French windows. Keep an eye on the children.'

'How are you, Dido?'

'We're well. We're much better. We've got to think of our two boys above all. Your children have grown and look very well. The country air of Kent, I'm sure.' How was she doing? She was so nervous. She had forgotten how to talk to Beth. She did not think she would be able to keep up the pretence.

'But you, Dido, yourself. You do look poorly...'

'I'm not my best at the moment. At least, I'm not coughing all over you.'

'Mr d'Aviniere, How's he?'

'He's well. We're both still distraught over Johnny's death, of course. He has to be at his work today. He sends his apology.'

'That's sweet of him...'

'Your man is at the door, Beth. I think he wants to say something.' Elizabeth felt that she would not be able to last the afternoon.

Beth turned to deal with the matter. 'Herbert, just rest it here near me.'

Beth's man rested a large lacquered box on a nearby table.

'Dido, I said I had a message to deliver and a parcel. Well it's this box and I've got here some papers we must discuss. Dido...'

'Elizabeth...'

'What did you say?'

'I call myself Elizabeth, now...'

'Really? You always were Dido, surely...'

'That's my name, Elizabeth...'

'We can't both have the same name. It won't do. How confusing.'

Beth was laughing all the time.

'You know Elizabeth is my baptism name and...'

'Yes, but surely. How can you be anyone else but Dido? That's who you are...'

'Well, I'm Elizabeth. Baptised. I prefer it. I never did like Dido. I'm not Dido...'

'Yes, but, really Dido! I can't believe after all these years.' Beth laughed nervously again.

'Yes, you must stop ...'

'How can I?'

'You must try...'

'This is a surprise. Why?'

'Why? A name given when I was a slave...'

'Dido! All that's so long ago...'

'Yes, but not finished with...'

'Let's not get on to this today of all days, I've not seen you for so long.'

Mr d'Aviniere was right. Beth had not changed one bit. She was relieved she was not putting him through this meeting. Except that Elizabeth thought she had changed from the young Beth, who in very special moments was the person she was closest to, and then not. All in a twinkle of an eye it could be one thing, and then quite another. That was the problem. She was never quite right, never quite who the household thought she should be.

So many memories of this woman, as a child, a young girl, a grown woman flashed through Elizabeth's mind all at once: companion, friend, cousin and most hateful person at times. There were so many voices in her head. She felt quite queer as Beth turned away from her to reach for the large lacquered box that Herbert had rested on the gateleg table.

It was the battle over her name. It came to represent years of repressed anger. She must control herself. She called to Lydia as she saw Beth standing now over the table sorting through some papers in the opened box.

'Lydia. Lydia. Come and help me, please.' Elizabeth had to call over the laughter and play of the children in the garden. 'Lydia,' she shouted as loud as she could.

Lydia came running across the garden into the room. 'Yes, Ma'am.'

'Tea, Lydia. The children need feeding.'

'Indeed, Ma'am, I'll get everything ready. You don't look good…'

'I'm fine. It's a little warm in the house.'

'How nice to see you again, Lydia.' Beth turned from her task of sorting papers.

'It's a pleasure to see you again, Ma'am.' Lydia was all grace and politeness. She understood the difficult relationship between these two women.

'A glass of water, Lydia.' Elizabeth was coughing uncontrollably, almost choking.

'Immediately, Ma'am.'

Elizabeth sipped her water and listened to Beth talking, while she watched Billy playing with Daniel and Louise in the garden. They ran back and forth through the light into the shadow and then they were held in the shadow as a cloud masked the sun. They were skipping and then playing with their sticks and hoops along the path.

Elizabeth saw herself as Dido, with Beth, running in the park at Caen Wood. They were leaping little girls down from the south terrace towards the Thousand Pound Pond, and they were calling to each other. She heard it now, that name, Beth calling her, shouting, *Dido, Dido, Dido*, ringing out.

'Dido, Sorry. Elizabeth. I must call you Elizabeth to distinguish you from myself. Is that what you want?'

'Those close to me call me Lizzie. But, yes, you can call me Elizabeth.'

Beth stood at the table. She had the large lacquered box open and had placed some of the papers on the table. 'There are these documents. But first, there is some news I must tell you...'

'News? Should we wait till after tea? The children are coming in from the garden. Here are George and Charles. Are the horses fed, boys?'

'Yes, Mama, and cousin George has shown me how to whittle a switch.'

'That's marvellous, sweetheart.' She pulled at the hair on his neck and straightened his white collar.

Lydia poured tea while the younger children were made comfortable on the floor with Billy's soldiers. George and Charles sat with the grown ups. Lydia had prepared large amounts of bread and butter. The children finished up every last scrap, greedily. There was a treat of strawberries and cream from the nearby farm where Charles had got the hay for the horses.

The cousins made Elizabeth's boys happy. Charles and George discussed school, the study of Latin and Greek, and what they thought of Napoleon, 'Boney' as they called him, giggling. Louise was particularly attentive to Billy. She was allowing him to play with her doll. But Daniel seemed a little isolated and was given a book to look at quietly at Beth's side.

Elizabeth overheard George saying to Charles, 'Was Johnny really your brother? You're so black and he was only brown with strange green eyes?'

'We're mixed race, you see.'

'Oh, yes we're kind of cousins, aren't we?'

'We are cousins.'

Elizabeth smiled and felt proud of Charles.

After clearing away the tea things, Lydia was good at helping to organise games in the garden. Elizabeth sat and looked at them playing at skipping and hopscotch along the path. What a family, she thought, her black boy and her clearly mixed-race child among Finch-Hatton's very white English children.

'Elizabeth, I feel terrible. I don't know what I've done.'

'What is it?' She recognised that look on Beth's face. She had not forgotten, like when she was repentant after being particularly selfish.

'I didn't tell you the news of Aunt Marjory's death.'

'My God!'

'Yes.'

'Why didn't you tell me? When did this happen?'

'I feel so ashamed...'

'Beth, what are you telling me? When...?'

'April 19 1799.'

'After all this time, I don't understand...'

'I'm so sorry. These papers will explain.' Beth unfolded the document in her hands, which she spread out on the table. Elizabeth leaned in towards her to view more carefully and to read what she was pointing to on the page.

'My father was executor of Aunt Marjory's will. This document and letter from him explain that you are a beneficiary. Look, it's stated here.' She pointed to the line in the will. 'Aunt Marjory, read here, has left you £100. This is the actual deed. You must sign here.'

Herbert had obviously rehearsed this moment because he was ready at hand, with a pen and ink.

'Miss Marjory, I can't believe it. I'm going to start to cry. Lydia, Lydia.'

Lydia came rushing in from the garden.

'Yes, Ma'am?'

'This cough, water, more water.'

'I've been so clumsy. I'm sorry.' Beth was rolling up the document. Herbert had dusted the ink with sprinklings of sand, examining it to see that it had dried.

Elizabeth sipped the water and choked back her tears. 'Miss Marjory...'

'She was fond of you...'

'Yes, she was a kind woman, important to me after Lady Betty's death. Left alone in that house after your marriage, to care for my Master. It's not just her death. It's the past. Our past upsets me...'

'Is that how you still think of him, as your Master?'

Elizabeth stared at Beth. 'He was for twenty-eight years of my life.' She painted a picture of what life was like at Caen Wood after Beth had left with her husband and she had to remain with the aunts. 'I was eight years as his amanuensis, as he called me.' Beth was trying not to catch Elizabeth's eyes as she spoke. 'Must I remind you? You visited with Mr Finch-Hatton.' She described for Beth the fetching and carrying. 'I wrote his letters. I was there at his bedside, changing the sheets, emptying the commode...'

'Dido...'

'I read to him from his beloved Cicero. You know this, Beth. Miss Marjory helped, can't say the same about your Aunt Anne. She was distant, did her duty. I needed to be loved. Miss Marjory loved me...'

'Dido. It was a while ago.'

'I remember visiting her in Twickenham.

'It was a strange time, Dido...'

'Yes, I was Dido then. But I'm Elizabeth now. You must respect that. The past, our past was so different in the same household, so different...'

'I'm sorry. We were friends once, companions, blood sisters. You remember?'

'Yes, I do, but I remember a lot of other things, you wouldn't know unless you stopped to imagine...'

'Dido, Dido...'

'It sounds cruel but at times I was a sort of a pet, wasn't I...?'

'No, let's stop this.'

'Yes. I will...Twickenham...'

Elizabeth described going there once, along the river, far into the country and the dirt roads winding down. 'We crossed on a ferry, quite a short crossing at the bend in the river. And as I paid the ferryman, I joked about the river Styx and having to pay a coin to go to Hades.' She continued her description of the embankment, and the boats moored alongside, and a visit to Mr Walpole's house at nearby Strawberry Hill. 'All quite splendid.'

'Yes...'

'I called her Miss Marjory,' Elizabeth continued, 'but yes, she was like an aunt. I wasn't accustomed to having aunts. I didn't have aunts.'

Elizabeth was conscious of Beth looking at her, as she was unable to cease her excitable speech, and eventual sobbing.

'How you've changed, Dido, here.' Beth offered her a handkerchief. 'She was your great-aunt, sort of...'

'Yes, sort of, you don't know what it means to be sort of, all of your life, do you? Now that I'm Elizabeth...'

'You'll always be Dido to me. The world has not changed that much...'

'That has changed. I'm not Dido. No, it hasn't, it's hardly changed at all. But it might. It will. Much is happening.' Elizabeth described the meetings she and her husband attended to support the abolition movement.

'You think it will help? I remember your regular visits to the Meeting House in Shoreditch, your giving up of sugar.'

'Your husband's in the parliament. Does he not tell you what goes on there? I know there was the disappointment of the Wilberforce bill failing. But we'll progress. Men like Mr Equiano inspire us.'

'Equiano? My husband tells me very little. I'm so caught up with the children and the running of the house.'

Elizabeth despaired of Beth. 'Yes, I suppose. Anyway, I won't be here to see it...'

'You mustn't say that...'

'I must, because it's true. I must prepare myself, prepare my boys.'

'Elizabeth, you must stop this talk.'

'We both lost our mothers in different ways, didn't we Beth, when we were little girls?'

Beth looked away. She went silent with Elizabeth's mention of her mother. She rose and went towards the French windows. She turned and said, 'I must just see what Daniel is up to at the bottom of the garden. I expect it's a worm or a caterpillar that's caught his interest.'

Elizabeth watched her descend to the garden and join the children in the bright light. Her frock of rose-coloured silk shimmered in the sunshine reminding Elizabeth of that absurd portrait of them as young women.

'Elizabeth, come into the sun,' Beth called out from the bottom of the garden.

At last, she's got my true name, Elizabeth thought.

'You must come and talk with me while Lydia keeps an eye on the children.'

'I prefer it here. There's a chill in the breeze.'

Beth returned to the house.

'Your writing box, it was once my great-uncle's...?'

'Yes, a gift...'

'You keep a journal?'

'Well, an attempt to remember how it all was.' She described that she wanted something for Mr d'Aviniere to have when she was gone, a story for the children when they were older.

'We shared so much, but in different ways...'

'Different skins.'

'Skins? You mustn't give in to melancholia, Dido.'

'You sound like Lady Betty instructing me when I was moody and keeping to my room, or lost, wandering in the park.'

'I don't remember any of that, you know.'

'Really?'

'I hardly remember any of that time.'

'A mercy, a privilege not to have to remember.'

'I don't seem to have a mind of my own.'

'What about your mother? Don't you remember her?'

'Hardly. I don't remember ever being in Poland or Vienna. Our mothers gave us away.'

'Is that how you see it? Your mother died. My father gave me away...'

'Your mother, she...'

'What did you know about my mother?'

'I do remember you going to visit her from time to time. When you got back to Bloomsbury, you would tell me stories about travelling on the river. Was it to Greenwich? You were sad when you arrived back. I remember you crying at night in your room.'

'There, you do remember something of that past. I'm sure you must remember more...'

'As I say, I'm so preoccupied with my children and my husband...'

'It saves me, my writing...'

'Saves you? What do you mean?'

'I'm hoping that it will help me to understand why I've never heard from my mother after her first letter. We exchanged letters only once after she had left and returned to Pensacola, despite me writing continually for years. It's been a mystery to me. She promised to write to me.'

Beth turned towards the gate-leg table and reached for the lacquered box.

Elizabeth got up and went towards the cabinet where she kept her precious mementoes and brought out a smaller chestnut box she had had since she was a girl.

'Beth, look, there's something I must show you. As I say, I had never had a reply to my letters, just this one when my mother had first arrived back in Pensacola. As you see, the paper is stained. I imagine with sea water.'

Her mother's words were swimming now as she undid the small parcel because her eyes were full. She began to read to Beth in her mother's tongue.

Dearest Daughter

I reach back in Pensacola after three weeks on the sea. My child. I sorry to leave you there with them people, your father people, but is for the good. You know that. You know I tell you so. I promise I go bring you. I promise. Your father self promise you that he go send you when I say I fix up and ready for your arrival. You remember Miss Hettie the girl next door where we used to live when you small small. She send to say how do... one of your father's men on one of the ships he say he go bring this for you... I can hardly speak to you my child — I can hardly speak and not keep crying my dearest daughter... I will write soon again.

Your mother who loves you.

'Dido...'

'Elizabeth.'

'Elizabeth, sorry, how old were you when you received that letter?'

'I must've been thirteen going on fourteen. As I remember it, my mother left for Pensacola in 1774.'

'Who gave you the letter?'

Elizabeth kept re-reading her mother's letter as she spoke, checking her tears, swallowing her sorrow. She could hardly read the words that said so little and so much at the same time. 'I think it was Lady Betty who brought it to me one day in the orangery at Caen Wood. *Dido, there's a letter here for you.* I can hear her now. It must've been delivered to the house in Bloomsbury. They were words I wanted to keep hearing. Waiting so long. It was folded like a little parcel as it still is now. As I began to read the first two words, I ran out of the orangery up the backstairs to my room and lay down on my bed reading it over and over and crying, reading it through my tears. Then I folded it back the same way it arrived and put it among my precious things with her blue kerchief and the small gold earrings she pierced my ears with.'

'You remember so much. It frightens me how much. What you remember must explain so much to you. It frightens me.'

Elizabeth explained how she stopped asking questions. Miss Anne and Miss Marjory as well had both been quiet on the subject when she had asked them many years later, still thinking that it might be possible that she could hear from her mother.

'Dido...'

Elizabeth had begun to speak again without stopping.

'I'd been so proud to write when my mother had first departed since my writing had come on strongly. I was thirteen then, proud of my writing. Even Master had time to read what I'd written and promised that I would have to be his amanuensis, as he called it, when I was a bit older. It was a word I did not know then and learnt the meaning later. I admit I was then perplexed as to his choice of word...'

'Dido...'

'I was to be within the reach of his hand, he said, to be there, always to fetch and carry and then to read and write and copy and copy again. A most trusted servant, I read somewhere of an amanuensis, one who had once been enslaved and was now free. Like in ancient times in Rome. It was in a book in the library I learned of such a meaning. Was it Cicero, who Master admired, and read so much of, who had an amanuensis like myself, copying and copying and being at hand to fetch and carry? Cicero had a slave whom he freed.'

Elizabeth looked at Beth who had been trying to interrupt her. She had been staring into the garden while she was telling her this story, talking on and on. Beth looked afraid and sad. Elizabeth had lost herself, going on and on in her own world.

'Dido. You must stop...'

'It's something I do now that disturbs Mr d'Aviniere and can amuse the children, or perplex them if I don't stop.'

'Your mind goes everywhere all at once. I cannot keep up. I'm moved by the way you tell it. You remind me how I used to ask you to tell me stories when you got back from visiting your mother. I could not imagine your black mother and how she spoke and where she had come from. When I crept into your room and sat by your bedside as you went on and on, I remember falling asleep at the edge of your bed and being woken by the wind in the trees, and the candle at the side of your bed had burnt right down, and I blew it out before creeping back to my room.'

Elizabeth smiled at Beth's story. 'So, you see, you do remember. Maybe you'll remember more. There's much that we both witnessed, heard, and saw with different eyes.'

'Yes, yes, there was. You telling the story now brings back the storytelling then. It confused and hurt me when I was little and then I grew up as I was meant to do and went away.'

'To marry well…'

'Yes, I've married well.'

Beth and Elizabeth smiled at each other, and in that moment Elizabeth remembered how she could feel and think of her as a kind of sister, not that she ever knew that feeling really.

Beth then went back to the lacquered box from where she had fetched the document and letter relating to Miss Marjory's legacy.

'This is such a coincidence. I've been delaying what has been the principal reason for my visit. Aunt Marjory's will was one thing. But since her death, there's been this other matter.'

Beth's hands were trembling as they hovered over the box, where she now stood at the table and began lifting out a bundle of papers tied with pink ribbon. She rested this bundle on the table and then lifted out another bundle tied with blue ribbon. Then she turned towards Elizabeth and spoke solemnly. Her voice cracked with emotion. Elizabeth had not ever seen Beth so overcome except maybe at the time of Lady Betty's death. Beth looked directly at her. 'You must read these.' She handed Elizabeth the bundle that was tied with pink ribbon, saying, 'The others you will both remember and be more familiar.'

Elizabeth reached out. Beth went towards the French windows and then stepped out into the garden. Elizabeth was left with the tight bundle on her lap. She put it down on the table. She turned to look at Beth as she walked into the light and then she became part of the shadow that the clouds made.

The children's voices came from the bottom of the garden.

As Elizabeth untied the ribbon, the small parcels fell apart. She knew at once what had been given to her. She dared not open them after all these years of yearning to know, to hear. She turned to look at Beth. She looked with incomprehension at the collection of letters. Beth was kneeling in the grass attending to her little boy.

Beth and Lydia and the children seemed far away as Elizabeth sat unable to open the parcels. She was looking instead at the house martins as they swooped and fed on the wing, darting into the eaves to feed their young in the nests, which were lodged there, small enclosures of wattle, part of the walls. She could just see one with a chick's head, a mouth at the mouth of the nest to be fed.

At first, she could only read *Dearest Daughter* as she began and then folded back the small parcel, the words that she had been waiting years to read. She knew now that she could not blame her for not writing. She began counting the letters.

Beth came in from the garden and found her looking hopeless with the letters still unopened. She sat next to her and began to explain. 'I must tell you what I know. I had it told to me by Aunt Anne...'

'Miss Anne?'

'It was originally your father's idea. He felt that after the first of your mother's letters, the one you have just read to me, it would prove too unsettling for you to keep receiving such emotional outpourings from your mother. He entrusted Lady Betty with the task of reading them on arrival. He wanted her to decide whether they should be given to you. They had the same reason for not sending on your own letters. They thought it best to stop the communication for your own good.'

'These?' Elizabeth reached out for the second bundle. 'My own letters never sent. My God! Not one other from my mother? How extraordinary. And, what did she get of mine?'

'Maybe one.'

Elizabeth opened one of her mother's letters tentatively, taken at random. As she turned the pages of this early letter dated 1775, a year after her mother's departure, she could not continue reading.

She could see herself now knocking at the door of Lady Betty's dressing room, delivering her own letters.

Beth did not explain anymore about the letters. Elizabeth could see that she was embarrassed and upset. She even looked ashamed, she thought.

'Beth, did you know about this at the time?'

Beth did not reply. She busied herself with closing the box, tidying the papers on the table. She turned to go back to the garden.

'Beth, I asked you, did you know that this was happening? It happened over years. Did you at any point know about this plan? Maybe, not at the beginning? You were a girl then like myself. But, later on? Were you complicit with them, Lady Betty, my father and my Master in this terrible betrayal, this plan to stop me hearing from my mother over all these years; to hold my letters back so she was left wondering? Not to upset me?' She could feel her anger rising.

'They did not want to...'

'Not upset me! Beth! Not have my mother for the whole of my life! No explanation to either of us?'

'Elizabeth, I don't mean...'

'And these, my own carefully written, penned by a child, a mere girl at the time.' Elizabeth picked up her letters and let them spill onto the floor. The breeze through the French windows lifted the pages and scattered them. Beth got on her knees scrambling to retrieve them in some order.

'I was proud of how I wrote. Do you know the emotion I expended each and every time I completed one of these, these yearnings for my mother, my dear mother who was to send for me? Did you know that she had promised to send for me? I was waiting. I was waiting for her to tell me when I should go to her.'

Beth could not listen to Elizabeth. She put the letters on the table and looked towards her children. Elizabeth's raised voice was alarming them. Little Louise was crying out for her mother. Beth went and picked up the child.

Elizabeth realised she was not going to get an answer. Beth was not giving her a chance to ask any further questions. She was terrified to begin reading her mother's letters, to find out what had happened to her, what things could she not read when she was a girl.

Elizabeth had too many questions. Her anger made her incapable of bending down to pick up the letters from under the table. She was beside herself at the injustice. 'Justice.' She kept repeating the word 'justice'. She tried to stand up and had to sit back down. Lydia came in from the garden noticing that something was the matter. 'Justice, justice, Lydia. How will I get justice?'

'Ma'am? Let me help you.' Lydia collected up the last letters.

Elizabeth noticed that Beth was at the bottom of the garden, the furthest she could remove herself.

'Water, Lydia, and a tincture. I won't survive this. I need some relief. My children. Look at that black boy and my little hazel-eyed Billy. How will they get justice?'

'Here, Ma'am, sip this.'

'Yes, that's better. My throat is so dry. Put the laudanum aside for later. Allow me to feel my pain.'

Elizabeth picked up the letters off the table with Lydia's help and kept arranging and rearranging each bundle. They were now mixed up. 'Do you know what these are Lydia?'

'Ma'am? Lady Elizabeth brought these, didn't she, Ma'am?'

'A legacy...'

'Ma'am, better to quiet yourself now for the sake of the children.'

'The children? Where's my black son?'

'You won't have just a tincture?'

'No, no. I want to feel this just anger. My belongings. My own letters. I cannot open them. I cannot bear to see those letters written when I was so young, when I needed my mother so much. What will I discover? Did you know about this, Lydia?'

'What Ma'am?'

'This hoarding, this deception.'

'No, Ma'am. I don't understand what you're saying.'

The rest of the afternoon seemed to have disappeared with the children running in and out of the house, the garden alive with laughter. Beth was now leaving. She said, looking worried and sad, 'You have the £100 from Aunt Marjory.'

Elizabeth looked at her with incomprehension and replied, 'I've my mother's letters. I'll read them all in time even if it kills me to do so.'

'Dido...'

'Of course, I'm grateful for Miss Marjory's gift. That's another matter entirely. What part did she and that Miss Anne play in this deception? Do you know?'

'Dido...'

'I now understand what has worried me all of my life. How will I contact my mother? She must be alive. She was a young woman.'

Beth continued, 'But the money must bring some joy...'

'I'll put it aside for my boys.'

'Dido...'

'You must learn to say my name correctly. You must go now.' She lowered her voice.

Beth looked embarrassed as she collected her children around her to enter the carriage. 'Dearest Elizabeth.' She kissed her. She looked flustered. 'We must get off. Ashford is such a distance.'

Elizabeth caught a glimpse of the young girl who had been her blood sister. 'Travel safely, Beth. You must go. Let us write to each other.' She wanted to part in a way that would not alarm the children.

'I'm not sure what I know...'

'Still, let us write. You began remembering.'

The children were bundled into the carriage amidst great excitement, turning and waving to their cousins as they moved off. They all waved, Charles running alongside the horses and Billy hanging on to his mother's skirt.

Charles was quick off the mark with 'Why does Mrs Finch-Hatton keep calling you Dido?'

'She was accustomed to calling me by that name when we were children.'

'But it's not your name...'

'Quite so. It's not my name. But it was what I was called at Caen Wood and Bloomsbury. One day I'll tell you more of that story. Not now, sweetheart.'

'Has she upset you?'

'You notice everything, my pet. Some of our past is upsetting when we go over it. I'll tell you all in good time. Run along now and give Seamus a hand with clearing up the mess the horses have made outside the front door. Get the broom for all those bits of hay.'

Elizabeth wondered whether Beth would ever learn how the world worked.

Lydia was wiping her hands on her apron as they kept on standing in the street after the carriage had disappeared. 'She hasn't changed at all, has she, Miss Beth?' She smoothed down her apron and looked up into the sky. 'What a summer's day, Ma'am.'

'Yes, we're fortunate with that.' They turned towards each other, arms outstretched to embrace. 'Dear Lydia, I've got you. You'll have to help me explain what has happened. I can't believe what has been given to me. I can't wait for Mr d'Aviniere to get home.'

11

'SO, AN AFTERNOON of extraordinary surprises Lydia tells me.'

'I'm so glad you're back. Lydia? I still need to talk to her.'

'What do you mean?'

'I need to know who knew…'

'What exactly? Tell me.'

Elizabeth related to her husband the afternoon's events from the very beginning of Beth's arrival with her children, her refusal to get her to change from calling her Dido.

'She wouldn't call you Elizabeth?'

'She did in the end, reluctantly. She said that's who I always would be, Dido.'

'That woman!' John d'Aviniere remembered the first time he came calling at the Caen Wood to see Dido. 'So haughty. She never allowed us time on our own. How would I have been able to be polite?'

'You would've been for my sake. But that's not all.'

When Elizabeth came to Miss Marjory's legacy, she handed him the legal papers. John listened carefully as he read the document and looked at the deed for one hundred pounds. 'You always said she was the kinder of the women…'

'Yes, but given what then followed I think it's most revealing. I've been thinking…'

'Revealing?'

Elizabeth then told her husband of how her mother's letters were given to her and the shock of seeing her own and the realisation of how she had been betrayed.

'None of my letters had been posted.' She placed the bundles in her husband's hands.

'*Mon dieu!* These people! Beth, did she always know? That they kept the letters. Why?'

'Can you imagine my mother's hurt, her puzzlement, her sense of betrayal? How was she to bring me to her?' Elizabeth choked on her words.

John embraced his wife. 'I can't believe this.'

'You're going to have to help me.'

'This is so intolerable. So intolerable.' John began to pace up and down the room. 'How was this secret kept? Accomplices?'

'Miss Anne lives in Brighton. What can I say to her? Beth must know more. She needs to answer my questions. She would not answer this afternoon. I just wanted her to leave.'

Elizabeth could see her husband's outrage on his face.

'Watch your health, darling. We must bear this together.'

'I must read all the letters. I must write to her. You have to help me find her.'

John began reading and the tears came quickly. 'This is your mother.'

'Sweetheart.' Elizabeth held on to her husband.

As they eventually began to plan they realised that the task ahead of contacting her mother was going to be more difficult than they had immediately thought, the world changing all the time with countries changing hands. After all these years?

'Darling…'

'Can you imagine how betrayed she must have been feeling all this time…still must…'

'Be realistic. Your health, our boys…'

'We must plan right away…'

'My employers in Gough Square may be able to help. They own

ships. They'll know the best way.'

Later that evening, once the boys were in bed, John and Elizabeth stayed up to talk.

'You seem far away.' Elizabeth reached out her hand to touch John's arm.

'It's the story of the letters, keeping you away from your mother. It brings it all back. As you know my father didn't allow my mother into the house at Coulibri, didn't allow me to know who my mother was. She was just there, down in the yard, in the huts at the edge of the sugarcane. A woman working in my father's house told me that. She said she would bring me to her. I thought I knew which woman it was. Martha thought she knew. I used to stare at different women who came up from the estate to work in the yard. Could that one be my mother I would ask myself? I could never be absolutely sure. Can you imagine her sacrifice? She knew who I was, who we were, her twins. She must've had no choice. I was not allowed my father's name and I was not allowed to know my mother. Think of Martha. Once I went searching all over the estate. I would ask women, are you my mother? *All of we is mothers, all of you is sons*, one woman told me. When I returned to the house, my father beat me. He had a tamarind switch for his beatings.'

'John, dearest, you know I know that story as if it's my own...'

'The stories keep repeating themselves. Can I ever leave them behind? I wanted to kill him.'

'Rage...yes, when will we be able to leave those stories behind?'

'Yes, we were saved and lost all at once, Martha and myself. Saved by Thomas d'Aviniere when he found us in the port at Bordeaux after that terrible ship...'

'Lost and found...'

'It's why we've found each other. It's sad that Martha has not found anyone and our foster father so very old now.'

They held on to each other, the boys in the next room, Lydia shuffling about in the room above.

Her mother's letters took Elizabeth back to the room where she remembered delivering her post.

⟫ LADY BETTY'S DRESSING room had been newly decorated after the taking down of the rather horrid, old green paper and the putting up of the new linen with the Chinese border that Dido loved to look at in what had now become the blue room.

'Is this another letter for your mother, Dido? Let me see.'

Lady Betty took it from her hand and, looking at the way she had folded it and addressed the front of the little parcel, she deposited it in the side drawer of her desk.

'You're a good girl, Dido, to keep writing to your mother.' Then she allowed her to admire her new room. They talked about some task that she needed done in her dairy. 'We must make sure our butter is better this year than Lady Southhampton's.' She smiled then. Dido felt honoured to be part of her confidence.

'Is there another letter from my mother? She promised to write. I've only heard from her once since she left England.'

Lady Betty continued smiling as she kept on with what she was writing at her desk as if not paying attention to Dido's question, and then said, almost nonchalantly, 'No, Dido, no. It's the other side of the world, you know.' She said this, not looking at Dido.

Dido stood her ground that day and said that she did understand the geography of the world, that it was the first thing that her father had taught her with his maps and she did consult the globe in the library at Bloomsbury. At this, Lady Betty lifted her eyes and turned towards Dido. She looked as if she did not know her, searching in her head for an answer to what she had been asking.

'Indeed, you do, Dido, indeed, and so you above all should understand how long it takes for letters to cross the ocean.'

Dido still stood her ground and said, 'But Lady Betty, it would take as long going the other way from here to there. It's the same distance that my letter has to travel as my mother's. Isn't it, wouldn't you say?'

'Dido, what do you want me to say...?'

'One would not fall off the edge of the world would one, not anymore, surely? My letters must be getting there? Except I haven't heard...'

'That's enough, Dido. Hurry on now, I must finish my own letter. This one has only to get to Hertfordshire. And this last, I'm about to write has to get to cousin Susan in Bath.'

❧ HAD THERE BEEN a flicker of doubt on Lady Betty's face to suggest the hoard in her desk, accumulating there for years, hidden just there in that right-hand drawer? Elizabeth did not remember any sign. It had never crossed her mind that such a thing was possible.

Sweetest Mama

I must still work each day at supervising the milking in the dairy and collecting eggs at the poultry at the end of the week at Caen Wood. I have a new entertainment which is learning and that I do in the library when I take down very heavy tomes, as they are called, from the shelves and read there stories of ancients — there are the Greeks and the Romans with their gods — you would be proud of my reading aloud and as you can see my sentences are coming on. My Master wants me to write for him, to copy for him. He dictates to me. The library I talk of is at Bloomsbury because the library at Caen Wood is not yet in order and all the books from Bloomsbury must be transported to that place. Master indulges this entertainment which he himself calls learning. I want to be with you. I am sure we could have some books in Pensacola to read together. When are you sending for me? I know I continue to ask this, but you have not given an answer and my father does not seem to visit his uncle and aunt so I do not see him to ask him for that information. I want to ask him why I have not heard from you.

They had not prevented her from writing. They must have thought it good that she wrote out her feelings. They must have read them to get to know her innermost thoughts. It was a way to keep a check on her. It was part of her capture, her bondage. It was a clever way as well to keep an eye on her mother. Above all, it worked to keep mother and daughter apart forever.

Which was more distressing, the voice of the young girl writing to her mother, or, the young mother writing to her daughter? Elizabeth did not possess the scales to weigh up such a contrast. She took one of her own letters out and then put it back. She was unable to read another. The things she discovered: *Mammy I cry all night...send for me. My father has abandoned me. He does not write.*

Elizabeth let the lid fall on the letters. Instead, she wrote to Beth.

Dear Beth

I keep reading the letters. I must write to you for I am sure there is more you can tell me.

Was it the plan by the original creators of this archive to gift it to me later in my life? Was it that after Lady Betty's illness and death my Master forgot all about the letters? Lady Betty's plan might've been: allow her this till she is an older woman and can cope with the separation and then she will see the benefits of it. Did I once hear something like that and not know what was being referred to by those words? I keep imagining things I think I remember hearing. You must fill in the blanks even though you tell me you do not remember much of our past. But you did remember when we began talking. I need to know the truth. My father's reason for not allowing me to see my mother's letters is one thing, But not a thought about the effects on my mother? Could he not have explained it to her? She kept on writing. What faith, what love.

You know what it was like at Caen Wood. There were whispers both at Bloomsbury and then at Caen Wood, houses full of whispers, a door ajar, along a corridor, under a train of satins on the stairs, lingering on the banisters of honeysuckle. You must think I'm going mad, speaking like this.

Well, I am going mad, raging within myself with the deep injustice done both to me and to my mother, and ask myself now, who will take responsibility? Who can take responsibility with almost everyone dead now? You were given this terrible task, but is that all your part in this stratagem? My mother promised that she would send for me. She promised. Did you know that? She will want to know why I didn't respond to her. Anger, when you think it has been stilled, rises unannounced. It rages at the injustice. My mother's endeavours and her concern to keep in touch from the beginning, even though she received only one of my letters in return, tells me how much she continued to love me. Where's my mother in this changing world? I think of the territories exchanged. Where's my mother in all of this? Where is she? Dear Beth, for the sake of whatever little sympathy you may still have for me, please tell me what you know, what and who can help me find my mother. You must've known about this. When did you first learn? Why didn't you tell me?

Excuse my ramblings, it is my anger and my broken heart.

Write to me.

Elizabeth

Elizabeth could see from the letters that at 13, in 1774, when she was Dido, she was not behaving herself. Her temper was beyond control. This was her contribution to the bargaining that went on between her parents. Elizabeth read of her own rage. After her mother had departed, she had told her mother everything folded into those small parcels. She now got to read her autobiography in the epistolary accounts. She related to her mother what she once overheard.

Dear Mammy

I overhear them in the kitchen. They say I must be beaten to be controlled. For she knows no better, little savage, they say...

Elizabeth felt she should surely have remembered such a deed. But it was there in her letter to her mother. *They beat me, mammy, they beat me*. Her child's voice sprang from her letters. She cannot not now imagine either Lady Betty or her Master performing such an act; neither her father, who was so intermittently at Caen Wood itself or at Bloomsbury. But the letter confirmed it in her child's hand. *They tie me up and beat me.*

Was it a child's exaggeration? Possibly this had been a voice overheard from downstairs, Mrs Burns, Mr Way, or Mr French, reacting to what they had heard of her tantrums. Maybe, it was something like, *she needs a good beating*. Something they might have said about their own children. *Keep her on the leash. Spare the rod and spoil the child.* Elizabeth had heard it said that men did it to their wives, but the stick they used could not be larger than the circumference of their thumbs. Did men all have the same size of thumb? She felt herself fortunate. Her husband was a tender man.

She had heard her father's lash before she saw him strike her mother across her face in the enclosure of the cabin of his ship. But later that day her mother was in his arms and being called *my darling*. It was the way of some men. They beat and then they had remorse. She was bound by that bondage.

She should be reading without stopping to make up for the time that she had not had her mother. She snatched at some letters, and left others unopened, or opened if she construed that they were everyday details — though these particularly could fill her eyes with tears, not to have known just the ordinary things of her life, her business in the market, her having to secure a fence that had fallen down, the white picket fence that she remembered and that her mother reminded her of, trying to bring her closer, include her in her present life.

Darling daughter — that was how she began almost every time so that she would be able to revive in her daughter her belief in her mother. On nights alone, Elizabeth could not imagine why she had stopped writing to her. Had she thought that she had died?

She wondered whether she should be mourning or pining.

Darling Daughter

I don't know what is best — to have you here with me or to know you safe where you is in that big house with them powerful people. Some mothers deliver their children beyond this life to make them safe from this terrible dark thing which labours free — free labouring — shackled and constrained — haltered and harnessed in the coffle passing in front of the house every day. Each of the wretched of this earth with iron on their tongue — iron pressing the head to look neither right nor left but straight down on the furrow — a straight line with the hoe, be it in the sugar or in the tobacco or among the cotton fields like snow fall even though it hot like hell. This is the south very different from the north. Even with the manumission papers they can capture you and take you back and sell you another time. Them does tear up the papers. I haves the manumission your father give. I has those papers — and since news reach me that he dead I think upon the fact that all I have is his signature write on the paper — John Lindsay. To see it so is to think upon you and know that whatever happen you is the best fruit off that tree the best from that seed he sow inside of me — no other — the best fruit of what we do. You must be twenty-seven years of age and I wonder if you marry — if you free and marry and have children self — have my grandchildren. I wonder about these things. I keep writing just in case one day I hear you get these letters. The miracle would be to receive back one from you my girl telling how you must be now. All else is well if I keep myself quiet on the land your father settle on me. You remember the white picket fence — I plant so much garden so much ground provision that I does sell. Any pretty flowers growing wild I let them be...

Elizabeth began to doubt her plan to write to her mother. Mr d'Aviniere had still to find out about the ships and post. Would her mother still be there? Would she herself be able to bear the expectation and the disappointment if she could not find her mother? She had this wild hope plaited in her heart to see her again and for her to meet the children.

'But Ma'am, for sure I remember very well letters coming to the house for you off and on over the years when you were younger, or letters sometimes being left on Lady Betty's desk in her dressing room addressed to you. You must've received those letters?'

'No, Lydia, that's just the point. Apart from the very first letter that my mother wrote to me, I've only now seen the others. Likewise, the letters I wrote to her were never posted, except the very first.'

'What a terrible state of affairs, Ma'am.'

'I've not yet recovered from the shock…'

'I understand Ma'am. What can you do now?'

'No idea, Lydia, but you're telling me that you knew nothing of this plan. Was there never any talk? Are you sure it was not an open secret?'

'No, Ma'am, not among the servants, Ma'am. You must not let this take you over Ma'am. It's so much more important for you to look to your boys. You need your energy for that and for your own health. You must not risk getting ill.'

'You're right. I must not let this spoil my time with my boys and my husband. How much time have I got left? Yet I must try to get in touch with my mother if she's alive and living there still in Pensacola.'

'You've got time Ma'am. I'll be here. You call on me. We must see what can be done.'

Elizabeth reached out to her.

'I do understand your loss, Ma'am.'

'Yes, your own mother still back in Ireland.'

'Yes, for sure. Will I get back there? She's very old now.'

I remember daughter the time when we first arrive in that England and it was snowing. I teach you about snow, remember. You so little then. I imagine is snow by you now and you coming to that time Christmas and I wondering if this reach you and if this time I get a reply to make your mother happy. I keep on with the letter — the writing of the letters help me to have you in my mind and to make me believe I and you still speaking. I can't believe you read these words here and it not turn your heart towards me. What is it child — what is it. Woman you must be no child but a grown woman and still not a word. What prevent you...

Elizabeth could see plainly that her mother was still hoping that she would write. That was part of the last letter collected as far as she could surmise. It was the year that she had left Caen Wood, the year that she got married in the December. She could still be alive, Elizabeth worked out.

12

It was a babble in Dido's ears, the arguments and debates back and forth while the country waited, the world waited, it seemed, for her Master's judgment as she read in *The Advertiser*.

'That confounded man does pester and persist.'

Her Master's irritation in his courtroom overflowed into the drawing room. Dido was under no illusion that he could be as stern, cold and forceful in his court. A glass of port fuelled the rising thrust of argument in the evening at home.

'Who's that dear?' Lady Betty asked. 'Who pesters you and persists, and with what?'

'I'm surprised my dear wife asks...'

'Granville Sharp, no doubt, must be that confounded man.'

'Those Sharps should confine themselves to their barge upon the Thames and to their music at one of their concerts.'

Dido's thimble fell to the floor. She pricked her finger with her sewing needle.

Beth was nodding over her novel, something Lady Betty was encouraging her to read dropped from her lap. She was no doubt dreaming of her horse-riding with her great-uncle.

If it had not been for her visits to her mother at that time, Dido would have learned very little from all those actors, politicians and artists who came to sit in her Master's drawing room, to drink coffee with lots of sugar and smoke tobacco, filling the room like a coffee house. They discussed the affairs of the King's realm and the trade upon which the success of the economy depended.

When she was only a little girl, much of it had passed over her, though some got lodged and was now becoming more meaningful. As she got older, she could not wait to be part of the company in the drawing room. She knew her place in the corner on a stool with her book, preferring that to sewing or working her pattern as Lady Betty would have wanted. She was more intent to please her Master by showing him that she was getting on with her reading, though she did have one ear cocked for what the gentlemen discussed. She tried not to be too visible, too inquisitive in her attention. She kept her eyes lowered on her book and followed the voices, once she had sorted out who was sitting where.

She would have formed a negative opinion of Granville Sharp and his family if she had not had the stories of her mother, had her talk of the streets; if she had not had the newspapers, if she had not gone with her mother to the Quaker Meeting House in Shoreditch and heard the abolitionists' talk. It was not always approved that she should be allowed the papers. It was very good that her Master had allowed and arranged for her to continue attending the Shoreditch Meeting House. He surprised her and contradicted himself at times, allowing her different influences.

'I've tried to prevail upon the godparents, if such they are, they who brought the *habeas corpus* to purchase the man themselves and solve the whole darn thing. Or, for that matter, Stewart, the owner, to offer to sell the wretched man.'

Dido could not believe what she was hearing from her Master. It was his tone that shocked her. She understood that neither side would budge. Her Master wanted rid of the whole thing. He wished to be relieved of making the judgment. The repeated postponement of the final judgment increased the anticipation on all sides for a verdict, which would vindicate their position.

The papers made much of her Master's postponements. They lit the fire beneath each of these positions, making the judgment much more important than it should have become. It was a *narrow* judgment, her Master kept saying. But the world wanted to hear something larger and more definitive on the question of slavery and its trade. They wanted to hear the rightness of it all. The papers wanted the big story. He did his job along the narrow lanes of the law. The system was *odious*. He meant the trade in live cargo, the commerce, the business of the property, and said it would need law to support it. But he would not intentionally lead the way to change that law.

This was an early education for Dido in who her Master really was, and in how she could both admire and learn from him through her reading and writing. But now she began to know that he would not be the one to free what her mother called *their people* whom she met at night at the Meeting House.

'We cannot run the country on emotion, but only on law. And I dare say, only on commerce. What would I say to his Majesty if I believed in it any other way? What if we lost the trade with some so-called principled moral reform in this matter? The world would come to a standstill.'

He explained to the company that different people would draw different conclusions from his judgments. 'What best furthers their cause and feathers their nest.' He explained again that he would keep to the business before the court. 'I'm not launching some abolition crusade. I won't be responsible for the collapse of trade and the economy of the realm.'

Dido found herself staring at her Master.

His mellifluous arguments continued with explaining the working of the West Indian lobby, those on plantations in Virginia who wanted the matter legislated for in law. 'They want to boost what goes on there.'

Molly came in with more coffee.

'What is legal in the colonies is one thing but not on this soil.' He sipped on his coffee adding two lumps of sugar. 'I would tell you friends that I would rather avoid it altogether. I wish the owners would be happy to think their slaves were free men and their slaves to think of them as their natural masters. A much more peaceful life would ensue for me.'

Dido noticed her Master glance in her direction with a benign countenance. Is that what he thought was their arrangement, or, rather what was his arrangement, and that she had little choice in the matter? She was always so amenable and had to be so grateful to him.

'You don't want to set precedent, Mansfield.' That was Lord Southampton.

'Quite so. One judgment can indeed overturn the other as we have seen with Yorke and Talbot.'

'Too many interpretations being bandied about when what we need is clarity and order.'

'Quite so.' Dido's Master nodded his approval to all the company.

She raised her eyes to catch Beth's. She was nodding again, unmoved by these conversations..

Dido put her book down. She could not concentrate to read. In the silence of her embroidering fingers, she travelled far across the countryside, hiding in ditches, escaping into the kindnesses of people in small towns in an effort to free James Sommersett, and thinking whether she could walk the streets of London and not be captured for transportation to the Americas or to Jamaica.

Master must free him, she insisted to herself, her needle almost pricking her finger, her thimble falling to the floor.

In bed, that night, she closed her eyes and listened to the wind on Fir Hill. She dreamt of her mother waving from a ship caught in a storm.

The days at Caen Wood were too short. Monday morning, and they returned to Bloomsbury Square. Mr French had prepared a nosegay for Dido that morning. He was growing fond of her, no longer *a little savage*. He had come to the Bloomsbury house to advise about some new plantings there that Lady Betty wanted.

Dido remembered how once when she had visited her mother at Greenwich, before she had left for Pensacola, she had told her what she had overheard at Caen Wood and she had replied in that inimitable way, 'Is more than rumour, child, along the lanes of Greenwich and Deptford, or up Saint Giles. It spreading across the wealds and moors, up and down dales.'

There was such a geography of clamour for a verdict, her mother told her. It stretched across the ocean and found its voice in the hills of Virginia and in the ports of Boston and the Carolinas. If only her mother could have a voice in the court, her poetry would move the world.

Dido was torn between her mother and her Master.

'That James Sommersett might as well set sail for Jamaica,' her mother said, 'and see if the sea breeze do him any good. Is not the air of England or the holy waters of their baptism go free him.' This was her repeated joke.

She explained that her people were crowding into the courtroom to listen and to hope. 'Even we people believe that man, who you call your Master, has the words of freedom on his tongue.' Then she laughed. Her mother could laugh so much. She too laughed and they went out to find some amusement in the streets down by the river.

Dido asked if she was going to leave her.

She stood and looked out on the river and did not answer her question. Then she said, 'You think there are easy answers for my predicament, child.'

That was a different answer to her promise from before.

Her mother kept saying, 'He thinking of you and how any Tom, Dick or Harry catcher could sweep you up outside Bloomsbury Square, bind your pretty wrists and ankles in irons and put you on a boat bound for Kingston. That is a place more dangerous than hell for a strong blackamoor as they call the fellas, so imagine a pretty child like you in that forsaken place. Just there on Holborn you find the devil in his hell.'

Dido believed her mother, and believed her more when she raised her dress over her shoulders and showed her laddered back of welts that told the story of when she was a child. 'I don't want this for you,' she said, looking over her shoulder at Dido as she fixed back her dress. 'I don't want you in some sugarcane field under the burning sun. I don't want you become some *belle* for no gentleman, nor have your head down picking cotton and tobacco.'

'We must remember that we do need these necessary implements, the free labour, I mean, if we are going to continue with the commercial success of the realm. The colonies need the labour. Jeopardise that with talk of abolition or stopping the trade and all will be lost. How could we compensate the planters for their loss if that ridiculous situation was ever to come about?'

Dido saw it was the planter who had arrived that evening with his little pageboy, just before supper was served upstairs. He was full of himself. The child had been put to sit in the pantry.

'You're quite right, how are we to get that necessary spoonful of sugar into our dish of coffee, tea, or even chocolate?' That was that poet. She had missed his name.

There was laughter. Dido's Master's friends loved this kind of talk.

'Quite so, quite so,' they all murmured.

'What do they say in Liverpool? Straw for bricks, negroes for sugar.' The poet was now trying to be comic. There was some consternation at his last remark.

Beth was again nodding. Dido was going to have to take her arm and walk her out onto the terrace to get some air. But she was too enthralled, so shocked that she pricked her finger again and almost smudged her pattern with her blood, As she moved towards Beth and took her arm to stir her she was detained further by what she then heard. She stooped near the fire as if to rearrange the dwindling embers, to stoke the flames. She shook the scuttle. What world did she see there? As a small child, Lady Betty had said she should look for a world of legends in the flames.

'I've heard it said that the bricks in that city on the banks of the Mersey, crowded with the ships especially constructed for the cargo, are cemented with the negro's blood. They say the very mortar is a negro's blood.' The poet repeated his lurid descriptions.

The shock around the room was now more marked. All did not think alike. Dido's Master cast his eyes upon her at that remark. Lady Betty offered more coffee.

It was only later that Dido thought it might have been a metaphor, the purpose of that figure of speech was recently learned with Beth in the schoolroom.

There was silence then, and Lady Betty coughed and Molly was at the door with some more coffee for the gentlemen, and Dido thought, yes, a spoonful or more of sugar.

That she was allowed to overhear these debates, the evening chat, was perplexing. If she had told her mother stories like these she would have howled the place down. Hers was a laughter of pain, a riot in my belly, as she once told her. *Laugh and dance, my child.* Her dances were always for freedom, she had said, *Even though it might never come I stamp my feet for freedom. I click my maracas in the ears of gentlemen for freedom. I laugh for freedom. Watch my stamping feet, my flamenco, learn from the Spanish. Come come dance your feet. See the African drum in my hips.* She was indomitable. It made her feel better to say the words.

'Stories of blood will feed the cause of Granville Sharp and he won't be silenced. We cannot condone murder. There's law to govern the behaviour on the slavers. Is it kept? That's another matter.' Her Master was wishing to return the conversation to some sobriety. It was the talk of blood cementing bricks that he thought odious. He did not think that way.

But Dido learned again and again he was a man of law above all.

'Let us get back to the judgment, my Lord.' One of his lawyer guests was pressing him.

'What will the consequences be if the owners in general, and all at once particularly, were to lose their property?'

'Quite so. Quite so.' The murmurs around the room echoed his words and sentiments.

'Planters in America not to mention the West Indian lobby want a ruling. I repeat myself. They want the legislation in black and white, I am not joking, no irony intended in my choice of words, and so does Mr Sharp as you say. He wants a precedent.'

'But there are...what is the latest estimate? Fifteen thousand blacks in the country at the moment. A total of £800,000. That is a lot of property, what is it? What are the consequences if that is lost?'

Dido could not distinguish the speakers.

'It would be most disagreeable if that were to happen. What will you do?' The voices of this opinion were in unison; each one singly stated, and then all together, in agreement.

'I will keep my counsel, gentlemen, as you know I must. I have adjourned the sitting of the court to give them all time to think. Let us sup, my dear, do lead the way.' Dido's Master rose to leave the room.

She caught Lady Betty looking at her. She thought she was telling her to go off to bed at that moment. Dido was ignoring her. She wanted to hear more. There was a philosopher in their midst. He was elaborating the views of Mr John Locke who said, 'That estate of man is most vile and miserable.' Dido agreed with the philosopher that 'It is opposite to the generous temper and courage of our nation. It is difficult to conceive how an Englishman much less a gentleman could argue for it.'

And they, those gentlemen, when they had arrived all smiles, were even bearing small gifts for their 'Little Dido'. Some had come to the house many times.

They talked and laughed with such a roar that the blood rushed to her cheeks.

'Little Dido, dear little Dido.' She had had to protect herself from one gentleman with his wandering hands in the corridors and on the stairs. 'Do you actually read?' he asked. He carried sweets in his pocket and used them as an enticement.

In the pantry she met the pageboy she had seen at the beginning of the evening. His name was Caesar, he told her, and he had accompanied his master from Barbados to be his valet in England.

'I was a birthday present from his wife.'

'Indeed.' Dido was shocked. She reached out to the child and touched his head affectionately. The extraordinary things that happen, she thought.

He said that he enjoyed his master's country house in the West Country rather than his house in town. He asked what she was doing at Caen Wood. But, by then, she had served him a slice of beef with some dripping and bread and left him to his meal. She had wanted to talk further but thought she should return to the drawing room. He told her, as she was leaving the pantry, that he was ten years old. She wondered how he would survive as he got older.

'I know the company you keeping in your pretty clothes. Is a new bonnet they should give you,' her mother had once said to Dido.

When she said that, she tidied up Dido's hair on the nape of her neck. Dido had told her once that she had overheard a gentleman, one of her Master's friends, commenting that her woolly hair was escaping from under her bonnet.

'Woolly! What a thing. You is some sheep? What business of his? Scoundrel. That so important to mention? We hair always seem to scandalise them. It not prevent them, though, wanting to interfere with we body.'

She looked knowingly at Dido, something she thought she should remember.

> ELIZABETH STARED OUT into her garden.

Maybe, Lord Mansfield, the Chief Justice, her Master, had thought of her, that girl Dido, as he pondered his judgment. Had he thought he could not risk that his grand-niece, legally his nephew's slave, his for safe keeping, his indeed, could be captured and deported? Elizabeth reflected on this from the distance of time and place. If that were so, she had not changed his mind about the larger question. It took ten more years for him to write down a statement to grant Dido her own freedom. His judgment on Sommersett never stopped the catchers. They carried on more than ever that year and the years immediately following as Elizabeth learned from the charming Mr Equiano. He spoke so eloquently and wrote so elegantly of those matters in his narrative.

It shocked her now how she had felt that it was impossible to leave her Master. It terrified her now to put it in so many words. Still she thought of him as her Master. It had been as if each night she locked herself in under lock and key. Then she discovered in a letter to her mother how she once did try to run away. She was found forlorn not far off in Kentish Town, her dress and apron torn with brambles where she had tried to hide in hedges. That she forgot that? Did she? *Miss Dido where will you run to my girl? You a runaway?* That was Hal who had seen her escaping under Sherrick Hole and then along Swain's Lane, trying to avoid the farmhands. He marched her back to the house, straight to the kitchen door where he delivered her to Mrs Burns.

Hot August and the lawn was parched. Her mouth was dry. Elizabeth had waited and waited for these letters. As she opened the box this time, the bundles burst from the constrictions of their ribbons, tumbling out onto the floor. The ribbons were old and faded, each parcel having been secured before being stuffed into a drawer and hidden away. Who had been the ones to spy on her mother and herself over the years, knowing all their feelings and all their plans: Lady Betty, Miss Anne, her Master himself?

She swept them up into her arms, and pressed them to her bosom. She was brave today as she opened the first parcel and smoothed it out on her lap.

Dearest Daughter... Elizabeth's eyes ran down the page... *I still waiting...* She chose another letter. She heard her voice and could not continue. Her tears were flowing down her cheeks. She returned to a former letter. She saw the words through a mist:

is weeks — months I not hear anything yet from you daughter. What do you child that you keep so silent — you forget your mother. I preparing to bring you. You must believe that. I will send for you when I feel it safe for you to come. Your father send me with a letter stating I is free. I have that letter. I don't believe that letter is proper manumission just his arrogance and presumption. I must secure my own freedom here. I must get that money together to buy my freedom. I can't have you here with me until I know I is free. Or some catcher hold me and take me to sell upon a plantation. $200 I must pay for my manumission. No matter the freedom your father think he bestow upon me. So I then have to start collect more money to bring you. Before I leave London your father secure that I have a piece of land. But he also demand that I build a house on that land. I don't know where you father think I getting money to build house. But I must build because I must keep this land. Is good land right here at the front of the town — right there by the sea. But that house where we used to live when you was a small small child have to come down. The wood rotten — the windows and shutters hanging off their hinges. When them storm come you mother get soak...

There was repetition in her letters; her need and her terror, insisting that her daughter knew what she was experiencing.

Elizabeth's tears ceased as she read and imagined her struggle. She saw at once why such a letter was not delivered to the girl, Dido. She remembered her young self. She would have been in constant expectation to leave England to travel to meet her mother. She would be running away all the time to find a ship on the Thames, some madness like that. They must have thought her mother's condition was squalid. Is that why her Master, Lady Betty and her father wanted to keep her in England? Her father had satisfied himself that her mother had her freedom, legally.

Elizabeth's anger swelled up. It was not as if her father cared for her. She had hardly ever seen him for years. He was not a constant man in the end. His own ambitions took him round the world and into battle, that young boy still who had once joined the navy.

Where were Lydia and the boys? Elizabeth sat among her roses and her mother's voice flooded the air and her mind. 'My children.' She woke in a panic, crying out for them. Was it that tincture of laudanum again? It was getting dark. It was almost time for her husband to be back.

She heard the front door slam.

13

JOHN D'AVINIERE, ON arriving home, went out immediately again in order to search for Lydia and the two boys. There had been no word of where they were since Mrs Halifax had come to the house that afternoon. She had come to say that Lydia had called in earlier with Billy. She had said she had to go looking for Charles who had not met them at the appointed place in Belgravia after school. She had seemed alarmed.

It was a summer's evening with two hours left of light. Elizabeth waited at home. Elizabeth told Mrs Halifax that she preferred to be quietly at home, but she would come to her if she began to feel she could not cope on her own.

The boys had been so eager to start this morning with Billy going off to school as well, so excited to be accompanying his brother, Charles. How they had both grown over the summer, shooting up above the pencil marks scratched on the wall of their bedroom by the door where their heights had been recorded over the years. There was Johnny's, whose last measurement had been used for his small coffin. Elizabeth traced his height with her fingers.

Where were they? What was Lydia up to, going off with Billy on a wild search? Elizabeth was desperate. She had only the letters, her story, the summer evening with its high, blue brightness, the orchestra of birds and the gulls from the river, circling. This pleasure contradicted the time, filling her with the foreboding that she had been having for so long, that her black boy would go missing. Would they steal her Billy, as well?

Dear Mammy

Who else is there for me to tell — I not hear from you, so I not sure you listening. But Mammy, I tell myself that this is where I talk to you and this is where alone I feel you close when I think I talking to you just so as I want to talk to you. I talking as my tongue feel easy as us on Mary Hill looking down on the river. You must not think I am a bad girl when I tell you these things. The other afternoon I take a walk among the elms in a part of the wood beyond where the new dairy build. I get loss there. Something alarm me. I was on my own when Molly find me. All I remembering now as I write to you is that I must stand brave. I stand and listen to the music of the strong wind rushing through the branches. It sound like the waves breaking on the shore by the rocks where you must be living in your house in Pensacola. I want to be there with you. When Molly ask me who it is that she see running through the woods I tell her that she make a mistake. No one in the woods but me. I lie. I did have to warn Hal at the dairy the following day that the next time he alarm me I go have to report him. But I frighten to do that because I think they go think is me doing bad things. Hear what he ask me. And you is not the Master little piece of pork — easy pickings on the street like the little negresses near Holborn — so, why you refuse me. What is that you say I ask. I call after him. Little nigger he call me. It was then he run off into the woods pulling up his breeches when he see Molly coming to meet me under the elms. But I never tell her what Hal do me. I can't find words for that now, for his hand under my dress for his fingers where they poking inside of me between my legs. Forcing himself. Him all shivering and whimpering and me cold cold. You must not think bad of me mammy. Who I go tell. What I go do — tell me please — tell me please. Where are you — send for me...

Elizabeth let the letter drop to the floor. She was struck how she had written in her mother's tongue as a girl, hardly a girl then, needing her mother, finding solace in her grammar. To see her words so raw upon the page shocked her. It was not her, now. She was not the person who was remembering so much, she, Mrs d'Aviniere, Elizabeth, Lizzie with her garden, the fragrance of roses, forgetting so much, remembering so much, having to think of her own boys, then having to remember the world and what was happening to so many who were still transported. Instead, in that letter she was that slave, Dido. What they named her and made of her for a time, and captured in that portrait, framed with her basket of fruit and flowers looking like a *belle*. The mix of the artists' pigments and applications of colour may have been similar, but their ideas were quite different. What a mess it turned out to be. Never hung. Disappeared.

Elizabeth remembered more of what had happened among the elms that day so long ago. She pinned down the chronology of Hal's wickedness. She was forced to recall the hedgerow where it had all begun as a girl of fourteen. She had lain terrified and dared not scream, but somehow managed to stop the fumbling boy, stop his business that first time. *Wipe yourself*, she remembered whispering. What she remembered most was the terror that lived with her each time she had to encounter him, which was every day when they were at Caen Wood, with her working in the dairy and the poultry and then every day after when they moved from Bloomsbury after the fire to be at Caen Wood for always. Every day she had had to give some part of herself to survive. She remembered now his words down at Sherrick Hole. He had kept to his word: *When I touch, you'll know*.

It was soon after that episode under the elms that she learned that Hal was going to be moved to the neighbouring Fitzroy farm. It was Molly who had informed her with a knowing look on her face, and it was Mrs Burns who, uncharacteristically, put her arms around her shoulders one day and told her that she would be safe. She still remembered her unusual words: *There will be respect now, Miss Belle.*

Your Master insists. She did not hear another word on the matter, neither from her Master or Lady Betty, whom she had assumed must have been given details by Molly or Mrs Burns on the direct evidence from Molly. But she did remember now that she could not look her Master or Lady Betty in the eye that night and for some time after.

They must have read her letter. Was that the way they knew everything, kept an eye and an ear on her always? *Miss Belle.* That was the only time she remembered ever being called so, politely. She was told that the new herdsman would be a Mr Edwards who lived with his wife and children in a cottage on the edge of the park.

The terror of Hal had worked its poison and had never left her. Still at times in the midst of the love her husband made with her was the image of that boy and his dirty business. *Belle, a pretty name for dirty work,* her mother's voice was on her shoulder reminding her.

Black Boy for sale. She was following her son now in her imagination like she had followed James Sommersett, the runaway. She imagined Charles trying to escape his catcher by running over the marshes, hiding among the reeds, hunkered down. He must not be put up for sale. The letter to her mother concerning Hal now seemed ironic, reminding her of her time close to capture. It brought her back now to Johnny's disappearance, the soliciting on the streets by that strange gentleman who offered Lydia a good price for her boys. Her anxiety now seemed more than justified. But she would not say, I told you so, to Lydia. She just wanted her husband to return to the house with her sons. She would not blame Lydia. What was she thinking, poor Lydia, at her age, searching on her own with Billy? She had not been able to return home saying that Charles was missing. Elizabeth was sure that that was the reason. She had been reminded so repeatedly not to lose any of her boys.

It was impossible to concentrate and then Master's voice seemed to be speaking from his portrait in the hall.

➢ 'I MUST SEE to her manumission.' Dido's Master proclaimed. 'I cannot have her assaulted or attention drawn to her presence. Only the other day at Highgate, some wretch caught and sent back. So much for my judgment. It was in *The Gazette* and *The New Daily Advertiser*. Did he think to come over the hill to my door for freedom? Poor wretch. No one understands my narrow judgment in the Sommersett case. They think I have bestowed freedom on every Tom, Dick and Harry in the Americas and the West Indies who sets foot here in England because I let the black, Sommersett, go. They are wrong. As I keep saying, a narrow judgment for the good of the realm and His Majesty's coffers. Only law can make such a thing so odious, legitimate, only another law can change it completely. People must be educated by the law.'

Dido stood at the door of his dressing room and overheard her Master talking to Mr Way.

'It must be stated in the will. Dido's freedom.'

'Yes, my Lord.'

➢ WHAT HAD IT meant, his law, his manumission, if today her son cannot walk back from school safely? Elizabeth raged within herself sitting alone with her writing box. And where were the papers, as her mother would say, the manumission? She never received any papers. A statement in a will, was that sufficient? Her husband, did he have those important papers? She began to imagine the worse. If they were not identified by the correct documents what of their boys? The nonchalance of it, it was the privilege of power in dealing with their property.

She fed the robins. The summer heat was at its zenith and her garden was getting dried out. Mercifully, the heavens had opened the day before, but the hot earth had soaked up the rains. It smelt like Pensacola, rain on hot earth. The dryness had been good for her breathing. Now there was a chill with the damp.

Charles would be so exposed to the weather.

Elizabeth had so wanted her mother's protection. She was hungry for it. Who was her real protection? Her husband became that protection. Could he be sure of being able to do so now? They were a household ready for capture. How could they protect themselves when any fraction of Africa's colour could get them captured and deported?

It had been raining again. The house was silent but for the drip, drip on the path. The light had faded. Darkness had come. Surely, they would return now with or without Charles. Her son will be soaked. They had to come and tell her what was happening. The oil lamp in the street was turned on. There would be that light for a while on the street, but not out on the marshes. That was where she imagined they were. Elizabeth began to pace up and down in the hall. The Van Loo portrait of her Master stared down.

Lydia was too old for this search.

Just a drop of laudanum and relief would come. She was too late to visit Mrs Halifax. She would have to wait on her own. She recalled now how often it was that she could not fall asleep after those drawing room debates. He was neatly seated, her Master, buttoned up, and with that nervous mannerism of knocking his heels against each other. She recalled all the gentlemen sitting around the drawing room. This night, this night with her black boy running away from capture was their invention. Was the *Ann & Mary* or some other ship waiting on the river to carry him across the Atlantic?

She wanted a ship to carry her letter to her mother.

Elizabeth woke with a start. She was sure that she had heard someone call out, like a seller passing in the street ringing a bell and shouting out *Black Boy for Sale*. Then the silence and the darkness closed in on her and she realised that she was on her own and her shawl and rug had fallen to the floor and she was cold. Her boys should be in bed. Lydia should have finished her chores and gone up to bed. Her husband should be here with her. She got up and walked about the house. The eyes of the Van Loo portrait of her Master followed her each time she walked up and down the hall. This had not been his plan, she thought. His legacies and now Miss Marjory's £100 were meant to protect and ward off danger. But they had not been effective. She wished her husband and Lydia would come back and put Billy to bed. They would need more people to help them search the marshes. She was on the marshes in her mind, searching, crying out her son's name. What story would they return with? How could Billy be helping in the search? Was this the future to which she was leaving her family?

Elizabeth woke again to the sound of the front door opening and being closed. She listened to the whispering on the stairs, and on walking onto the landing, she came upon her husband holding Billy asleep with his head on his father's shoulder. She pressed her hand on her youngest son's back. 'My darling, Billy, up so late.' She kissed the sleeping boy's forehead. 'Put the mite to bed.'

Behind them, still at the foot of the stairs was Lydia and Seamus. She had not thought that Seamus had been alerted to join the search party.

No one was speaking.

Her eyes took them all in, but she kept searching beyond them as she passed her husband, protector of his boys, on the landing. She could not read the story in his eyes.

Then it burst from deep inside of her, a cry of desperation, 'Charles, Charles, where are you? I don't see you. Where are you?' At the bottom of the stairs, breathless with her crying she was held up in the arms of Lydia and Seamus. She turned towards them and called out to her husband, 'Where is he? Where is my black son? Why doesn't anyone answer me?'

'Here, Ma'am, here, come with me,' and Lydia and Seamus helped Elizabeth into the parlour, where, in the darkness, she could just make out the small form wrapped in blankets on the sofa.

'Darling, my darling, what have they done to you?' Charles lay as if asleep.

'He is concussed, Ma'am. He's received a blow to the head and needs to rest.'

'A blow?' Elizabeth knelt at the side of the sofa and put her arm around her son. 'A blow? What wicked person did this?'

The story of Charles' disappearance came out slowly. The entire family had received a shock. Lydia and Seamus were needed more than ever to keep the household going so that the parents could spend all the time they could with their two boys and with each other. They went out to Ranelagh Gardens together. August had disappeared and September continued with the hot weather. They would on some days go out to the riverbank to fish and to have picnics. Mr d'Aviniere was allowed to have time off from his stewardship. Elizabeth made sure that she kept her strength and would recline in the shade while her husband taught Billy to fish. Together with Charles they brought in the catch with great excitement. 'Mama, Mama, look!' Billy ran up the bank to show his mother his first catch.

The period allowed Lydia to recover. It allowed her to deal with her own sense of guilt. Elizabeth knew that Lydia blamed herself for what had happened, even though she, herself, had been careful not to blame her, cautioned by her husband who had been the first to see her distress when he found her with the boys on the search.

'It was Billy crying out, Ma'am, that he had found the scarf...'

'Lydia, you must not distress yourself. No one thinks it was your fault.'

'Oh, Ma'am. I know your worry about those boys...'

'Yes, Lydia but they're safe now. You did your best...'

'His scarf, his satchel and then where he had been dragged. I can't get it out of my mind...'

'Lydia, please, we must stop because as you know it is my continual nightmare that one of my boys is going to be snatched sooner rather than later...'

'Yes, Ma'am, sorry. I understand so much more now. You, your husband and your boys always having to be aware, always looking out, worried... They're just children...'

'Yes, it's how it is, Lydia. Black children. We depend on good people to change it.'

14

DIDO WAS TWENTY. Beth and herself were no longer girls. Dido did not ride but Beth still rode in the park with her great-uncle and at times with her suitors. Dido watched them from her window, leaving the path, entering under the elms. She was jealous.

The fun of dressing up, like when Beth and herself were little girls, was a distraction that particular morning. The trunk had been taken down from the attic. She had had nightmares about this dressing up lark. What did they want to make of her? She had seldom slept well, often jolted into consciousness by some alarming incident in her dream to do with her mother, usually of being abandoned and left to find her way through threatening alleyways, or through the shadows and mists of a dark wood. And just when she thought she herself was going to be found, or to find her mother, she was left totally alone.

The dressing up trunk for charades was opened with delight, Dido reluctantly agreeing to give herself up to her Master's entertainment. This was what she always did. The scene became a circus for Lady Betty, Beth and the maids, crowded at the door, enjoying the show.

'Mr Lindsay says that when she's dressed like that she looks just like her mother.'

Whose voice was that? When had her father said that? It was something she caught, half listening to the chatter behind her in the drawing room.

To learn that her father was still thinking of her mother surprised her. Dido's father had not visited the house to see his uncle and aunt for a long while. Comparing Dido to her mother was both puzzling and touching. She seemed a person long forgotten by the family. Dido had only recently written to her mother, though she still had not had any reply. She had been sad about that as she cleared up the pieces of costume, which had not been chosen, and packed them back into the trunk.

The idea that Dido should be part of a portrait of Beth had been a topic of conversation from time to time, entertaining Lady Betty and her Master when he chose to listen after supper and a hard day at the courts, with that avuncular ear and voice: 'Oh, but you must, Dido,' when he saw a look of reluctance on her face. 'You mustn't allow the opportunity to be lost. Mr Allan Ramsay would be so disappointed. You know that he's famous. I know he has a thesis in his mind. He's already begun the painting of Beth. I told him you must be fitted in. I want both of you to be together. I would be so disappointed if you didn't oblige.'

Dido had learned not to disappoint her Master but to return what he thought of as his affection with her own. She had not the means by which to disagree with what then was his fantasy. Disagreement did not pay off. She had learned that since she was a little girl. She had had to quell her tantrums.

Therefore, when the fantasy, the entertainment, became a definite project, Mr Ramsay was invited to Caen Wood for supper and afterwards for coffee and chat when Dido joined the family in the drawing room to discuss the desires of her guardians. Dido liked the elderly artist. He did not patronise her. She was then left without any alternative but to satisfy everyone's wishes.

From the start, she had dreaded the whole affair. She, at first, did not fully understand what was really afoot. The artist did not explain his thesis, as her Master had called it. She was glad that he did not seem enthused by the old, glittery costumes from the dressing up trunk when Beth suggested he look at them. How was she to be added to the composition?

'She could be just fitted in, added for effect,' she overheard her Master say to Mr Ramsay.

'Oh, no, I don't think that would be appropriate. There should be some purpose to this endeavour.' Dido heard the kind artist's reply.

'The silk would be good for you to wear, Dido?' Beth was excited by the project.

'What will you wear?'

'Well, Mr Ramsay has already started on me. It's rather wonderful what he's chosen.'

'Let me see.'

When Beth showed Dido the wonderful outfit of her pink hooped skirt, Dido said, 'I have no dresses quite like that. You know that. How could you possibly think of dressing me up from those pieces in the trunk? What would I look like next to you, fitted in?'

'Come on Dido, it's like dressing up when we were girls.'

'I don't think so.'

Mr Ramsay commented as if he had been listening to the young women. 'I can paint you, Dido, as I paint the Queen.' He was standing behind her with his brush in one hand and the other on her shoulder, as he mixed colours on his palette. He showed her what he had done so far of Beth and she thought it was splendid. She wondered what she might wear though. 'Something matching that says who you are, the friends and companions that you have been over the years,' Mr Ramsay said, choosing his words carefully.

She did not know what he meant at the time, mentioning the Queen. Later, Beth told her that Queen Charlotte had been whispered about after Mr Ramsay's portrait of her. 'True mulatto face and much else.' Beth related the story and giggled.

'Is that like my face?' Dido asked.

'Dido, you're much prettier. But yes, you're a mulatto as well. You know that.'

Then Dido remembered her father joking at Greenwich with her mother about the African in the Queen. Some had thought, with relief, that her Majesty's ugliness had quite faded when another portrait was produced erasing any trace of African. Other people were raking up ancient histories to attach the Queen to a line from black Africa.

'There was a Moor, Madragana, and a Portuguese royal family.' Beth was hurrying beyond her usual self with her history. Or was it just gossip?

'Really?' Dido asked.

'Yes. Mr Ramsay is reported to be something of an abolitionist, and this was part of his plan to paint the Queen thus to help the cause.'

'I don't trust any of those stories, and, I like him. I think Mr Ramsay wants to do something quite original. And I'm pleased he does not want to drape me in all those glittery, silken cloths and feathers my father brought back from India. Anyway, if he's really an abolitionist I'm in good hands.' Dido was a little surprised at Beth talking of abolitionists as if she was well informed.

'No, he's not to be trusted. He might spring a surprise,' Beth said. 'He eloped with your father's sister. Didn't you know? He's your uncle. They were persona non grata with the family for ages, but apparently now all is forgiven. They've been welcomed back into great-uncle's house. Family loyalty is everything to him.'

'Am I family?'

'Dido. You know you are meant to be half family, but...'

'But...'

'You know, your mother...'

'Always, my mother.'

Beth frowned. She did not like it when she seemed to be getting on to subjects that made her uncomfortable. Dido's mother was always such a subject.

As it turned out, days before Mr Ramsay was to begin his work he had injured his right arm and hand and was not able to handle his brushes easily. Mr David Martin, an assistant in his studio, was employed instead to complete the portrait.

'It's fortunate that we have the light today. We're not always so lucky. That will be good for you Martin. I leave it all to you. I know what I would do, but they're in your hands now. I've started you off.'

Dido was disappointed and a little nervous as to what was now to happen. Beth giggled, taken up with the dashing, younger artist with his auburn hair. She and Beth had both grown fond of the older man and enjoyed his play, but they were both excited to sit for David Martin.

He immediately commented on Dido's accent. Not only her accent, she thought. He was a little flirtatious. She found that quite irritating and perplexing. How else did she know how to speak? After all these years the telltale was still there.

She heard her mother's instructions: *Child, speak with your own tongue, is that what I tell you. And I is your mother. But when you see the time is proper speak how they expect you. But I tell you, you not go fool them. But you mustn't fool yourself.*

Dido wondered whether they might've been better off with Mr Ramsay. She was distracted and worried. She had felt so comfortable and confident with the older artist. He had been her Master's first choice. He seemed to know what he was going to do. David Martin was already experimenting with the contents of the dressing up trunk, which had been brought to the orangery that morning. 'Yes, we can do something with that,' he said, folding a length of silk and extracting a string of pearls from a box he had placed on a table next to him. 'Your skin being quite different needs an altogether different approach,' he said to Dido. She had been made to wear a series of get ups. She ceased to bother. None of these costumes would fulfil Mr Ramsay's idea of something matching.

Beth and Dido were not allowed to view the work after the last sitting that day.

'It's forbidden,' David Martin teased, as he peered over his easel above his spectacles. Beth and Dido had caught on to his teasing. He was pretending. He was a romantic figure. They, in turn, pretended to be intimidated, and then their smiles drove away the clouds and they shared the charade to their own delight. They were all having fun. But Dido remained a little alarmed.

Later that evening while the family and guests were still at supper, Dido left her unfinished meal upon the table in the pantry while Molly was already clearing away and clattering with the washing up in the scullery. She refrained from offering a helping hand that night. She crept away quickly and quietly with an even tread upon the backstairs so as not to disturb the family at their meal in the dining room. They would be expecting her to join them with their guests after supper in the drawing room as usual.

She tiptoed across the corridor, past the music room to the orangery where Beth and herself had been sitting for hours, it now seemed. Indeed, since after breakfast, then a break for luncheon, and then they sat again till tea. David Martin had taxed their concentration exceedingly. Dido's shoulders ached. She had had to make fun of it all, but now she was agitated and tired.

The late evening light still lingered in intense pools upon the orangery floor with an illumination that varnished the bright green leaves of the orange trees to the sheen of enamel, and lit the fruit as if they were lanterns in Mr Marvell's poem hanging among the leaves, *as in a green night*. She had been reading Mr Marvell at that time. There was a wonderful pungent fragrance from orange blossom all that day in the heat, which was still pervasive. Outside, the parkland was a quilt of shadows, of clouds, and the branches of the plane trees rising and falling in the breeze where the piebald herd with their curled horns stood in the shade of the full copper beeches grazing, having been recently let out after milking.

The easel stood shrouded in the middle of the orangery with a white sheet flung over it to protect the paint from the intense sunlight.

Dido stood and stared and thought hard upon her intended action before she went towards the ghost in the room and lifted off the shroud. It was daring of her and she looked around to see if anyone was at the door or perhaps peering in through the glass from the terrace.

She pulled on the white sheet, the shroud. It fell crumpled on the floor. She stooped and picked it up and hung it on the back of the painter's chair.

What she saw appalled her. It was not her. It had nothing to do with her. She thought she should cover it up and leave the orangery immediately. As she turned away, she nearly stumbled over Mr Martin's box of paints, the brushes in their bottles, the tubes laid out on the small table, excretions of all colours like caterpillars crawling on the artist's palette. As she looked around the room, the scene of the morning: the artist's chair, the easel, costumes falling out of the dressing up trunk, she felt sick with the memory of the morning and what she now saw.

As she stood there staring at the portrait, she began to understand the artifice. Mr Martin had made the most of the dressing up clothes, which Mr Ramsay had not approved off. Where on earth had that turban and the dyed feather, to so expertly set it off, come from? They and the glittery stole had come from that confounded trunk full of the junk her father sent and brought back from the far reaches of His Majesty's colonies. She was so angry as she thought of the hoarded fine old silks, a treasure trove from the East India Company where her father had worked, mediating between Nawabs and Englishmen? He used to bring her back glittery materials as a gift, always a bauble for sweet little Dido.

Who was she? Dido frowned. Who was this turbaned, bejewelled, bare-chested, dusky, tawny woman being ushered forward by Lady Elizabeth Murray's gentle coaxing hand? When did she or her mother ever look like that? Was this David Martin's Dido, Queen of Carthage? Was she being ridiculed, subtly? Was she being egged on, as it were, to rise from her seat in haste? To go where? That was not shown. It had to be imagined. Lady Elizabeth, Beth, could caution without looking. Her gaze was straight ahead, not like this charade that was her, in flight, as it were, pointing, in a silly way, to her face. Why was she pointing? She remembered that he had asked her to put her finger up to her cheek, not knowing then what was the reason. Why that smirk, that ironic smile upon her lips? She was furious at the outcome and felt helpless as to what she should do about it.

She returned the portrait to the darkness of its shroud and left the orangery to the dying light of evening and walked along the long corridor to the drawing room, firstly looking in on the library to compose herself before joining the family for coffee and a chat. She would not show the slightest sign of her discomfort on her entry though she seethed inside and felt alone, utterly isolated. She felt betrayed. This betrayal was something she seldom showed to anyone. What had Mr Martin done with her Master's permission, with Mr Ramsay's commission, to make her so different after all these years compared to Beth, so quintessentially a perfect English lady in her hooped skirt?

One day soon after, she let her mask slip with a remark to Beth, overheard by both her Master and Lady Betty, 'They must think I'm their performing monkey.'

'But didn't you think David Martin was dashing, with his auburn hair?' Beth giggled.

❧ AS THE EPISODE now returned to Elizabeth in the quiet domesticity of her Ranelagh Street home all these years later, she found that she now understood much more about the portrait. She had learned quite a lot from viewing her Master's paintings and listening to him and his learned friends' discussions. It had indeed been some stratagem of David Martin's. It had not been Mr Ramsay's thesis that had been executed, which her Master had talked about, though she was never fully aware of what that had really been.

She could hear her mother laughing. *Don't let them fool you who in the end go have stop this appalling business. It will fail. It will fail to give them money when we burn down every plantation and great house, when it is no use anymore to their economy but a waste.* Her mother's words frightened her, coming to her at this point.

She mused on what she could remember of the portrait. She began to laugh to herself. Where were her milk pails, her basket, not of fruit and flowers but of the warm eggs she had collected each morning? Where was little Dido? Where was the real Dido? Where was the butter and the cheese from Lady Betty's dairy? She was a milkmaid after all. Where was her bonnet and woolly hair that had so offended that American gentleman, Mr Hutchinson, whom she overheard at coffee one night?

What had they done with the portrait? Had David Martin even signed it? It had disappeared. It had never been hung in the house. Had Mr Ramsay disapproved of the outcome so that all it became was a portrait of Lady Elizabeth Murray and a negress?

15

HER HUSBAND HAD been up all night nursing Elizabeth. She had coughed up a lot of blood so was feeling terribly weak. They had tried to keep this episode from the boys though Billy had wandered into their room at some point calling out, 'Mama, are you dying?' That was his fear. How much worse was his mother's nightmare? His father took him back to bed and then returned to complete the wiping up of the bloody evidence before Lydia found the sheets and had to spend the morning washing.

All these bedside ministrations and ablutions brought back, for Elizabeth, those dark days at Caen Wood, nursing her Master. Then it had been her wiping up the blood.

Autumn, then winter, made the coughing worse.

She rested. Her husband's affection was more valuable than ever. His touch had always healed her sadness.

'You must leave off from the reading of those letters and write to your mother,' he counselled.

'Yes, darling, I must.' She folded away the first letter of the day.

Dear Mammy

I hate them all. I know I never show it. I am always most obliging and thankful, but the hate that springs in me hurts me because often they are so kind — in their way. I read of the accounts of capture and abuse on London streets and along the hedgerows of England, and so have to be

thankful for this place where my father has put me, where I am captive.
Please write me. Please, please write to me…

Nearly losing Charles had banished any fear Elizabeth had of failure in this endeavour of writing to her mother. She was prepared now to risk any nervous anticipation, any disappointment that there might be. Dr Featherstone had been very kind ever since Johnny's death. He had made Elizabeth comfortable with a homeopathic remedy. Also, she and John had been able to get advice from him about the post and its reliability when sending letters outside of the country. He had had reason himself to send a letter to a cousin who was living in Boston. He advised them to contact the captain of the ship, the *Dover*. The changes that had taken place with shipping to Pensacola, now that it was no longer a British colony, meant that they had to be more certain than ever of the ship's destination. Ship post was the best rather than the packet post, he had explained.

Mr d'Aviniere had, with the aid of Seamus, made contact with the captain of the *Dover*. Captain Richardson was happy to be their messenger though he did not hold out great hopes. 'So much has changed in those parts,' he warned. The ship would sail within the fortnight. He had agreed to deliver the letter to Maria Belle on Wharf Street, her mother's address mentioned in one of her letters to her daughter.

It was now left to Elizabeth to write to her mother. She had to put her fears away and write at once in order to catch the Dover before it sailed.

My Dearest Mother

Are you alive? I've been so lost and now that I have found you in your
letters I must find out that you are still there. I cannot believe I am writing
to you again with so much distress at what has happened and with such
hope. You will receive this letter safely within the month. That is my hope
and then that you will write to me. I feel wretched. You must not think ill

of me. You must wonder why you have never heard from me since our exchange of letters when you left these shores in 1774. I did receive that first letter. In the last few months your letters together with my own have been returned to me by Beth. You must remember Beth, she was the girl who came to live with the Mansfields, my Master and his wife. I am sure you remember my difficulties in the early days with her, which I would tell you about at Mary Hill in Greenwich. But so much time has slipped away. Are you there? That is all I need to know. The complications and the reasons why your letters were never given to me, or mine to you, are beyond me to explain as is so much that has controlled our lives for decades. I do not wish to waste time with that matter now. I will only rage. So will you when you hear the reason. I will tell you all later. Hopefully. Are you there? I want to know that you are well. I want you to know that I am married to a dear man, John d'Aviniere, I have two sons, Charles and William Thomas, our Billy, who wants to see and hear from his grandmother. Charles' twin brother Johnny sadly died a couple of years ago. I have always told them about you. I live in Pimlico on the other side of London. I am not so well. As you know, I was at times weak as a child with that persistent cough. I am worse with that, but not to worry now. As you must know I am 43 years of age. And you? I can't believe are more than 59. That you are there is all my concern. Please forgive if you ever felt I had neglected you. I never did. This is a trick they have played upon me, upon us, for mine and your own good, I am told. But no, let us not give in to rancour. I want you, if you receive this letter, to reply at once. I understand ship post is best. Even better, if actually delivered to the captain of your ship. I have all the evidence that you know about post, so what can I teach you. I am hoping this will sail safely to you. I live at No. 9 Ranelagh Street in Pimlico. Please, please write to me. We live in continuing troubled times. But I am sure if you are there we can begin to talk through our letters. Dare I wish for more? I do. I do. I do.

I have given up the name of Dido. There is much to explain.

Your ever dearest daughter, Elizabeth, Lizzie as some close to me call me. You may want to call me Lizzie, never Dido.

She folded the letter, her eyes brimful, as her mother's small parcels had been sent, her own less expertly. She heated the wax and sealed it at the folds. She gave it to her husband who went immediately that afternoon to convey it to Captain Richardson.

Elizabeth told Dr Featherstone he had to keep her alive. To hear from her mother filled her mind with too much wakefulness. He had to give her something for a good night's sleep. She worried about what she saw as her unexpected and imminent death due to the erratic behaviour of her illness, which saw her healthy one moment and then quite ill another. She worried whether her mother would be able to travel. Her husband told her again that she must prepare herself for disappointment. She should not be surprised at any delay in a reply. Captain Richardson might not return for at least a month or two. She might not hear anything before the end of the summer.

Time in the hourglass on the pantry dresser was slipping through with the falling sand. She worried about what she had heard of storms and wars. She dreamt of shoals and rocks and prayed to the god Hurucan, who she remembered her mother talking of, to be merciful.

Billy and Charles were frustrated and irritable with the rainy weather not being able to play outside. While she still feared every moment that Charles was away from home, she and Mr d'Aviniere wished to build the boys' confidence in going out. She had to keep her anxiety from the household so that they would not guess at her worry over her mother and about her own health. She had told the boys about the letters that Aunt Beth had brought and about the letter she had just written to their grandmother. They were curious and had begun to ask questions.

Elizabeth and her mother had both been writing into a void; just the longing and the plea, asking for each other, inquiring why are you not writing? The difference now was that her mother did not have her own letters nor her daughter's.

Line upon line across the empty sea, an empty page she received with each breaking wave upon the shore of Pensacola, an empty page returning to her daughter in England on the tide.

Today, Elizabeth was led to the story of the ship the *Zong*, mentioned in her letters to her mother. She did not want to be near to that story. She remembered that it had been Mr Equiano who had alerted Mr Sharp to that fateful ship and the story of the murders. It was the first time she had heard the writer's name.

Her Master had fallen from his horse that year. Why was that inserted there in her memory now? Might the injury have affected his judgment? Her mind was suddenly on fire. It was while she was nursing him that he mentioned the name of Olaudah Equiano, the African.

Names and facts shrieked at her with the persistent clarity of the insane she sometimes could hear coming over the marshes from Locke's Asylum.

She eventually found what she was looking for. She remembered that she had written to her mother at the time of the *Zong* case. She recalled it well after all those conversations during the evenings over coffee. She still refused at that time to have any sugar. It was all she could do to keep Beth awake and insist that she listen to these extraordinary stories they were hearing. Returning to the desk in her room, she would sit up late, beginning under candlelight, day after day until each letter was completed and handed into Lady Betty for posting.

She now knew that they must have read her thoughts on these matters.

Dearest Mother

To whom can I speak openly of this matter? I cannot sleep. When my Master paused in the court, it was portentous. I too shuddered. What was it that would make a courtroom shudder? This is what we are told in the papers. The name Zong tolled like a death knell. Another word was Tobago, the small island. Do you remember, in the distance? I sneaked a look at maps in the library with my candle. I spun the globe. Was it not on that journey on my father's ship, that journey to Cartagena when I was a small child? Do you remember? My father pointed. It surprised me all these years later to hear that the Zong was lost off Tobago, adrift, miles from its destination to Kingston, Jamaica. I remember the swell of that sea. Have you had the news of the trial? Do you get wind of these things? Maybe a captain on a ship speaks to you as you walk along the seafront where I imagine you. I heard my Master say that we are property, speaks of hundreds, thousands as property. I have known it. But now it makes me shudder as those in court who heard it and knew it of themselves. Am I still property? Freedom from being property? Is that what will happen? Is that what happened to you before you left? Might you become property again? I long to hear from you even after all these years. Why don't I hear from you?

Your dearest daughter, Dido.

Elizabeth saw it plainly now. Lady Betty had paid little attention anymore and just gestured that she should rest her tight parcel of words on her dressing table. She had stopped looking at her when Dido brought her a letter. Elizabeth was certain she was not imagining it. She was remembering the moment as if yesterday.

Dearest Mother

The ship was bound for Jamaica. Captain Collingwood lost his way, this time between Hispaniola and that island. It had been a packed ship when it set sail with 470 souls. Too packed for the size of the slaver, as they call the vessel. Many had died of a sickness early in the voyage including seven of the seventeen-man crew. This was a fated ship. I listened gravely over coffee after dinner, even Beth was shaken into consciousness, even she shuddered. Supplies of water were running out. Luke Collingwood thought the sick should be thrown overboard. He ordered the crew to dispatch the bodies into the water. It was seen even as a mercy because of the severe disorders among the ill. My Master depended on facts and these were the facts that he was given. One hundred and thirty-one of the live cargo was thrown into the sea. The fast moving vessel was deaf to the cries of women and children, arms raised from the swell as they floundered, drowned. There is more I must write, but for now, I rest.

Your dearest daughter,

Dido

As a girl, she had told herself the story as a ghost story. She thought she could hear the cries like sea birds upon the waves where they fed on the drowned in the wake of the vessel, blood rising from those fathoms. Now there were the gulls overhead from the river, gulls circling and keening above her garden, their cries sounding like a knife scraped against porcelain.

Dearest Mama

Facts, Master asked for the facts. Some were thrown from the deck in the sight of their kindred, some shackled who revolted at their fate were thrown fettered into the swells, ten with loosened chains freely throwing themselves into the brine. They chose their own death as the best freedom they might achieve. It was reported that one man grabbed a rope and pulled himself aboard to freedom. I can hardly continue with this story and must leave off to go and supervise the milking. But I must tell you more as soon as I learn more facts.

Your Dido

To freedom? What freedom was that to climb aboard a slaver? What a man was he to find in the fury of that sea a rope swinging?

It was during one morning in the library as Elizabeth saw it clearly now, conversations overheard. It was not long before milking. The voices would not stop. And to stop it she had had to tell her mother the madness in her head that those gentlemen conversed about.

Dearest Mother, dear

My Master says that there was deception in the owner's case. That was my Master's voice in the library across from his dressing room. I talk of the house as if you know it. But of course you did not come here. I came to you along the river. I hold to those meetings, go over them in my head and have your voice for comfort and counsel. Caen Wood has disappeared into fog this morning. Master and Mr Way talk of the men you first told me about, Mr Granville Sharp and Olaudah Equiano, the African, who is the one that alerted Mr Sharp who then brought this case to my Master. It has not pleased my Master. The water shortage was to blame, and the sick. These two facts would threaten the entire cargo. That's what they call it. This was the captain's reckoning. No sooner had the captain chosen the first 54 infirm from below deck and ordered them thrown into the sea that it began to rain. Water was plentiful. He continued to argue that the sick were still a risk to the safety of the remainder of the live cargo. He convinced himself it was a mercy to throw them to the waves so to ensure the safety of the remainder of his cargo. This makes it that the insurers have been wronged. This is the case that Master must judge. If there were enough supplies of water, there was no necessity to jettison the live cargo. These are all Master's thoughts. I learn this vocabulary. If of course there was no water that would be another matter altogether. They might then jettison the property, the cargo. He speaks of the likes of you and me, dear mother, as cargo. This is exactly what he must look into, he says.

Elizabeth looked at her boys playing, and at Lydia preparing the supper and felt so fortunate to be where she was now with her husband and her children.

Dearest Mammy

The captain, Luke Collingwood, had died soon after the ship arrived in Jamaica. But there is a witness who says that within sight of Jamaica another batch of cargo was pitched into the water from the deck in full sight of those brought up onto the deck that morning for washing. He also witnessed that it rained again. The slaver, as I now know to call the ship, was lost twice. Who can argue that we have solved the problem of longitude? Do you remember my father always talking of longitude and Mr Harrison's clock? The Zong arrived in Kingston Jamaica with 420 gallons of water on board, 132 live cargo jettisoned upon the ocean. Master and two other judges have ordered a retrial. The law is the law Mr Way kept saying while he drank coffee with Master. He uses spoons of sugar in that coffee. Did I tell you that I do not use sugar anymore? It is my protest. The girls in the pantry giggle. Have you lost your sweet tooth, they say. They know I like cakes. I must confess to the tiniest portion of cake at times. In Master's court there were cries, not property, not property, meaning that the cargo should not be termed property. But in law it is so. Slaves are property. We know. I expect that was what provoked the description of 'shudder' in the Morning Chronicle, imagining those cast as horses or furniture into the salty waves of the Atlantic ocean. Had cast you dear mother, had cast me? They shuddered at Master's remarks. The original judgment favoured the captain's assertion that there was no water. That is my Master's view. To hear Master speaking like this forces me to ask, to whom do I speak? Beth was asleep I had to wake her. I must try and sleep...

Elizabeth remembered sleeping and then rising early before milking to complete her letter.

I continue. But what is clear is that there was plenty rain water for drinking, sufficient, so no need to jettison the live cargo. So there must be a retrial as it would not be lawful for the owners to get away with thinking that they were owed compensation. That is what Master says. I kept spinning the globe in the library as I listened to them across the corridor in Master's dressing room. The ocean blue is so vivid in the story as it is upon the globe. What Mr Granville Sharp wants is a judgment that will aid the argument for the abolition of the trade. Planters and the American lobby want a judgment that will back them in continuing with their trade and the development of their plantations. Master says that if there were such an abolition it would help no one because the slaves would then be treated badly on less regulated ships by foreigners. There is no doubt that the merchants in Liverpool and Bristol will lose revenues. He says that we can't risk that sort of catastrophe. Every owner from the little widow in Aldershot with her two slaves in Antigua, to the rich planter with numerous slaves and carriages in the West Country will lose according to their investment. Even a vicar in Hackney in need of his investment would be ruined. How on earth could they be compensated for such a loss? That would be something they will have to think about in the future, he says, if it ever comes to that. As you can see, dear Mammy I'm overwhelmed and wish you above all were here to advise me.

Your dearest, Dido.

PS I am beginning to hate myself. My good fortune worries me when so many die. And not to have sugar is the least I can do. Lost your sweet tooth, Dido, Master said the other evening when Molly came in serving cake to go with our coffee.

Elizabeth glanced at another of her mother's letters and read: *I can send for you now. But where are you? I never hear back from you.*

She had never heard her Master talk of a retrial. She did not believe there had been, in the end, a retrial. She had not heard of one at any time thereafter. Her inquiries had been ignored.

She now remembered when Mr Equiano had come to speak at the Shoreditch Meeting House. It was packed to the rafters, she and Mr d'Aviniere squeezing in for a seat. They were already courting. It was like one of those early meetings, which her mother had taken her to, to learn about abolition. She was inspired to speak and she felt bold to ask a particular question concerning the retrial of the Zong case. He had answered briefly but then, after the meeting, when she got a chance to meet him with her list of questions he confirmed her belief that there had not been a retrial. She had needed to have that confirmed. No person had been held responsible for the murders. *There never was such a trial, dear lady, and of course there should've been one. Justice can easily be done. And maybe they thought they had done the justice. But to do right is not easy. We must do the right thing. To do justice is easier, to do right, much harder.* Elizabeth had marvelled at his eloquence and wisdom. She and John thanked the African gentleman for his undying work.

My Dearest Mother

In the last months it is the weather that has consumed everyone's attention. The strange, unusual atmosphere we have all been noticing has become a national conversation. Newspapers up and down the country report it. To me it is the gloom of the trial...

Elizabeth, as she thought back, could not reconcile her regard for her Master's wisdom in other matters, his affection, that chuckle, that laughter in his eyes which made him so human with his legal logic. There was the law as it stood, but could he not have, with his power, altered it? He was known for reforming mercantile law and the law of commerce. That was always the overwhelming concern, the loss of profits, which determined his view, the view of the age. This problem was still present. How much longer the struggle for freedom? Certainly Mr Equiano was asking that question. Elizabeth remembered looking at her Master years later, on his deathbed, and asking herself, was there ever a reckoning in his mind on these matters? Or, was the law always, as it had been, a narrow place to hide?

Dearest Mother

I must keep writing to you to keep you alive even though I don't hear from you. 1783 has us still reeling from that terrible weather and more importantly from the almost inevitable diagnosis that Lady Betty is indeed very ill again. We had had experience of these bouts, which she suffered in

'74 and '78 but this is much worse, sudden and violent. Master's distress is visible. Against the strict instructions of the very good doctor in Kentish Town, Lady Betty has refused swallowing remedies of bark and the taking of asses's milk which she had imbibed on the other two occasions.

Elizabeth was alone in the house when Beth's letter was delivered.

Dear Lizzie

Forgive my delay. I have not known how to reply. You said that those close to you might call you Lizzie. I do feel close to you despite all that has happened to us, all that has been done. To undo it is to change the world and my little head is dizzy with such large questions. I leave it to Mr Finch-Hatton as I manage his house and his children. I still do ride. You will smile. But it is so important for me to ride out on my own and gallop away my worries. How do I answer your letter, your plea, your need for answers? I cannot fill in all the blanks. It was when I was coming of age, being prepared for marriage, that Lady Betty let me into the secret. I did wonder about your mother's letters before since I never saw you reading them. I knew they had come to the house since I often collected the letters both at Bloomsbury and at Caen Wood and you did not speak of your mother in Pensacola. I did not know then about your letters not being posted. I saw you writing them and presumed they had been posted. But the original plan of your father's and then carried out by Lady Betty came to me at the time of the portrait. I know you were angry about that, but to have told you about the letters at that time and to have broken my word to Lady Betty seemed impossible for me to do. Yes, you were different. You were lovable but you were different and we treated you as such, a sort of cousin. Your anger, your rage, is reasonable, Lizzie. No one thought of your mother's feelings and no one thought it would be better for you to be with her. Everyone thought they were offering you a better life. Personally, I'm sure that it was always Lady Betty's intention that eventually you should have the letters. But I think she just did not know when was quite the right time to do that. When Lady Betty died and then I got married I never thought of the matter again, until I was entrusted with the task by Aunt Anne of bringing Aunt Marjory's inheritance and the letters to you. I suppose they thought that they all belonged to you and what harm could be done now. I cannot offer any other explanation nor help with the ways to contact your mother. Your life was not your own to determine. I suppose that is the truth of the matter. You belonged to your father, to my great-uncle and that was how they saw it, how we all saw it. You were just Dido. I can only hope that now you have the letters and you have your husband and children and with some inheritance from my great-uncle and Aunt Marjory you can begin to determine your own life with your husband, though the world has not changed sufficiently for me to be secure in that view. You will always be Dido, I suppose. That sounds harsh, maybe. I cannot imagine it otherwise. I'm sorry your heart is broken.

Your cousin.

Beth

Postscript

The children seemed happy enough together. Perhaps they'll meet again. Then, what do children know till they are taught. They must be taught. I was taught. You did not eat with us, Dido, that made all the difference.

16

ELIZABETH DREAMT THAT night about the house at Caen Wood, the great white house. She was on the path down by the Thousand Pound Pond looking up at it. There were only two things in an empty room, the portrait of Beth and herself and the box of letters, one a false history and the other a true history; two contrasting archives. She was sitting on the floor in front of the portrait reading the letters, which were strewn around the floor. Her mother and herself were trying to sort them out, trying to find some order. There was someone knocking at the door to get in. Elizabeth woke in a panic. It was Beth breaking down the door to come into the room.

Elizabeth woke her husband.

'What is it, darling? I'm here...'

'The letters, I'm sorting the letters...'

'What letters?'

'My mother's letters, of course. She was here and we were sorting out the letters at the Caen Wood house in a room with that dreadful portrait of Beth and myself hanging on the wall.'

'That's a nightmare...'

'It's that letter. I've got to write to Beth again. What a thing to say. She can't accept who I really am. Is that her conclusion to the matter?'

'How do we settle the past?'

'You ask me that...'

'My love, come here.' He took her in his arms.

Charles and William Thomas were being schooled at home by Mr Bridges, a private tutor. Elizabeth and John had decided that would be the best way, for the moment, to deal with Elizabeth's anxieties, which had increased with waiting for her mother's reply. It was also a way of dealing with the danger the boys were in on their way to and from school and with the bullying in the schoolyard. Charles had gone back to school after the ordeal of his capture only to be persecuted with taunts and fights. He was now enjoying classical stories and quoting from Mr Shakespeare and Mr Marlowe:

Was this the face that launch'd a thousand ships
And burnt the topless towers of Ilium?

He was impressing Mr Bridges who had been recommended by one of the Quaker elders John and Elizabeth had met at an abolitionist meeting. Billy was working on his sums. Elizabeth overheard the lesson in the parlour. Charles' recitation reminded her of Mr Cowper comparing the fires in London in 1780 to those of Troy:

When the rude rabble's watchword was destroy
And blazing London seemed a second Troy.

'Tell us that story,' Charles demanded later that evening. 'Tell us how you escaped from the fire.'

> THE STORY HAD saddened the whole household at Caen Wood in that unforgettable year, 1780. They were told that Master's coach had been broken into pieces by the mob, Mr Cowper's 'rabble', outside parliament. Her Master's face had been besmirched with mud and he had been shaking where he had been sitting on the woolsack. The news had been brought to Lady Betty in Bloomsbury Square. Why did the messenger speak in poetry, Dido remembered asking herself, saying that her Master, once he had been conducted safely to parliament, *was quivering like an aspen?* It seemed such a contrast to the other messages that had been coming across the town about the

destruction. He arrived to what the family thought of as their oasis in the busy town, their beautiful Bloomsbury Square. He told Lady Betty and Beth, Dido listening on the stairs, that he had been mercifully allowed to escape through a back door of parliament leading down to the river. 'They threw about me this disguise of a green coat and this bob-wig.' From parliament he had been rowed under cover and conveyed via the Strand, then along Holborn by coach to the Square.

Dido was sent off to fetch a basin of water as her Master was still so dirtied by the mud that had been thrown at him. Mr Way brought him some brandy. How lowly he seemed to have fallen as Dido looked up at one of his portraits where he was resplendent in his ermine, wig and crimson robes. She pitied him. But no sooner were they taken up with making him comfortable than the news arrived ahead of the mob that they were converging upon Bloomsbury Square itself.

Dido understood very little of the events at the time, about how to assess the Catholic question of the day, which her Master had championed and was now pilloried for. She missed her mother's ear to the ground. It did seem a good thing to be on the side of liberty, each and every kind of liberty. Dido could hear her mother's voice: *Who it is giving liberty? You see anybody giving liberty? Is take you must take it.*

There was concern about Lady Betty, Beth and the household. They were told that they had to be removed to Caen Wood as soon as possible. Dido was fetching and carrying all that was easy to transport. There was very little time left as they could already hear the roar of the rabble and some were now in the Square and in front of the house, hurling cobbles dug up from the pavements. It was nearing dusk and some were carrying lit torches. Windows were broken at the front. The fear was fire. Already reports were of flames from torched houses left in the wake of the mob as they came through the streets from parliament. They had originally congregated in St George's Fields on the south bank. Newgate Prison was reported breached and prisoners were on the rampage, some joining the original mob. What freedom were they in search of with their roar?

The household had descended to the kitchens. Dido had never seen such a congregation of Master and Lady Betty and Beth with the servants. She was anxious about her own safety. She heard one of the servants say, 'Is everyone to be trusted?' Was she talking about her? Dido wondered.

Two carriages had been ordered for the family. The servants were to make their way on foot or by getting a lift on a cart or horse, the best they could, north to Kentish Town. Every effort would be made to see what could be done along the way for their safety. It was then that her Master said, 'Dido, you must come with me.'

She had about her person some essentials of her Master's present work, copies she had recently made, which had been left on his desk. She was indeed his amanuensis. She was nineteen in 1780. She knew her place and all her efforts were to serve him in this travail.

Beth attended to Lady Betty along with her chambermaid Sarah who was to accompany them. They all escaped through the back door of the kitchen. Someone shouted, 'Fire!'

The journey out of the city, while a relief, was also terrifying. The speed with which the mob moved meant that they were almost upon the household before they knew what was happening.

After supper, Dido joined the family as was usual in the drawing room at Caen Wood. London faded into the darkness beyond Kentish Town. There was a red aura in the sky as if a sunset in the far distance towards Harrow Hill, which they could see from the terrace, forcing them to imagine the still burning houses. They were all shaken. Master, Lady Betty and Beth talked among themselves. Dido listened attentively for any errand her Master might wish her to do. Mr Way joined the company as coffee was brought in by Molly. He had had a report from town. The news was not good.

Lady Betty looked quite pale. She summoned her chambermaid who was told to wait at the door that evening. No one wanted a repeat of her illness. Dido saw Beth take her great-aunt's hand and attempt to soothe her.

Mr Way was beginning to describe what had happened at the house in Bloomsbury Square after the family and servants had escaped. He could not contain himself on this occasion. He told about the iron railings outside the front, which had been uprooted and used as weapons to smash down the front door. The rampage through the house was absolute. The fire was consuming in the wake of the mob coming through the house. It was pillage, incendiary damage, books flung from the windows, the library emptied onto the street below. Parchments floated in the air among the flames and the wonderful harpsichord was dropped from the large windows at the front down to the pavement of the Square beneath.

Her Master's face was lined and sad as Mr Way spoke in a fevered state.

Dido's Master looked to her and said, 'My Cicero, my papers, the records of my cases, a life's work over years, now lost.'

She noticed for the first time how old he and Lady Betty looked. She remembered them as so gay and youthful in their sixties when she had first met them. She was sitting at her Master's feet ready to fetch. He leant towards her, his voice hardly audible, 'My Cicero, my Horace.'

She looked at the reaction from the company at these chosen words so intimately addressed to her, everyone shocked at the story of the vandalism of the library in the house at Bloomsbury Square. He continued to speak what Dido did not understand immediately, 'Pope, what would Pope have thought of this destruction?' He was speaking to himself though he leant towards Dido, his words a whisper: *Again? New tumults in my breast? Ah, spare me Venus! Let me, let me rest!*

It seemed to her that in his references he felt that both himself and his country were threatened by this riot of people taking the law into their own hands. The law, above all, was in his hands to be administered. But he was now helpless. Before he turned away to speak to Mr Way, he spoke to Dido again, 'I have no books to consult.'

Dido thought that her own liberty was also being diminished. The library had become her refuge, particularly after her mother's departure and her learning became all that mattered, and to which her Master had exhorted her, *reading and writing, child*. She had tried in her letters to her mother to show that she understood this.

❧ How extraordinary that someone thought to save the letters from the fire, Elizabeth now thought. All her Master's papers had been lost, but the letters saved. Who had been the saviour, or, was it coincidence, a random picking up of things to take with them to Caen Wood that evening of the fire? Elizabeth thought she must ask Lydia whether she had been aware of anything. She felt sometimes that the past was fading for Lydia. Had Beth saved the letters on Lady Betty's instructions? She had not mentioned that in her letter.

Elizabeth sought a simpler version of the fire for her boys. How might she distil adventure from such fear and cruelty? Billy had mercifully fallen asleep, too heavy for her to lift and carry any longer. She gave him to his father to put to bed. Charles, who had been wide awake, was also closing his eyes as he collapsed where he sat on the window seat, still eager for his Mama's story. The last of the evening light was piercing with its final shaft; the lawns dappled with shadow cast by the foliage, robins and tits taking their last feed in the shade, skittish in the water of the birdbath.

After their father had put the boys to bed, Elizabeth and John sat and continued the reminiscence. He had heard versions of this story. He of course had not entered the country till four years later. So her successive recitals had always contained some new detail or some nuance he had not caught from previous accounts.

'I liked the story of how his Lordship's judicial robes became the masquerade of a beggar...'

'Yes and a chimney sweep was seen to dance down the street in Lady Betty's hooped skirt?' Elizabeth laughed. 'No, it was terrible.'

'Some silly illiterate fellow thought the name Pope written in one of his Lordship's books was reference to the Pope in Rome. This enraged the anti-Catholics to even more fury...'

'Yes, absurd...'

'There was retribution though, two culprits hanged on gallows facing the ruins of the burnt house in the Square...'

'All true. But you know, my Master did not seek retribution on the people nor recompense from parliament or the king...'

'A man of some principle and heart, then. But he was a very rich and powerful man. What a story!'

'The whole library was lost and all his papers. And there was more to the story...'

Elizabeth and John had hardly slept a wink with all the excitement of these reminiscences. She was exhausted in the morning.

'You must want to hear from your mother, Lizzie.'

'I try not to keep thinking about it...'

'As I said before maybe not till the end of the summer, sweet.'

'It's late. You must be off and become a steward. Kiss me.'

'But Lydia, I've been thinking. How were the letters saved from the fire? I was retelling the story last night to Mr d'Aviniere and the boys. The whole library was lost, all my Master's papers.'

'That time the Master trying to save the rights of us Catholics...'

'He had his principles. There was his Jacobite past.'

'I thought a good man on that count, Ma'am...'

'Sorry, Lydia, I just can't get the letters out of my mind. I was there at the time, gathering up a few things for Master and Lady Betty. Who saved the letters?'

'You know Ma'am. I see how upset you've been since Lady Elizabeth's visit, her bringing them letters.' She explained how when she first saw the box that Lady Elizabeth had brought she thought she had seen it before. 'I keep watching you sitting there reading. I don't say anything because I wasn't sure.'

Lydia explained to her mistress how Lady Betty had given them to her as the servants got onto the cart to race through the night to Kentish Town and into the hills. 'Defend it with your life, girl,' she had said, 'placing the box on my lap.' Lydia went on to describe how when they arrived at Caen Wood Lady Betty took the box of letters back from her, saying, 'I'll look after these.' She saw her place the box in her dressing room. 'I've not given it a thought till I saw Lady Elizabeth deliver it and her man Mr Herbert put the same box on the table.'

'What a thing, Lydia. I've got you partly to thank for this late gift.'

'I glad you get them, Ma'am, but you have me thinking what a terrible time that was for us Catholics. People in The Rookery where we lived had all their furniture taken from their home and put on a bonfire in the middle of Leicester Fields.'

'Yes, people high and low suffered. I think my Master was on the side of right with the Catholic question...'

'Indeed, Ma'am.'

17

WHEN HE WAS not with Mr Bridges, Charles was helping his mother arrange her letters. Few had been dated. By finding a chronology, he was learning about his grandmother. Elizabeth could now attach some dates to her memories. She was taken back to 1783. So much had happened in the '80s and in that particular year. With Beth on her mind, she returned to her last years at Caen Wood.

Elizabeth had found one of her own letters of the same year when she asked her mother to advise her. Had she thought that this letter, after all that time, would provoke the reply that she had been longing for?

My dearest Mother

I think Beth will marry soon. They are making arrangements. Suitors arrive at the house. Beth visits Bath for the season, as they call it, where she can be seen. I am excited and part of me is pleased for Beth. I help her choose her dresses. I feel jealous then. When she returns from Bath she tells me stories about the men she has met…

Elizabeth remembered going to bed desperate to know what would happen to her. She scribbled a note down to be included in her story, finding one of her letters, which belonged to that time. She needed so many answers.

Would Dido not marry? Would there be no romance in her life? Would Mr John d'Aviniere ever become a romance? They had allowed her to keep her visits, after her mother's departure, to the Meeting House in Shoreditch where she had first met him. Her Master had even insisted that she have a carriage for the long journey. She had offered Mr d'Aviniere a ride back to Hampstead where he lived in the village. Romance was what Beth had told her about though she knew that marriage was quite a different matter. It was a matter of money. How would she meet someone to marry and how would it be allowed? How could it be afforded? It was then that she wrote to her mother.

Mammy. Can you tell me what I should do? Lady Betty does not talk to me about this matter. There is never any talk of arrangements being made for me. I do not know what to say when the young maids who are also excited at Beth's prospects say to me, Who'll marry you, Miss Dido? What will I do? I am as beautiful as you Mammy. Who will make me a lady? This is my home now. At least write to me now. I need your protection more than ever. My father is nowhere to be seen. How can he find me a husband? There is my Master and there is Lady Betty but I am embarrassed to ask them of this matter.
Your dearest daughter,
Dido.

Elizabeth still raged to think how it was then.

> 'WHAT ABOUT YOU Miss Dido, will you find a husband?' That was Molly and the other maids.

They went off sniggering together and Dido did not know what to say. She knew that they still giggled about the colour of her skin, the crinkle in her hair. These were girls up from Kentish Town whom Lady Betty employed to do some heavy cleaning. They did not stay long, not permanent members of the household. There was always a new one to get accustomed to her. 'Maybe we get that fella Hal who used to work here to come and marry you.' She was the same girl who had once touched her to see if the black would come off. When Lydia was there she always leapt to her defence.

It occurred to Dido one day, while she was musing on her quite different state, that Beth, poor girl, was up for another kind of auction. She began to see it that way. It was not the auction block her mother described when she told her of how she had first met her father, not the auction block on the waterfront at Pensacola, but nevertheless, still paraded to be sold. Not branded, though. While Beth herself was concerned about how she looked, for she was pretty, the preoccupations were to do with a dowry. Mr Martin had made her pretty in his portrait, two years before. Or, at least, some thought so. In the portrait she was someone up for sale. Where did Dido in the portrait come in? Did she help? Did her presence there increase Beth's sale, seen as a woman of property? Lady Betty was trying her best to match her great-niece so that the gentleman was someone who would both care for her as well as make her prosperous. It had to do most importantly with money that was settled on Beth in 1783. Dido heard it spoken of, the sum she would inherit from her great-uncle, what she would be able to have on marrying Mr Finch-Hatton. It was substantial. This settlement would get her married well. She was worth a fortune. Dido was not worth anything in the marriage stakes.

'And love, Beth? We talked of that when we were younger,' Dido said to her when she had arrived back from a visit to Bath.

'Love? And a cottage? No, Dido. No. It must be a grand house with a park.'

She overheard that Beth's dowry would be substantial. Dido had been sitting near to her Master copying and listening to the arrangements between himself and Lord Stormont. Beth's father had another daughter, Caroline, to eventually marry off. Master had said he would help from his considerable wealth. And, of course, Lady Betty had arranged that Beth marry her nephew. It was all within the family, all hanging from good trees.

Dido knew more than she should. She always had, all ears, all eyes, and her Master's amanuensis, copying and delivering messages on the stairs. She was present in the drawing room, in the dairy, out at the poultry, listening and noticing everything in an effort to understand where she fitted in.

In whatever way they pretended, she was always on the outside. She survived by always trying to please.

Dido was called into the library to sit with her Master, a number of papers on his desk, one particular roll brought in by Mr Way and left, and her Master saying, 'You can leave us now, Mr Way, for it is Dido I must spend some time with this morning.' Dido saw the steward nod. He looked as if he already knew that this would be the case. He did not seem surprised that he was being asked to leave the room to his lord and Miss Dido.

'Come Dido, come and sit here with me.'

At his knee was his preferred position for her. She had sat on a low stool, as a child, on his footstool, and ever since with papers or a book opened on her lap, handed down to peruse and to follow at his instruction, repeating the information she found there. These were the morsels of story fed to her from his precious Horace or his learned Cicero.

It was a spring morning and Dido saw the first daffodils embroidered there beneath the library window and in myriad bunches and clutches on the bank, scattered everywhere through the pasture down to the pond, clogged with the nearly opening water lilies that promised a sunny morning.

'Come, Dido, this is what we must read this morning,' her Master said as he unrolled what looked like a document drawn up by lawyers.

In his face and hands she saw the strain that had begun to show since Lady Betty's illnesses in the previous year. It may have been a consequence of the fall from his horse in '81. No doubt that was one cause for his decline. But also, Dido thought, the stress of the *Zong* case, his judgment or ultimate lack of it, this very year. Had that perhaps taken its toll on his conscience?

The library at Caen Wood where Dido and her Master were sitting was being filled with the newly purchased tomes. These were no longer the originals, those signed by Master's dear friends Pope and Dr Johnson. Dido had spent hours here, this was her classroom when allowed to enter and to run her hands over the embossed bound volumes to take them down and read.

In the past he had instructed her. 'It's these stories, Dido, that will take you somewhere on the voyage of this life. To understand history, it is Herodotus. For law, for clarity and certainty, it must be my dear friend Cicero. For the beauty of the poetry, Horace, and for further inflections of poetry and drama in tales you must acquaint yourself with Ovid. And, if I can say so, for satire, my dear friend Pope, himself, and of course Martial and Juvenal before.'

Today it was another matter. Their attention was on the document in his hand. 'This is my will and last testament, and here there are some words pertaining to you, Dido. There are some more, but it's not those others that I wish to bring to your notice this morning. Time will be sufficient for that.'

'Yes, Master.'

'You'll learn of those in good time but these few are the ones which I would like you to read out to me now.'

His slender fingers, with still a relic of their youth in their slenderness but crabbed with the arthritis of age, pointed to the lines he wished her to read as his blotched hands handed her the document to hold upon the lectern of her knee. Dido had to lean into the page to decipher the spider's scrawl of ink across those documents. There was so much that she learned in those eight words.

She looked up to him with a request for permission, as it were, to continue for her eye had perused the sentence in one go before she came to enunciate it for him.

Dido read, quoting what was there written:

I confirm to Dido Elizabeth Belle her freedom.

Her thought was that he should have read it out aloud to her himself. But that thought was overtaken by both the weight that these eight words carried and yet, also, how ordinary and concise they were. And then, the thought that it should have taken so long for them to be said, twenty-two years, to be written and to be legally so written. She felt for a moment the urge to let her tears fall but instead kept control where she felt them welling and blurring her vision.

Had she ever known absolutely that she was not free before this moment? Had she been a slave for twenty-two years? When would this knowledge be proclaimed publicly so that all would know that she was free now, in case it was ever mistaken? Was it to be as here enshrined? Just that? Or, was it only to be at his death? Was it only then that he would release her? She wondered and wondered whether to ask. Was he offering her a sight of the reward to come but saying at the same time he must keep her to himself, his Dido, till his death? For it was a will upon which the words were written, not what her mother called *papers, manumission.*

Dido was angry inside. She was torn this way and that. How did he come to have her freedom, she thought, so that it was in his power to give it, or, should she say, return it to her? When had he acquired it? The thought passed through her mind whether her father had sold her to him. Was there a bill of sale filed somewhere, she, property, some document where she was linked to her mother, she a slave, therefore Dido also enslaved?

She was confused as to what to say. She did not wish to say thank you. She kept her silence and felt all the time that that was the proper thing to do. Her gratefulness lay elsewhere, in the intricate and the complex history of her emotions, which were there since she had come to live in his house as neither fish nor foul nor good red herring as Hal had been accustomed to tease her and then to insult her.

Her Master looked at her gravely. She kept her eyes mostly lowered apart from intermittent glimpses she allowed herself as he took the document from her hands and rolled away the contents from her view. It was not as if she was asked to put her signature to it, to agree. It was not that kind of document.

She wondered why this was happening at this precise moment in this year and not before. And then her Master spoke seeing the many questions of doubt and anxiety playing upon her face.

'You must not worry yourself about this just now, Dido.' He smiled then. She remembered how he smiled, like those smiles hardly breaking from his lips, but playing there as in his portraits. He always seemed another self beyond the self in the moment. He then went further to promise her a portrait of himself, which was in the keeping of Lady Betty's intimate friend, the Dowager Duchess of Portland. There were so many portraits of him, this one, by Van Loo. 'I wish to have you hang it in your room, Dido dear, to put you in mind of me when I'm not here, one who has known you since your infancy and whom you've honoured with your uninterrupted confidence and friendship.'

Dido listened without interrupting for she did want to ask, must I not worry? Then she asked. 'Must I not expect...?' And then she stumbled. Then she caught herself and repeated, 'Must I not expect my freedom *now*?' She had hesitated because of this gift of the portrait, which was bequeathed to her. She could see that he wished her to say something, to be grateful for the gift, at least. Too much was happening in that moment, happening yet and not happening, but told that it would happen. What was her present state to be? And him honoured by her uninterrupted confidence and friendship? These words were spoken surely to both silence any revolt within her breast and to woo her to him for life's duration, keep her as his property, his slave, till his death.

Next to the king he was the most powerful man in the realm, one of the richest. She looked out of the window where the wind was blowing among the daffodils and she thought then of their freedom in the breeze.

She could see that her Master had begun preparing to leave, shuffling his papers, tightening the roll to be returned to Mr Way to be stored, then rising to walk to the window to look out to his folly bridge. It led nowhere. Things were not what they seemed. All was a charade as in Mr Martin's portrait.

'What a genius, Mr Wren,' her Master said, looking into the distance of London. He was again at the window with his back to her. Then he turned to her where she had continued to sit on his foot-stool. He looked down upon her, as it were, from a great height as she used to experience his portraits looking down at her when she was a small girl. He seemed to grow taller and taller and her looking up to him made it difficult to hear or to be heard. And as if guessing her tortured self-questioning, he said, 'Freedom, Dido? To do what? Where would you go?'

She kept looking at him steadily in a way she had not done before. She could feel she was retreating. She sensed that he saw that retreat. Indeed, what was this freedom for, and besides, she, a woman? What was a woman's freedom?

'I will protect you, Dido. You cannot be taken. You must stay here. Here is your freedom. But I repeat, you cannot be taken. You are free. You are legally free. It is here written. Any capture or transportation would easily be contested in a court of law on the producing of this document that I have shown you.'

That possible capture that was mentioned so explicitly, and the scene of transportation imagined, shocked and terrified Dido. Her Master seemed uncertain at that point about the assurance he was giving her. He let the scroll fall from his hands, the entire last will and testament reaching the ground, written with his wealth. As he spoke, he pointed and continued to indicate the words written there which confirmed her freedom. 'I have seen to it,' he said. 'My judgment has made it plain that no one can be captured and put in irons to be returned to the colonies. But this above all, this statement, relating to your particular freedom, goes even beyond that judgment. Rest assured.'

Had he protested too much? Dido thought.

'Will I not go to my mother? Dido felt suddenly emboldened to ask.

'Your mother?'

'That was the promise a long while back, but not kept.'

'How can you think of leaving me Dido after all these years?' He knew her conflict and how to silence any thought she might have of running away from him. Was that what he thought? 'You ran away once,' he said ominously. Then he smiled. 'You were a girl, then.'

Dido did not reply, abruptly reminded of her skirt caught in brambles on the meadow at Brookfield and the awful memory of Hal marching her back to the kitchen door.

'My mother, why have I not heard from her for all these years? Just one letter, no more.' She felt her voice crack.

'That was for the best, Dido. Was it not?'

'She promised to send for me.'

'As I say, it was for the best. You must know that? Let us finish with this business now.'

She felt it was a verdict and a judgment. She felt that she might lose control. She did not want him to see her cry, not at this moment. She rose to leave and managed a smile and a curtsy.

'Come, come, Dido. None of that.' He put out his hand to raise her from her knees. He was always so charming and eloquent.

⊰ ELIZABETH NOW KNEW this might have been *the* opportunity for him to have returned the letters to her if it had indeed been her freedom he was granting her.

'He was my Master and my teacher, both my gaoler and liberator.' Charles listened with astonishment at his mother's words about the man whose portrait he was accustomed to look at hanging in the hall. Bit by bit he was learning his mother's story.

Mr Bridges coming into the room reminded Elizabeth that Mr d'Aviniere had left his wages on the sideboard to be given to him.

Miss Marjory's inheritance was a blessing to be used for the boys.

18

IT WAS THE first time that Dido had noticed her own breathlessness since she was a child. While climbing the stairs, running on short errands to Lady Betty's room, she had had to pause to catch her breath. All the meals had to be transported from the kitchens. There was bedding to be changed and laundered, basins and commodes to be emptied. She paid such little attention then as a young person. She had too much to do to waste her time in complaining. Lady Betty had retreated to the upper floor, vacating almost entirely her dressing room near to the orangery. This was a pity because Dido felt that the more fresh air and sunshine that she could enjoy better.

It was a melancholic account that Beth gave her that morning of Lady Betty's health. They had lived through this before in '72 and '82 when she continued to reject the bark medications and asses's milk. But this was much worse. She was deteriorating before their very eyes and there was little to be done according to the doctors from both Highgate and Kentish Town. They came repeatedly with their prescriptions and remedies, which did not prevail.

Her Master was in shock. Dido had to be attentive to his every need. 'Dido, come here, girl. I want you to do your very best now. I cannot lose her.' She had been told that he had invited relatives from Perth to help with the nursing. They were not to fetch and carry. They were to share in the supervisions, which had been the responsibilities of Lady Betty.

'So, you're the girl, Dido?' The voice from the top of the stairs greeted her in this way, looking her up and down, eyebrows arched.

'I am, Madam. They call me so.'

'They call you so? Is that not your name? Very well. I'll call you so, also. Lady Mansfield is failing fast. I'll now take the reins. Oh, dear, you seem to have smudged your face. Or, am I mistaken, perhaps?' By then the lady was standing over Dido.

'Madam?' she queried. Then she understood, yet taken by surprise. She could feel the blood rising into her face.

'You'll account to me about the business of the poultry and the dairy. I understand that those are your responsibilities. I'll be keeping the accounts. I'll collect and I'll dispense. Do you understand?'

'Madam, may I ask...'

'No, not now, later, possibly.'

Dido was left on the stairs to wonder at this new mistress of the house. She was going to ask whether she might ask her name. The lady had not stayed for the continuation of her request.

The following morning, there was almost a repeat of the scene, but with a difference. It was again on the stairs. Dido was so often either walking up or down the stairs, or simply lingering, catching conversations from beneath and above, always on the ready to fetch and carry from either direction, ever prepared for the call, 'Dido, Dido, are you there? Can you help me?'

'Yes, Madam, what can I do for you?'

'I'm lost.'

'Lost?'

'The house is so large and unfamiliar. My cousin is so much more confident with the domestic geography I dare say.'

This must be the other one of her Master's relatives from Scotland, Dido thought. She had guessed that her encounter the day before was with one of them.

Beth confirmed later that had been her aunt Anne, the daughter of her other great-uncle, David. He was her great-uncle William's brother. She explained that since her father's remarriage she had lost touch with the family.

'Where would you like to go, Madam?' She had Beth's story running in her mind as she looked at this lady who right away seemed much more friendly.

She smiled and she spoke gently. 'I must have some breakfast.'

'Has that not been brought to your room, Madam?'

'I wasn't aware that that might happen.'

'But you can also have it in the breakfast room. I can take you there straight away.'

They descended the stairs, Dido following and making sure that the lady whom she was escorting did not trip on her skirts.

'What should I call you, Madam?'

'You may call me Miss Marjory.'

So this was Miss Anne's cousin, Dido thought.

'Miss Marjory, you can sit here.' She seated Miss Marjory Murray at the dining-room table while she went off to the kitchen to remind Molly of the lady's breakfast.

On returning to the dining-room to reassure Miss Marjory that all was now sorted concerning the order of her breakfast, Miss Marjory said to her inquiringly, 'And what should I call you, my dear?'

She looked surprised, imagining by now that the good lady would have been informed of the young girl with the smudge on her face. If that were so Miss Marjory did not show any sign that she knew of her.

'They call me, Dido, Miss Marjory.'

'Dido?'

'Yes Miss Marjory.'

'Dido. Now that reminds me of one of my favourite stories when I was as young as you are, though a sad one. It is the story of Dido and Aeneas, a great love story, the queen of Carthage and her lover...'

'Yes. It's a sad story. I've read it in my Master's library...'

She was about to add that her own story was also a sad story but she did not progress with that idea. She saw that her answer had accumulated a sufficient number of other questions in the mind of the lady from the look on Miss Marjory's face, who was bold enough to ask quite different questions.

'In the library?'

'Yes. What's your relation to my Master?'

'To your Master?'

'Yes.'

'Whom do you mean? "My Master" William Murray, Earl, Lord Mansfield, Chief Justice in the good King's realm?' She laughed teasingly. 'He's my favourite uncle. Is that what he's called by you?'

'The very same, Ma'am.' Dido was enjoying the twinkle she saw in the good lady's eyes that she sometimes saw in her Master's eyes.

'So he has you calling him Master? I can't believe it.'

'No, Ma'am. I don't really know what he might have me call him. He, nor any other, has contradicted its usage. I made up my mind that if I continued to be called Dido, I would call him Master.'

'I see. And, Lady Mansfield? What do you call her?'

'She asked to be called Lady Betty. I called her that from the start and she was very happy. But of course now we're very sad at her condition.'

'Indeed. And that's why my cousin and I are here to help. But I can see that you are doing everything there's to be done. And here's my breakfast.'

'Let me leave you now, Ma'am. If there's anything more I can help you with...'

'And if there's ever anything I can do for you, you must call on me.'

'I will, I will Ma'am. I'm most grateful.'

Dido's Master had become quite a different person with the worry and obvious grief. He was not like the judge on his bench, in wig, crimson robes and gleaming white ermine. He was not the affable gentleman in conversation after dinner. He was not the jocular uncle out riding with Beth. He was not the learned scholar debating with the poets and legal men of his age, a converser with Dr Johnson, when Dido first heard with surprise of a black man in that gentleman's household.

Her Master was no longer the careful letter writer at his desk in the library dictating to her and lifting her efforts on the page close to his eyes to read the sentences he had composed.

He was now seldom the silver-tongued, truly eloquent Master. He was hollowed out as he sat by Lady Betty's bedside, his head turned to the door when Dido entered with a tray, his fingers to his lips to insist on silence. So it continued as she stood at his side and he spooned nourishment to his wife's lips, coaxing her with affection, his only words hardly audible, 'Try a little, my darling. It's a good broth that cook has prepared and Dido's brought up from the kitchens.'

So they, both husband and wife, now married for forty-six years, Beth had reminded her, desired no other world but this small tented bed, dimly lit. She noticed that he allowed the Miss Murrays to rearrange the pillows while he held Lady Betty's head. But she also noticed, jealously, she had to confess, that it was for her that he called and confirmed to his cousins, 'It's Dido that I need,' when they asked.

Was it affection or that long learned service on which he had become so dependent? Was it that confirmation that it was she, Dido only, that must fetch and carry? A perverse thought. She took his attention as kindness and in those moments hers to him was complete and absolute no matter the state of the world and what she thought about it.

Elizabeth knew now that they were all part of the great deception. But she just could not believe that Miss Marjory was also part of that conspiracy. How it all came back, so vividly, like a story, a sad story; Lady Betty, yes, the hush of the house, the tread in their steps on the stairs and along the corridors. *Dido, stop running.* That was Miss Anne with her ledger under her arm insisting on quiet as she descended the stairs. A pall of sadness had fallen over the entire household while the weeks and months ran into each other. Almost a year had passed without her noticing. Though the tedium of it all came back to her. Tedium and a kind of melancholia till Mr d'Aviniere spotted her at the Quaker Meeting House.

Elizabeth remembered what she learned from her early days with her mother: *Stay close. He has the power.* Pain did embitter her vision, a just position, she taught her to rage against the unimaginable. She had kept tutoring her. *It is the construction of their mind that has planned this. How they call it, enlightenment? That is what is frightening.* She was still writing to her at this time.

Dearest Mother

The nights are the longest and Master sleeps sitting with his head upon the edge of the bed, his hand in Lady Betty's to judge each and every move and request. I'm ordered to be always stationed at the bedroom door, and some nights I sleep on the floor at the foot of the bed, wakeful slumbers, ever ready to fetch and carry at his requests. Last night the Miss Murrays and Beth were not asked to keep vigil in the night. When it came to the end it was left to me to say to him with his wife's hand in his, she's stopped breathing, Master, to then tiptoe with the announcement to the rooms of both cousins and Beth that Lady Betty had departed this world. Master asked to be left alone to ponder for a long while before he descended to his dressing room and asked for Mr Way to come in, and for the arrangements to be made for the funeral, the undertakers called and the church of Highgate notified for the service and the burial in the nearby cemetery. All those who worked on the estate lined the drive to see the cortege on its way and followed to the hilltop village with its pretty church. They followed with bouquets, which were flung upon the passing hearse. So much will change here now. She was not a mother to me but she was a kind person. Only you are my mother. Who else can I write to but you my silent confidante? After all these years you can still write to me. I am here.

Your dearest Dido

It was now almost twenty years and Elizabeth relived it as if it were yesterday, that day in the spring of 1784, daffodils and violets on the banks along the way.

Later, Lady Betty had been transported to Westminster Abbey. Dido had been allowed to be present but to stand a little off from the family. She had felt her passing very deeply. Her Master had said she was to ride in the carriage with Miss Marjory and Miss Anne. But at the church she was to sit at the back not like in the Meeting House where she would sit equally with the rest of the congregation.

Elizabeth had noticed two children, a boy and a girl, at the front with Mary Milner, her father's wife. She did not know then whose children they were. She had learned afterwards that Mary Milner had not had children of her own. Were they her half brother and sister from another woman? She had kept her eyes averted from the direct gaze of the many cousins at the front. She had recognised ladies and gentlemen who had visited over the years at Caen Wood. Some had turned their heads to look at her where she was standing, *the black girl of Caen Wood*. It had been whispered so by some. But she had heard in the kitchen under their breath what those who hated Master had called her, *Mansfield's nigger, and you know what it is he has her there for*. It had not only been Hal who spoke like that.

Her husband's heavy breathing woke Elizabeth. She sat up and looked at his face. She studied the lines about his eyes. Crow's feet, they called them, where the sun had burnt him as a child, and the skin had dried. Those lines and the grey flecks at his temples made him distinguished. She touched and traced with her fingers his crow's feet. These expressions she had learned.

Then her mind flew to winter, the snow thick along the terrace at Caen Wood and the crows' feet there as she looked down from the window, a series of hieroglyphs on the white page of winter below, a sentence left by a flight of crows for her to read and to ponder and then to translate as she fancied. She kissed her husband on his brow and he breathed more regularly. She kissed his lips and the boyhood scar on his cheek. She lay back. Time was running out.

There was the tick of the clock upon the mantlepiece and there was the standing clock in the hall with its chimes, the hourglass on the pantry dresser. Its flow of sand mocked her if she cared to look and turn it over where Lydia had left it after baking. It was not to her a mere timer for the boiling of eggs and the baking of pies, but the seconds and minutes of her passing life and the time spent waiting for a reply from her mother, or some news from the captain of the *Dover*.

Elizabeth stood in the kitchen and stared at the sand's flow. It was a Sunday and the household were out to their different churches. Then, in no time, it seemed the family were back. Lydia was preparing lunch. The boys were with their father. Billy had graduated from his pull-horse to arranging his regiments and animals. He was either being a soldier or a farmer. Their father was going through the beginning lessons on the spinet with Charles who showed an aptitude for music. Mr Bridges had detected this in the boy and had the instrument transferred from an old aunt's house. John d'Aviniere had himself been given this opportunity by his foster father in Hampstead. They went through a simple fugue. Charles was still happy not to have to go out to school. He had not yet recovered from the trauma of his capture. His mother wondered whether he ever would.

Then she thought ahead to the future of her boys. Could Charles be a musician? Or were their futures foretold in the ranks of soldiers arranged by William Thomas and his growing empire over the carpet, regiments marching and horses galloping towards the drawing-room door? She would not be part of their future. Maybe she could tell herself another future, one with her children and their grandmother?

Dearest Daughter

The rain is heavy like when them storms come into Pensacola from the islands. You too little to remember your father's stories — his ship caught

many a time in voyages down south coming up from St Kitts, Antigua and
Dominica. Them get catch in the eye of the storm. Is the god Hurucan the
people say. Hurucan come last week. I lucky the house still standing. The
rivers swell up with landslides, mudslides, as if the whole place might sink
into the sea, dwellings flattened, crops destroyed, many bodies of those the
storm catch working in the fields washed out to sea and then brought back
onto the beaches on the waves and the tides…

Elizabeth put the letter aside. She found it difficult to forgive the great
deception, which had caused her so much pain. Another of her
mother's letters brought back an early memory, hearing her father's
voice and feeling the hammocks swing to and fro to the rhythm of
her mother's lullaby, its creak as the rain dripped from the roof to the
path beneath. There had been sweet moments then as now looking at
the healthy William Thomas, her husband, and Charles.

Lydia called them all to lunch and Elizabeth insisted that she and
Seamus join the family at the table. 'We really are all one family now.
Come on, sit.'

There was a single robin foraging among the dry leaves just outside
the French windows, the seasons turning over so quickly and still no
news from Maria Belle.

19

HER ILL HEALTH had made Christmas another quiet one, as she was laid up. Rest was always the best medication. Winter was the worse time for her condition. Martha had come to stay from Hampstead where she now lived with old Mr d'Aviniere, returning there to look after the old man who had rallied and then had now declined again and was near to death. They had invited Mr Bridges and he was pleased to see Martha again whom he had met at the Meeting House in Shoreditch. They entertained the boys, going out to play and to enjoy the cheer of the streets and the entertainments in Ranelagh Gardens. Charles, at last, was willing to go out with them, joined by Billy, who was more than eager for the excursion. There was snow and this excited the boys even more.

Elizabeth had joined the family in the parlour for a short while on Christmas morning. The children had decorated the windows with evergreens, holly and laurel. They all joked about bringing in a tree into the house and decorating it, a custom apparently introduced by the Queen at court, a custom from her own home. Elizabeth remembered when they said the king was mad. She thought of him and the Queen out at Kew — she must be able to distract herself with the new plants coming into the country from across the world.

Martha cooked a goose with the help of Lydia. They all sat at table together. Elizabeth tried a morsel. Martha struggled to keep things as usual for the children with trinkets and boxes of their favourite sweets, though Elizabeth was still insistent that she keep to the embargo on sugar at all times. She had to continue, if only symbolically, her support for the abolition cause. She did not force it on others. She was grateful to Martha, who was prepared to come again to lend support to Lydia and keep her company.

The new year of 1804 had her thinking, how much longer must she wait?

The boys were now both more settled with Mr Bridges. They had their lessons in the parlour and Elizabeth sat by the French windows looking onto the garden. Lydia now also had less to do with the boys and could take more time at her normal chores and attend to Elizabeth's needs. She also had to care for her own mother who had travelled to England from Dublin and was living in The Rookery. Elizabeth remembered Caen Wood becoming a house of illness after Lady Betty's death and the beginning of her Master's decline.

It must have been something from the apothecary, some powder or julep to remedy the diagnosed scrofula of the lung, her disease of the chest that made her so absent minded and forced her to drift. Elizabeth thought these so-called cures might kill her, put her to sleep forever. She held on to her mother's letters on her lap.

My Daughter

I fancy you must've decided to abandon your black mother for her ladyship and grow into your father skin... In that same letter: *Is some white man they choosing for you. Or they leave you to your lonely self. Something on a shelf, they say...*

Elizabeth woke from a reverie, caught between her mother's letters and her expectation of the one she was waiting for. She surfaced through the mists of medications.

She remembered now that it had been Lydia who had pointed to a column in the *London Chronicle* of the 7th to the 10th of June in 1788. She had overheard Mr Way reading it aloud. She had saved the paper and brought it to her. She still had the cutting from the paper. As she read it, it took her back to her story.

On Wednesday last died, at Marlborough, on his way to Bath, where he had been for the recovery of his health, Sir John Lindsay, Knight of the Bath, and Rear Admiral of the RED, to which latter rank he was raised in September last. Sir John Lindsay was nephew to Lord Mansfield; he has died, we believe, without any legitimate issue, but has left one natural daughter, a Mulatto, who has been brought up in Lord Mansfield's family almost from her infancy, and whose amiable disposition and accomplishments have gained her the highest respect from all of his Lordship's relations and servants.

❧ DIDO READ AND reread the lines. The familiar facts of his decorations and rank assumed a kind of mythic tone written down there, the story of someone else. This was her father and yet a figure out there with nothing to do with her, had had nothing to do with her for so long. She conjured him from the ship, peeping between the cracks of the partition where he had held her mother in his arms, kissing her mouth. Was he the same man, he who had teased her and taught her his geography? But then for her to be described so deliberately as illegitimate and a mulatto surprised her. Natural daughter? Of course, she knew these things but seeing them written down about herself made her think again about her situation in the family and not of the family. There were four lines about this illegitimate, natural, mulatto daughter, natural but not legitimate. From whom had these sentiments come? They were kind, she supposed; amiable, accomplished, and having gained respect from relations and servants. Dido looked up at Lydia who kept looking over her shoulder as she continued to read.

'Respected, for sure, who respect...You're well respected my girl.'

Lydia laughed affectionately.

Dido thought of Hal and his hands running up her skirts. His fingers like ferrets undoing buttons and ribbons, fingers everywhere. *Ferreting out* had been one of his expressions, the mice and rats among the apples. She thought of the girls from Kentish Town giggling as she spoke and touching her hair. Miss Anne asking her whether she had soiled her face, smudged it with black, like boot polish. Lydia and Molly even had been astonished that she was black all over. Had the journalist heard that part of her story, that the natural, illegitimate daughter had suffered those things?

'You'll inherit,' Lydia said excitedly as she deciphered the text with her poor reading.

Dido did not respond and then wondered if what she said might be true. But what of Mary Milner and the children she had seen sitting with her at Lady Betty's funeral?

Then Dido found that her eyes had misted over remembering her father as her fair captain on the deck of his ship, his efforts to protect her. But she was unsure of what her emotions were telling her. He had also abandoned her, not given her his name. They had not said she had been his slave or what the rest of her story was concerning her mother, or, Mary Milner. It was odd the selection of biography, which had been learned and chosen for this obituary of her father. She lifted *The Chronicle* from the table and left the pantry to ascend the back stairs to her room at the top of the house.

'What is it? What worries you, Dido?' John d'Aviniere whispered seeing her looking distressed in the porch of the Meeting House the following Sunday.

She had kept the cutting from the paper to show him. He read and said: 'It's why I've chosen you, yes, and this,' as he kissed her. 'You are accomplished, more than amiable to me — truly loving. Respect? I do that.'

'Lydia says I'll inherit…'

'We'll know soon enough. Don't trust it…'

'It would be good for our marriage…'

'Undoubtedly, but we must wait for the old man to die.'

There were footsteps and someone opening the door into the Meeting House. They parted abruptly.

Later, back at Caen Wood, alone, with her room drenched in June sun and dust trapped in beams of light falling through the window in shafts and broken shards upon the floor, she sat on her bed and reread the notice in the newspaper. She wept for herself and for her mother. She had no tears for her father. She then threw open the sash window and leaned out taking gulps of air, at the same time looking up to the swifts which had recently returned from Africa and were circling in spirals higher and higher into the heights of the hot blue sky with their clicking calls feeding on the wing. They roosted beneath the eaves of the house outside her room, their nest a brood of chicks with open mouths.

> ELIZABETH HAD NOT grieved then and she did not do so now. She had not attended the funeral. She had not inherited a farthing from her father. With an ancestry of being bought and sold, she now lived on her Master's legacy, Miss Marjory's gift and her husband's honest wages.

'I'll get the door.' Billy, bored with his reading for Mr Bridges, was running out of the parlour to the front door. 'Mama, Mama. There's a gentleman for you.'

Elizabeth was startled at Billy's shouting.

Mr Bridges could be heard trying to retrieve the boy. Billy ran rings round his tutor at times.

'Lydia, Lydia, can you see what it is?'

Lydia was coming down the stairs into the hall. 'Yes, Ma'am. William Thomas you must get back to your lesson.'

Elizabeth overheard the conversation, the voices nearer now. She could not make out all that was being said. 'Yes, Mrs d'Aviniere is here. Captain Richardson, Ma'am…'

'Captain Richardson?'

'The captain of the *Dover*, Ma'am…'

'Captain Richardson, of course, my mind, I'm losing it.' Elizabeth extended her arm to shake his hand. 'Excuse my feeble mind at the moment. My memory is elsewhere at times. You must've some news for me from my mother, a letter?'

'Your husband, Madam?' the captain of the *Dover* looked around the room. The two boys had left Mr Bridges in the parlour and were peeping round the door from the hall into the room, awaiting the message from overseas. They knew that their mother had written to their grandmother and was anxiously awaiting a reply. Mr Bridges was frantic to have them back at their lessons.

'My husband, Sir? My husband's at his work. He won't ordinarily be back home before this evening.'

'I would've preferred your husband to be here with you for what I've got to say as I expect you to feel some disappointment, though there's hope in what I've found.'

'Hope, yes, tell me of the hope. I'm all hope now, truly hopeful…'

'That's as it should be, Madam.'

'But disappointment? I know it well. We knew it would be like that. But, I had to try. At least, I know that I've tried. Disappointment…'

'No, Madam, there's hope. But it will take another voyage to complete my errand.' The captain's voice was authoritative.

'Tell me your news, now. I can't wait for the arrival of my husband. I've got strength enough for this.'

Captain Richardson described how he had found where Maria Belle lived. 'I was assured by the young woman who had come to the door. She spoke in a tongue I'm unaccustomed to hearing. She broke up her sentences and mangled the grammar.' He went on to explain, 'Those voyages they've made across the ocean, Ma'am. What has it done to them? There are sights I won't now describe to you, men and women in states of...'

'Who was she? The young woman at the door?'

'Quite young. A girl...'

'A daughter?'

Captain Richardson did not know. He described the black girl as darker than Elizabeth. He supposed her to be an African. 'One of the many brought over on the slavers and then bought and sold.' He told the girl that he was the captain of the *Dover*, which could be seen in the harbour from the door of the house. He also described how she had become very excited when she saw the ship and learned that it was from England. She had said that her mistress had been waiting twenty years for a ship to come from England with a letter from her daughter.

'Tell me more.' Elizabeth could feel herself beyond excitement now, deeply moved within, but she did not want to embarrass Captain Richardson with her tears of longing, now that she was on the cusp of discovery.

'When I asked about Maria Belle, your mother, she said, "She not in residence." Those were the words of the young woman. She then told me her own name was Glory.'

'Glory, not a daughter? Where was my mother?'

'She did mention a place and I wrote it down because I thought maybe you should know. Maybe it's a place I need to go to next time I make a return voyage.'

'Where, where was this place?'

Captain Richardson removed from the inner pocket of his jacket a piece of paper with the name of the place written in his own hand, which had been dictated by the young woman, Glory. He handed it to Elizabeth.

Lydia was standing next to Elizabeth. She helped her back into her chair. She offered the captain of the *Dover* some refreshment. The boys were inside the room now. Mr Bridges had given up hope of trying to persuade them back to their lessons. He was himself hovering just outside the room in the hall, also anxious to hear the news. He had been in Elizabeth's confidence since their acquaintance at the Meeting House where she had continued to go for abolition meetings. For Mr Bridges this was a story of abolition: Elizabeth d'Aviniere's freedom granted to her when she was Dido, and now, to find her mother, they both having been slaves, yet still in bondage because of their separation and their loss.

The company looked on as Elizabeth read what was written on the piece of paper handed to her by Captain Richardson. She read it aloud for all to hear, looking up at him, 'El Paso de Arroyo Ingles.' No one immediately understood the significance. But Elizabeth's tears which she could no longer restrain and her repetition of the name of the place, 'El Paso de Arroyo Ingles' kept everyone in a state of suspense. 'It was my father's estate outside of Pensacola. I lived there with my mother and father when I was a little girl.'

Elizabeth turned to speak to her two boys who were now seated on the floor near to where she sat by the French windows. 'I remember the house well, the *ajoupa*, a small cottage as the Spanish called it in those days. The fields were all tobacco, sugarcane on the boundary and cotton. My mother told me that when the cotton flowered it looked like snow had fallen on the fields. I sort of remember seeing it myself.'

All in the room, the boys on the floor, Lydia standing next to Elizabeth, Captain Richardson of the *Dover* in front of her, Mr Bridges eager for the tale she told, were silent and beseeching, not one daring to interrupt.

'But tell me Captain Richardson, did the young woman, Glory, tell you how my mother was keeping, her health?'

'I presumed it well as the young woman did not mention to the contrary. As I reported, she said that Maria Belle, your mother,

Madam, had been waiting for a long time to see an English ship enter the harbour.'

'Yes, waiting for a letter.'

'I gave the letter to the girl, Glory...' The captain was beginning to repeat his facts.

Lydia reached to hold Elizabeth's hand, to be even nearer in a bond of daughters who knew what it was to lose a mother. 'She still thinks of you, Ma'am...'

'She still thinks of me, Lydia.'

'She does, Ma'am.'

'Captain Richardson, you bring disappointment and hope. But what can I do now?'

'The young woman will deliver your letter when Maria Belle returns from that place. You must wait till I return from my next voyage. I expect to embark in a fortnight. Then there'll be another fortnight to make the journey depending on the weather. I'll not sail if there are any storms brewing.'

'I'll write another letter soon and have it delivered to you by Lydia's brother Seamus or my husband himself will come to the port.'

'That will be excellent, Madam. I'll endeavour to deliver your letter safely and hopefully bring you something more than hope from your mother on my return.'

'Oh, one last thing, Captain Richardson. Do you carry a Harrison clock upon your ship? I mean do you measure your longitude? I would not wish your ship to lose its way or founder upon some rocks.'

Mr Richardson looked at Elizabeth a little puzzled at what seemed an odd comment in the context. 'We do indeed measure our longitude Madam.'

'Good. It was my father, you know, who captained a ship, the *Tartar*, that carried the Harrison clock to Barbados on that first voyage.'

'Indeed, Madam...'

'Captain Richardson, my thankfulness overflows. Have you had sufficient refreshment?' Elizabeth could see that he was still puzzled as he accepted the last piece of Lydia's cake and a drink of cider.

'I'm replete, Ma'am.'

Lydia showed the captain to the door. The boys, excited to hear about his ship, detained him outside the front door with their questions of being on the seas till Mr Bridges eventually succeeded in persuading them to let the captain go. He, himself, eager for the stories and an opportunity to talk with Elizabeth allowed the boys out to the garden to play.

Elizabeth and Lydia hugged each other. The boys had many questions for their mother but all she could respond with, was, 'Later, my darlings, later.'

The following morning Mr Bridges abandoned Latin conjugations and mathematics which usually filled the second half of the morning. He replaced the rest of the day's curriculum with an impromptu history lesson concerning the Atlantic slave trade and the abolition movement. Elizabeth stood outside the parlour door listening to him instructing her two sons. The door ajar allowed her to see her two eager boys more attentive than ever. She smiled at the irony of the scene, the white gentleman instructing his black pupils in their story of capture and property.

Elizabeth's daily life had now become almost entirely the interior of her house. Weakened by her illness, she was caught now between the expectation of an almost certain letter from her mother and the past that kept interrupting to hold her in its bondage, still corralled by the prison of events. Her only prospect was the perspective that extended across her garden; always her little forest, as she called it, growing against the immensity of the sky and the neighbour's brick wall, between the chimney stacks where the shadows of taller trees played and the sun burned an orange path, if bright enough on mornings. Mrs Halifax and Mrs R visited faithfully bringing jams and custards and continuing to contribute to the knitting and sewing.

But it was essentially inside where she spent her time drifting between her more awake moments and the slumber that was now more frequent. She lost her children in her drifting, hearing their recitations of the Latin nouns declined and the verbs conjugated, their times tables sung with the rhythm that mnemonics required. She walked among the polished tables and chairs and delighted in the colour of the still life in the fruit bowl, the lemons in a bowl glazed with the tint of lapis lazuli in the dining room, or the pheasants with their bright feathers that hung in the scullery awaiting Lydia's culinary skills. They all brought the colour of outside into her interiors.

Eventually, she focused her mind on her principal task, her letter to her mother.

Dear Mother

I now know that you are alive. My heart is full of joy. You will now have received my letter with the tale of our undelivered correspondence that continues to grieve me, and I must confess makes me exceedingly angry at the injustice you and I have suffered. But your words tell me how much you love me. Captain Richardson, who bears this letter, will tell you of his visit and his relating to me the results of his last visit to your house. We, my two sons, Charles and our Billy, Lydia and Mr Bridges, the boys' tutor who is a new addition to our household since I last wrote, were the audience for Captain Richardson with the tale to tell of the young woman Glory in your house and your visit to El Paso de Arroyo Ingles. My dearest husband John was at his work. That you are there where our lives first began amazes me. It made me cry to read of our ajoupa written on Captain Richardson's piece of paper. Mr Bridges, by the way, tutors the boys in the morning and early afternoon since our decision to keep them at home rather than send them to school where they had been beset with insults and endangered by the possibility of capture on the roads back and forth. Not much has changed, as you can hear. Particularly Charles, who is my black son, as black skinned as I remember you, is affected the most. He has been threatened with capture. I can't risk losing another son. Mr Bridges is a member of the Meeting House you introduced me to at Shoreditch where my husband and myself have gone for meetings on the abolition of the trade and hopefully the casting aside of the entire invention of human property. Please write to me. I long to read a new letter. I occupy much of my time with your past letters learning of you, reading them over and over for things I may have missed in my first reading, moved and excited to hear your voice. I grieve that you never received my words written throughout my time away from you. I keep them for what they are worth now and to give them to you when we meet. I long to hear from you and dare I wish I may see you. I must see you. Please write.

Your dearest daughter.

Lizzie

'I wished you had been here, my darling, to meet Captain Richardson, to hear him talk of going to the house and meeting the girl, Glory. How my mother has been waiting for my letters, waiting to hear from me. I've already written to my mother. You must take the letter to post tomorrow.'

'What news! Your mother is alive...'

'I'm so hopeful, but fearful too...'

'Take it stage by stage. I'll take your letter to Captain Richardson in the morning. Your health is paramount. It's going to be at least six weeks before anything new can be planned.'

'You're always so practical, dearest.'

Elizabeth returned to the letters with greater excitement than ever as if to find things that she could now imagine more vividly since the glimpses allowed by Captain Richardson's report about her mother's life with the young woman, Glory. She flicked through the pages that were at the top of the box, one of her own filled with nostalgic curiosity trying to locate her mother back in Pensacola. *Dearest*

Mother I think of you and want to ask this little bit of information. Is the white picket fence still there?

She sorted the letters that had been left in disarray. Charles had given up sorting. She kept reminding herself of her husband's advice that it would be at least six weeks before there was any chance of news. The past with its double bind of bondage and release pursued her, her more recent memories brought back the last years at Caen Wood.

20

MR D'AVINIERE HAD gone to look for a house for them that afternoon. He had told Dido of his plan on the Sunday after meeting her in Hampstead. She imagined him now as she sat by her Master's bedside reading to him from his Cicero.

'That piece, Dido, from *de Senectute*, which my learned friend says he had lately included among his other works,' her Master chuckled. Dido had brought some of her Master's favourite volumes up from the library to his bedroom just so he could see them there and stretch out his arm to touch their spines and run his fingers along the leather and gold leaf of their binding and illumination; not the originals, all those having been burnt in the Bloomsbury fire. He hardly ever descended at that time to the ground floor of the house or to walk along the south terrace. His health was much worse.

'I wrote of old age as an old man to an old man.' Dido continued reading. She enjoyed that turn of phrase. 'Is it Cato talking in the dialogue?'

Dido was distracted in her reading as she imagined Mr d'Aviniere and his search in Pimlico. His letter was in her pocket, describing to her one of the houses he had visited the previous week, which had a good parlour and a room with a blue wainscot panelling on one of the walls. Another room was hung with paper. A house of their very own, he had called it. It seemed a dream that would never be. He wrote it in a letter that she could take out in the privacy of her room and read it over and over and so always have it, a kind of love letter, his desire for her, even though a dream, to remind herself what was going to be their reward once her Master had died and she would be free, free of the vigil that she had been keeping for eight years; her labour since a little girl, her freedom confirmed in 1783, not acted on, *no piece of paper*, as her mother would call it.

Their secret, Mr d'Aviniere's and her own, was loud in her head as she continued to read from Cicero's dialogue. His measured sentences were so much like her Master's: 'But my present purpose is to write to you something of old age.' Dido had to fetch water to his dry lips. 'A burden we have in common,' she continued reading.

'Indeed,' her Master agreed.

Dido continued, 'There must, however, of necessity, be some end, as is the case of berries on the trees and the fruits of the earth.' Then she saw that he had dropped off.

How they got through that last winter she did not know. That morning she was so distracted. Master had opened his eyes again. 'Carry on, Dido. Your pauses, my girl, obscure the meaning. I must look again for them in your voice so you must increase your volume, my child.'

He kept imagining her as little, always little.

She had to apologise for her lapse in attention, her voice growing weaker. And then there inevitably was some task to be performed. He had to be assisted to the commode. Then not left for long as she went from the room to empty the sewage from the bowl once he was comfortably back in bed with the pillows again rearranged and sheets straightened and clouts picked up for laundering. She was always particular to have one of Mr French's bouquets from the walled garden arranged on a side table and to have a nosegay of lavender at the bedside. She had one for herself and one for him as he declined and as his body collapsed with odours that needed a fragrance to remove them.

How would she have survived the long evenings, the long, long days of fetching, carrying and watching his decline without the secret of her love for Mr d'Aviniere? 'Keep it discreet,' her Master had required from the beginning of their courting. The measured sentences of Cicero, those sentences that carried her from the house to the dairy, from the dairy to the poultry and back to the house again, a wearying treadmill, culminating with the vigil at his bedside also saved her.

Her only joy, at first, was to be taken in the arms of John d'Aviniere in the porch of the Meeting House before the other Friends arrived. He had then begun to travel back with her in the carriage that her Master had said she could have at her disposal. Then there were their meetings on the Heath. He began to walk her home along the narrow hidden paths that ran between Hampstead, Highgate and the Caen Wood estate. This freedom, trysts on the heath, allowed Dido to transcend the hours of service so as to return refreshed to make an old dying man comfortable.

> ELIZABETH DOZED AND woke with a start, calling out, 'Mammy.' Was that her mother at the door?

She had to check that her husband had delivered her letter to Captain Richardson.

How much longer would she be able to go up and down the stairs? Mr Bridges was just finishing his lesson and she could hear the boys getting ready to burst out of the parlour. 'Stop fighting, lads.' Poor man. Her boys could be terrors as well as darlings. She would sit and have tea with them. She sat and waited and thought how they would be without her there. Then she heard Lydia taking charge.

'Your mother isn't well.' Elizabeth heard Lydia explaining to the boys. 'Let us go out. Wrap up. It may snow this afternoon and perhaps you may be able to go sleighing on the slopes near Belgravia. We'll be safe,' she said, as she patted Charles on his head.

Elizabeth scared herself with her doses of laudanum. What else could account for the memory of an experience so vivid?

It was when she was a baby, her mother's words telling her of the bright day, the green sea, the blue sky and the burning ships sounding like a lullaby. She was a baby, her mother's *pickney*. It was now a kind of hallucination, being suckled by her mother below the deck of her father's ship.

What had she stored, hoarded in her mind, that was now manifesting itself with the expectation of her mother's letter, her mother's arrival? Would that be possible, a black woman travelling on her own without protection? She had not thought through the practicalities of what she was hoping for. Would she be able to enter the country? She did not know anything really of her mother's condition. As Mr d'Aviniere had been telling her, she must be calm and await Captain Richardson's return with some definite news.

❧ THE WRITING OF the will was in her Master's own hand, followed by many pencil-scribbled codicils over the years and last months and weeks, conscience and duty pursuing him to the grave, all kept in a tin box and brought out at his command. 'Dido, Dido, fetch it down.'

She had been up all night, watching, mostly crouching on a stool at the door of his room, sometimes at the foot of his bed. She had to leave the intimate ministrations to Mistress Anne and Marjory, the intimacies that allowed them to kiss him on the cheek; but they had to sleep. He called all the time for her. 'Where is she? Where is Dido?'

This was not to Miss Anne's liking, positively against. 'That girl. That he can allow her to get so close to him. It's unnatural.'

Miss Marjory put a restraining hand upon her cousin's arm to protect Dido. She checked what could be her sharp tongue. Dido understood, had understood from the first, and followed Miss Marjory's cue. Dido was there to fetch and carry from the room to the corridor where one of the servants, either Flo or the young girl from Kentish Town, Susanna, recently arrived at the house, managed the back stairs with pails and slops and the emptying of the commode; something Dido was driven by necessity to do herself on occasion, swilling out and making all clean to be returned to the bedroom. Mistress Anne and Marjory had never left their uncle's side, as they put it to guests and relatives who called and were refused an audience.

Miss Anne's fingers counted out the pounds, shillings and pence, counted the guineas, a small fortune which Dido put away from her payment for the work in the dairy and on the farm during the last years at Caen Wood and saved for a life with Mr d'Aviniere.

This imprisonment in his sick bed had been a severe trial for her Master. Miss Fanny Burney called one day and was distressed to see his decline. She was allowed that time to ascend to the first floor for a short visit. All sickness had had to be tidied away and her Master washed and dressed for the visit, with a new nosegay brought in by Mr French. The house was in a buzz. Dido made it her business to delay her time in her Master's room to catch a glimpse of the novelist, to hear her stories.

But apart from that exceptional visit, he had not even been able to stroll in the corridors, his custom since deciding to withdraw from his room on the ground floor and take apartments on the first floor some four years before. He could not get to the sash window which overlooked the park and his favourite view towards Lincoln's Inn Fields and the inns of court where he had spent so much of his life.

'I left my home at Scone on the banks of the Tay when I was a boy of fifteen.' Dido's Master had a way of speaking that sounded as if the sentences were written in his autobiography, or sentences handed down. His was a voice accustomed to making judgments and proclaiming truths, at least as he saw them, publicly. He spoke almost in pentameters: 'Listen to the water rushing over the salmon beats at Scone under the willows weeping.' Was he going mad, losing his mind? Like the King? Dido sometimes wondered.

She sat and read by candlelight, absorbing herself in her Master's Cicero, interpreting as she heard him talk. She was torn this way and that by both the language and the assumed wisdom, the assured justice of his view, which competed with her mother's voice, always in her head, as a satirical and cynical corrective: *And he's your Master, and he sit on the right-hand side of the monarch.*

Dido could not remove herself for long periods from her post at the door because he might call from the bed, 'Dido? Is Dido there?' She did not always hear his voice, weaker than it had ever been. His inquiry would be conveyed to her in whispers by either Mistress Anne or Marjory, or both, each tripping over the other to be the one to most assist, or to give the impression of assisting when it was she, Dido, who had to do the chore or the errand. While one might be whispering for her attention, turning from the side of the bed, the other was whispering her Master's inquiry, while stepping silently across the floor towards the door. It was the rustle of their skirts, which caught her attention, because she could doze or be distracted by the work of the servants further down the corridor. It could be such a bustle and a crush, with much to do, with both her Master's nieces making towards her at the door at the same time.

'Dido, Dido,' he whispered. It was unnerving. Then she had to reply at once so as not to force him to repeat his inquiry,

'Wasting his precious breath,' Miss Anne rasped in distinct tones which were carried across the distance to her posting through the room from the curtained bed where her Master lay shrouded as it were in the very interior of a sultan's tent, as Dido often thought of the sumptuous bed with all its drapes. Though, as Dido corrected her simile, not a good mix of metaphors because of the Chinese motifs in the wallpaper hung on Lady Betty's instructions at the last refurbishing of the rooms; the bed, then more a couch for a reclining mandarin.

She guessed he liked to know that nothing had changed and that she was always there close by if he needed her, his amanuensis, the scribbled codicils in pencil falling off the side of the bed, distributing affections to family, trusted advisers and servants; making all right before his departure, distributing largesse for affection and duty, scribbled and then rubbed off to be amended. The things she saw when she read the letters that she replied to taught her about the world and the business of the King's realm. They were things she read and did not think about their import. Mr d'Aviniere would tell her that it was like a steward's job, to read and not to always comment; to know when to question and when to be silent, pondering the ways of powerful men in matters of life and death, of gifting and refusal, of condemnation and acquittal, execution and mercy. It was in these papers that she read to him that she learned of his reaction to the French king's execution in the January of that year. He had followed the events of the previous year, the attack on the Jardins des Tuileries and the imprisonment of the royal couple in The Temple and the abolition of the monarchy, he so close to their own king. 'Where is justice?' he asked.

Dido pondered that question. It was a question she had often wanted to ask him herself.

Dido's Master died that morning, 18th March in that year of 1793. Much of the spring had forced itself out of the earth.

> ELIZABETH REMEMBERED TWO magpies had appeared outside her room at Caen Wood, perched on the magnolia tree as if an omen. The memory returned as if today itself. Not a day had passed that Elizabeth did not think on it, the immediately engulfing absence, the great void made by her Master's last breath and then the momentous opportunity which took all the breath out of her: her freedom. That afternoon she had fled to Hampstead to find Mr d'Aviniere to tell him the news. They would be able to marry.

They had respected the period of mourning for it was a complex mourning, a sorrow most peculiar, and yet her shoulders had felt so light as she walked out of the room, out of his house, leaving him dead and being attended to by Miss Anne and Miss Marjory, all because of illegitimacy and the colour of her skin. She was excluded by Miss Anne particularly, having, she supposed, always resented his affection for her and allowing her near his person.

The African in her blood, the state of the world, the construction of the mind, as her mother put it, accounted for this. Mr Way had come in and relieved her of her duty to her Master. He had been both her Master and her champion protector, an uneasy combination that was now ended.

I once was lost and now am found, John Newton's hymn entered her mind with the many images of bodies thrown from the slaver into the Atlantic's waves. She thought of the one man that was reported to have rescued himself from the cruel sea by pulling himself aboard the *Zong*.

Elizabeth thought again, whenever she thought of the Zong, that there had never been a retrial. Justice had not been done. Anyway, it was never considered murder, it was simply an insurance matter, whether it could or could not be given for the loss of property. He did not go far enough. Narrow was his word, always. He followed the narrow lanes of the law. He was not the reformer that she had wanted him to be.

Elizabeth got up and walked into the hall to look at the Van Loo portrait. Did she still want it to hang there? What would her mother think? And she still referred to him as her Master, the terrible effect of it all on her down the years. Things were going to change. Things had to change.

☽ DIDO WORKED AT the milking on the morning after her Master's death, many thoughts racing through her mind. She would be a free woman. The eight words in the will, he had made her read in 1783 ten years before, had now to be enacted. *Make sure you get that piece of paper. You hear me, what I call it, manumission*. Her mother's words reminded her of the duty she had to perform, *Get that piece of paper.*

That same night she went with Mr d'Aviniere to a meeting in Camden where Mr Equiano was to speak. There was great excitement in the hall when the gentleman arrived on stage and was introduced by Mr Clarkson. His book had become a best seller. It was as exciting as the meeting in Shoreditch when Dido and John sat close together in the crowded hall as Olaudah Equiano described his recent visits to Bath and Devizes and the great following he was having all around the country for the abolition of the slave trade. His new wife was with him. The couple exuded in their closeness, sitting on the stage before he spoke, the humanitarian compassion that Dido believed in, seeing the black man with his white wife and their two daughters working together for freedom and the end of the trade. There was a hush when he rose to speak. Individuals in the crowd called for him to tell them of his travels. He spoke of the strides that had been made and that he expected that soon there would be an end to the cruel and worthless trade. But it was as he spoke and read from his narrative of his travels through the islands that Dido was taken back to her own voyages on one of her father's ships, her memories full of her mother's voice with tales of her own passage from the African coast.

The coincidence of the meeting with the death of Dido's Master emboldened Dido and John with a greater sense of their own personal freedom as they left the meeting excited about their future, Mr Equiano's words ringing in their ears. John walked Dido back to Caen Wood from Highgate. They stood out on the terrace and looked out over London in the distance and planned their future. As he left her he said, 'The house is bought. My foster father has loaned me the money.'

'We'll have to see through the time of mourning and then we can announce our intentions.'

They held on to each other. 'I'm scared. I hardly know anywhere else but here,' Dido said.

'Don't be,' he said. 'I'll protect you. I'll provide. This has been a special night for us. Think of the future Mr Equiano has spoken of that lies before us.'

Dido and John married later that year, on the 5th December, in the presence of John's sister Martha and their friend John Coventry who had secured her husband the stewardship. It was in St George's Church, Hanover Square.

❧ ELIZABETH DID NOT have that piece of paper, that manumission, as her mother had insisted. She did not have papers. She thought of Lydia and her concern for her settlement. She had only those eight words *I confirm to Dido Elizabeth Belle her freedom* written in her Master's will. She did not have a copy of that will. Such was the arrogance and power of the mighty. She remembered that her mother did not trust the freedom that John Lindsay was supposed to have granted her in 1774. She bought her own freedom for $200 on her return to Pensacola as her mother mentioned in one of her letters. She bought her own freedom. She did not trust his.

It was twenty years since those events which now haunted her.

After sleighing, Billy and Charles had gone to the Saint Bartholomew's Fair with their father. The boys loved the wakes. She had felt too weak to accompany them and stayed at home with her letters and her writing.

Dearest Mammy

Is Dido. Please send for me. I feel the time is so long since you gone. Send for me now. I do not know how much longer I can stay here behaving myself the way my father want me to conduct myself with his family, the way you say I should be and not stubborn or harden as you used to say. I can hear you speaking to me. I try and try. Beth is not like me. I don't get the clothes she gets. She has a new dress and Lady Betty say I must have

*the one she used to wear. The boy on the farm frighten me. The girl in the
kitchen hiss at me. Send for me. I try and ask when my father coming but
he does not come since you went away. He must be travelling round the
world. I go in the library and spin the globe. I see where you are. There is
the big sea between you and me. Please send for me.*

Your dearest daughter

Dido

Is Dido

The cry of a child: they knew she was suffering. Yet how well behaved
she had been.

❧ DIDO LISTENED TO the amounts counted out in the main will and
then the additional gifts in the codicils. Her Master's will was read out
in the drawing room by Lord Stormont, her Master's nephew, the new
master of Caen Wood. He was not Dido's Master. Mistress Anne and
Marjory were there, given £6,000 each and another £300 a year. Dido
understood that Beth was to attend with Mr Finch-Hatton. They were
held up on the way from Kent. They arrived in time for Beth to hear
of her £10,000. Dido's father, John Lindsay, had his £1,000 bequeathed
to Mary Milner and to his two other children, quite illegitimate, but
white, Dido thought, as she listened intently. Her father had only had
illegitimate children, how odd. Yet, they carried his name. She had
never carried Lindsay. So it was not only illegitimacy that prevented
her getting her rights. It was this colour, the human stain they thought
she had upon her skin. She did know this but it was plainer than ever
now. There was an inheritance that they all, the assembled, had
received on this occasion. Mr Way bowed at the announcement of his
£1,000. Mr French of the nosegays, the gardener, led the retinue of
the different servants, Flo, Molly, Lydia and Susanna, the cooks and
all the staff of Caen Wood assembled, crowding the door. Lord
Stormont read out all what was left by her Master, his gifts and

legacies. Many got £50, some £100. Dido had seen these gifts stabbed out with a pencil in the codicils, the computations changing daily at the whim of her Master, at the pricks of his conscience.

Then she heard her own name called. Dido was to receive an annuity of £100 from the main will and two codicils stated two further amounts, one for £200 and another £300. She thought of Mr d'Aviniere's house, his gift to her. That might get settled now and the loan paid back to his foster father.

Only Dido knew about the agonising rehearsals of her Master over the years as he tried to weigh on the scales hanging in his mind the balances he had conjured, the services and the favours, the rights and the wrongs as he saw them. *Dido, where's Dido?* She thought she heard him calling her, a voice from the top of the house, requiring her service, as Lord Stormont read out the will. Then he added, 'I quote from uncle's will, *I confirm to Dido Elizabeth Belle her freedom.*'

The company turned to look at her. She stared ahead. The room gradually emptied.

She and Lydia stood together holding hands.

⟩ COULD THIS HAVE been another occasion on which she should have been bequeathed the letters, her mother's letters and her own, that archive of correspondence that belonged rightfully to her, Elizabeth thought. Only now, Miss Marjory's gift, and the letters wherever hoarded, at Miss Anne's in Brighton or with Lord Stormont at Caen Wood. Poor Beth, only now had she been given the painful duty to bring them to her.

21

ELIZABETH CLEAVED TO her husband in the night. She woke and lay in the dark close to him hoping she would not begin to cough. He would have to rise soon to make his way to work. For how much longer would she have the comfort of his warmth and the knowledge that her boys who were sleeping securely in the next room would always be safe? She rose to stir the embers of the fire in the parlour and get the house warm for her sons and her husband, and let Lydia, who was accustomed to be down before her, rest. She wanted time for herself before the house was a clamour of voices over breakfast and Mr Bridges arrived to tutor. She had woken feeling better than she had for some time and hoped to have the still dawn to herself and her mother.

Dearest Child

I must write at once and send to you this letter which the kind captain of the ship Orion I travel on to Pensacola tell me he will personally see is delivered safe to you my darling. It's a while since I see him in the harbour. You too small to remember this place. It change in the last ten years. The house your father build and you come to live in with myself and your father as baby and little girl was still here when I arrive but in terrible repair what with storms and the daily sea blast. The grain of salt is everywhere. I am bound by agreement with your father to build a house so is build I build and that first house blow down and I must build again.

Each year a mighty storm lash the coast. People in the islands call the god Hurucan. You not going remember that. No protection even from Santa Rosa Island. Now I build with new timbers I buy from the Creek and Choctaw traders. All along the street is cottages the British build in building this same town of Pensacola. I build with the same timber clapboard and brick. It go be a strong house. So when you come you go see what a good house I build for you and me. It right here on the wharf. I want to be near the port. That will be good for trade. I will let rooms. I must survive. I have two young girls helping me now. Little wretches — they was runaways. They run far some from Georgia some from Carolina. The Spanish have another law here. Once they are Catholic, freedom does come with baptism. They run from the lash of the whip. I count the stripes on their back and on their legs. They lift their skirts showing off almost like trophies of such cruelty what they had to take from overseers and drivers on estates on their arms and legs cut up by the serrated leaves or bent bending to pick cotton and tobacco. Before they fall into the catcher's net I take them in. I might've been one of them. I know well what they talking bout. I was their age when your father find me standing in the middle of a market place showing my backside and having my teeth examined like a horse or some hog put on scales like a piece of meat. How much was I worth — I must stop with these stories. When I get going is only rage that fill my heart that this thing going on and on. You know you father never thought it safe for you to be here. But I will keep you safe when you come. The bay is busy with ships and Santa Rosa Island across the water have the lighthouse. I sit and watch the world entering into the emerald bay with those tall tall ships. One day I will see you waving from the deck and I will be here standing waiting for you. You will know me my darling. I am your mother.

Elizabeth read and let her mother's voice bathe over her in the quiet dawn where she sat by the French windows. How would she have survived reading that letter as a girl? How could they have let her read that letter? How would she have settled? Had she ever settled, though?

She had no way of knowing what would have happened to her. How would they have constrained her? She would have always been packing her belongings to run away to her mother. Might she have hung herself upon a willow tree down at Sherrick Hole?

Just one letter more she said to herself before her husband came down for his breakfast.

Dearest daughter child

I not get no letter from you — no reply. I expect you have restrictions on what you do and cannot do. I don't know what they make you do. I wait for your words. I sure that Lord Mansfield will find a way for your letters to come to me quickly. His nephew your father know the place I living. It right here on the wharf and I only watching for a ship flying the British ensign and my heart does lift. The other afternoon a flutter as I see one ship round the point on Santa Rosa and enter the harbour. When the captain come he does stay. He tell me next time you will get a letter Mrs Belle. He call me that — what these people know, Mrs Belle! He is a kind man — and he not fresh. I has to watch them young seamen — fresh for so with their hands and their sweet talk. I does keep a couple of rooms for them.

Elizabeth picked up just one more letter before she had to cut bread, and not forget Lydia's marmalade stored since the summer. She read and stopped and then picked up yet another letter. She began to piece together the quilt of her mother's life, her brave mother building and trading with Indians in the Americas. Why they should cut me off from her I shall never know. Not for my own good as Beth continues to say. No, it was not for my good. She spoke to herself, whispering aloud her feelings of rage and injustice, putting aside her understanding of the good sense of wanting a child or young woman to settle. I can't forgive them. I had no choice. They offered my mother no explanation. My father could have written her. The only way to stop the rage would be for her to stop reading the letters and that she could not do, She fed her rage. Such rage burnt plantations to the ground. Such rage burnt down the great houses.

Sweet child

Still no letter but still I must write because to write is to believe that you are there and you going speak to me soon. Is like talking to you. If I was to walk down the street talking so people will think I is a mad woman. I take a rest from supervising these fellas who replacing timber and brick and one Choctaw fella say he going bring me good timber from inland. Then I sit here by the window and write my letter. I remember your father hiring these young Choctaw men when we first moved to Pensacola. I trust them. Nitushi is the one I trust the most and he stays here in a room I build for him in the yard where I have chickens and pigs. He works through the week and returns to his people on a Friday. Your mother has become a frontier woman a black woman with her own house and men working for her like so many yellow women here. I seem a stranger in this land and other women look at me with suspicion in their eyes. I think of the women I meet on London streets those in Shoreditch and I wonder who is more free. The house almost complete. Is waiting for you. Months seem like years my child. You must be a woman now.

How could they have read those cries for a letter from a mother and not themselves write to explain to her what was happening, at least that, so that she would not be going mad with not knowing and the continuing grief that the woman, Glory, reported to Captain Richardson? Where in the end was that human feeling? Was this handing over of the letters now meant to be some kind of reparation, putting things right?

'Sweetheart, what are you doing? I'm late. I must be off.'

'You scared me. Sorry, sorry, darling. I meant to have breakfast all ready and I lost myself in my mother's letters. Are the boys up?'

Elizabeth hated it when Mr Bridges arrived and the boys were not ready. She was frantic with getting breakfast for her husband.

'I'm in a hurry.' Her husband ate his porridge Elizabeth had quickly cooked.

'Don't forget Captain Richardson...'

'Yes, I must check the sailing of the *Dover*.'

'Can't bear the waiting. You must go. Kiss me.'

'Sweetheart, be strong. You need a distraction.'

John d'Aviniere wanted his wife to help Mr Bridges with his work for the Abolition Society, writing to lawyers and parliamentarians, getting pamphlets prepared for publication. 'Talk to Mr Bridges.'

Elizabeth got the boys up with difficulty. Charles was finding William Thomas far too demanding. He never stopped talking and showing off. Lydia came down to help with their breakfast later.

Charles was immediately down to some work that Mr Bridges had set and which he should have completed the night before. William Thomas, on the other hand, was reluctant to do sums or reading and just wanted his mother's attention. Why could he not go out with Lydia as he used to do and insisting all the while on playing with his soldiers marching to war against Napoleon on the breakfast table.

While Charles was flourishing with the personal attention of Mr Bridges, William Thomas wanted to be running around in a schoolyard and being with boys of his own age. It was a dilemma that Elizabeth and her husband would have to confront in the spring.

Elizabeth left them to it. Lydia was already sorting out Billy's clothes. He was naughty, but also charming, a combination difficult to tolerate or ignore at this hour of the morning. 'Come on, Billy, you must help yourself, Mr Bridges is waiting.'

Later, Elizabeth would speak to the tutor. It was a good idea of her husband's to help with his work. But this morning, before lunch, she returned compulsively to her mother's letters, her new drug, her solace, not withstanding the pain.

Dido girl

You must wonder why I not write all this time. To tell you the truth is a sickness that take me for weeks. There was panic here with talk of typhus and even some captains of ships talk of plague. And what you know is who first to die — but then they find sickness got no respect for persons and is the master that catch it as soon as the slave — that is a mystery to some who have us down as animals. Then a slave upon a morning mourning his master for that is his livelihood till he find another to own him, feed him and for him to dig and plough his master's field — what a life — what a life — for to runaway is to go where and I wonder bout yours you pretty girl. What a life unless you can escape or buy yourself north — for is north now when before they was running south here for the Spanish give them freedom with baptism...

Elizabeth was interrupted by Mr Bridges, who had crept out of the parlour. He had left the boys alone, seemingly dead quiet at their study. Shutting the door behind him, he indicated to Elizabeth as he came into the room not to say a word, putting a finger to his lips as if he were hushing her. 'I've set them a test,' he whispered, looking very pleased to have gained control of the boys.

'That's clever,' Elizabeth smiled. Mr Bridges was a good man, like so many of those men and women at the Meeting House or at the society working for abolition. She could not have hired a better tutor. But he did not find it easy to discipline Billy.

'They both enjoy the competition in different ways. Charles likes to test his knowledge and William Thomas likes to win. They're so different.'

'Yes, Charles seems to have an aptitude for numbers and William Thomas the mellifluous tones of my late Master and a tendency to rule the roost.'

'Are these your mother's letters?' Mr Bridges was finding it difficult not to pry.

'Yes. I can't keep away from them…'

'Valuable documents…'

'Yes, a treasure for me…'

'Yes, of course. But I was thinking what a treasure they might be for the cause. What does she tell you?'

'She's doing some of the work you're doing with helping runaways. How to save people and to set them free…'

'Exactly. You could write something based on her letters to further the cause. Maybe there's a letter that we could publish that would illustrate the conditions, those terrible stories of capture…'

'Oh, I don't know.' She talked to him about her husband's idea. 'All this time I have and then time running out and I must keep writing.'

'It sounds a wonderful idea. When you hear from your mother…'

At that moment, Billy was at the door saying that he had completed his test first and wanted to have a drink of water. Mr Bridges went off with him. 'Let's see what you've managed to do.'

'All of it,' Billy shouted.

As she settled back to the letters Elizabeth remembered what she was thinking about when Mr Bridges had interrupted her.

She was again Dido, among the elms at Caen Wood. She was focused on something she had not thought about for years. It was a dress that her mother had sewed for her and asked her to wear the day she departed from Greenwich where she stood with her father on the port. It was a moment that she could hardly recall without feeling some of that desolation she had felt then. She had kept the dress after she had grown out of it, the waist and sleeves too tight and the length quite impossible. Her mother had told her the story of how she had, with her savings from her father, bought the material from a merchant who was selling pretty cloth from the east on his stall in Deptford. It was a blue silk with a flower pattern down the front and around the hem. She made the stays with good white cotton so that her shape was right.

You must have deportment child and you is a lady? This was to tease her father even at that moment. *You never make me a lady but she you must look out for.* Her father had held on to her as her mother mounted the gangway to the ship, which was to take her away. They stood, her father and herself, the whole long time it took for the ship to begin its voyage down the river, till it was out of sight beyond the Isle of Dogs.

When the dress was far too small for her, she had folded it and kept it on a shelf in her room. That dress together with the gold earrings her ears had been pierced with and the blue kerchief were what was left of her mother after she had departed for Pensacola. She remembered now that it was not only that she had grown out of the dress. It had got dirty among the elms with Hal tearing off the fine mother-of-pearl buttons with his soiled hands. She had had to hide herself beneath her shawl on meeting Molly in the wood, and Hal running off pulling up his breeches. She had repaired, laundered it and folded it away. The dress as a relic of her past contained both the consolation to have what her mother had made and given her and the awful memory of what Hal had done to her as a girl.

The letters now were her solace and her pain. Her mother at her side was all she wanted now to make her whole.

So much had been happening since the dawn had parted the curtains and its sound was the homing call of ducks in their chevron flight from the river inland to the feeding ground among the marshes. Gulls swooped and wailed in the high, clear blue of the winter morning.

Sweet Dido to talk with you is solace

All week I wait for the captain that I know well the one who bring me to this place. But his ship not anchor here anymore and is long time he not stay and I have no news — so who to bring this letter to you who to bring my words to a daughter who don't write and I getting like a mad woman who does write without knowing if what she write ever reach ever read. Is a kind woman — who know what she doing here — her husband bring her on some mad adventure and she befriend me one day by the port and I say please will you take a letter to my daughter she does live in England in London town Highgate Hampstead. I know you move from that house in Bloomsbury which get burn down. That news reach here about the mob and the hanging. The lady smile when I mention those names in London, for true she looked lost here on the wharf in Pensacola and say she will return to London on a voyage starting the following week and will make sure this letter reach where you daughter living — she will make it her business to inquire if there is a difficulty.

Bless that woman who loves to hear the sound of London town. What a thankless task it was in the end. Elizabeth fed herself another morsel as she watched the blackbirds that inhabited her garden forage under dead leaves for worms.

Dido

I tear the pages from a writing book I keep that hangs on a nail by the table near the window. Why go on so as I have in letters past — but why not go gentle with my own soul and tell you stories child — tell you tales to put you to sleep to tell you how much it is that a mother love a daughter even one as wretched as you who become a lady in some English gentleman house in fancy clothes and reading books and — maybe — who know I must believe you are still my sweet daughter and there has been some terrible mistake that happen along the way. If I could only know — my captain used to tell me the letters all safely delivered so why why why — I must be ready if you arrive suddenly. For that is a hope sent by your father long ago. I will be prepared for you.

When Mr Bridges had completed the lessons of the day, they talked over what Elizabeth could help with. He would bring her some pamphlets to correct. He would value her assistance.

She might have been working with her mother if she had gone with her and not stayed behind. Her mother could not have known what she might have managed to do. Elizabeth could not regret what she was imagining and have her husband and her children. She could never regret them. She continued to read:

I have taken to this new work now. Is because I tell myself one day I build rooms but no one to fill them. So I keep looking out for those young girls. I don't ask too many questions. But them on the run and I give them a place to rest. Everybody want to head north. Is a hope that driving them. They say that is where the liberty coming. They are not in place of my daughter to fill the empty rooms, the place at the table I build for her with a window to the sea and curtains that flutter in the breeze and does rise like sails on a ship. I want to see a sail that bring letters. Only gulls this morning in the sky. I stare and stare at one single sandpiper pecking and running from the wave breaking on the shore. I think some of the captains and soldiers that rent rooms think these girls are here for their service. There are such houses on the wharf and some of them same girls want to escape to my pretty house with my girls who work at selling and scrubbing and sewing. I have to explain that I am no Madame as they call such ladies that keep such houses as I hear from travellers there is in the big towns of Louisiana on the Mississippi. The one the Spanish and the French keep at New Orleans. No — some tell me it is a good business. No — I am educating myself and helping to educate these girls teach them to sew and make quilts — then I get them work as a seamstress. I hire them out so that they seem to be mine and not taken by any catchers as theirs — they are preyed upon. They will feed themselves with their needle and thimble I tell them. I must save money for their manumission. Child you must come and help your mother with this work.

Elizabeth wanted to go there and to work with her. She was indulging herself with unrealisable fantasies she was unashamed to entertain. She dozed between letters, between the poetry of her mother's words and the lyric of her life — all this so long ago — her work with her runaways. She was alive. When would she hear from her?

Spring began to arrive with its gradual changes, her garden unfolding through snowdrops, crocuses, daffodils, bluebells. The new life mocked her for her constant dwelling on her passing. She had amassed through the winter a number of shirts and warm waistcoats for her sons and even some shirts for her husband. Between her sewing she had corrected a number of pamphlets, which were preparing for another bill to come to parliament after the failure of Mr Wilberforce's first effort. She helped Mr Bridges with letters to members of parliament. Would she see the abolition of the trade?

A message had arrived from the port that Captain Richardson's ship had eventually sailed, risking bad weather, but there was still no word. They had no idea now when he might return.

The boys were skipping on the garden path and they had brought in a friend from down the street and Charles was playing hopscotch with him. Charles was much happier. Billy looked left out. Then he was provoking the friend. Elizabeth could not bear a fight. 'Billy, Billy.' She hated shouting. 'Come, I need you to do something.' He came reluctantly. He was becoming quite uncontrollable. 'Let Charles play with his friend for the moment. I want you to help me sort my letters. I've got them all out of order again.'

'Do I have to, I'd rather play...' Billy began to check dates. 'When's she going to come and see us?'

'Well, that's what we're waiting to hear, hopefully soon.'

'The friends I had at school all have at least one grandparent. I don't know what to tell them.'

'You just tell them that she lives in Florida.'

'Then they'll ask why she's there.'

Billy had quickly sorted the letters.

'That's a good boy.'

'Can I go and play now?'

'Yes, but don't provoke Charles.'

'He needs love, attention and above all a firm hand.' Mr Bridges gave the first two requirements for a good education. The latter was beyond the soft-spoken gentleman who was more accustomed to quiet consultations rather than speaking from pulpits. Elizabeth noticed he mainly kept silent at the Meeting House the last times she had been able to attend.

She and her husband had managed a favourable compromise over the return of the boys to school. It had been Mr Bridges' idea. He would continue with a day of tutoring and on the other days he would take the boys to school and fetch them back in the evening, staying on to help with their homework and even extending his time for supper on occasions when Mr d'Aviniere had late evenings. He and Elizabeth could then work on pamphlets and letters. It seemed a perfect solution. She would also have more time for her own writing.

Lydia had had to rest after repeated fevers. She had become very concerned with her future despite all the assurances both Elizabeth and John had given her that their home was her home. Her old mother was also poorly. She feared she might have to give up work, lose her right to her settlement. Elizabeth had to keep insisting that this would not happen. She could have all the time she needed to be with her mother. Her hiring would not be broken. Elizabeth understood her anxiety.

Sweet child

I got to thinking and I must tell you the story of Lizzie — a shortened form of your own baptism name. She come to me and is soon I know she carrying a child — hardly child herself — so what I must teach her is to rock cradle and properly attend to her pickney and then I get her work like I used to have with that English lady from Kent I tell you about a long long time ago who tell me the story of snow — is that make me think of you just so as I looking out to the sea and thinking that I go see you walking up from the wharf — in fact is one day not so long ago I see this girl so nicely dressed that I look at her again and she looking for a particular house and I just crazy for she to be you. I really think is you and I go up to her and then has the extreme disappointment to find her looking at me as if I am mad. Is okay child I tell her. I is just a mother grieving for a daughter. Is a long time I grieving.

Elizabeth wished that she had been that girl her mother saw upon the street by the wharf. She imagined herself and her mother in her timber and clapboard house with her girls sewing quilts falling upon the floor from the bedstead — so many daughters she had now.

Elizabeth had delayed replying to Beth. She read to her husband the short note she asked him to post.

Dear Beth

Forgive my delay in writing back to you. I must accept your word. I cannot now keep going over what took place and what did not take place. You know my disappointment, my anger and feelings of injustice. But also I do understand some of the reasoning to protect a child's feelings though I think my mother should have been told of the plan, given an explanation to help her with some consolation. I write to tell you that the letters prompted me to write to my mother in hope and we have been fortunate to locate her through a kind captain who delivered a letter. She was not there but she is alive and well as far as we can tell. I am waiting for a reply to my letter. Life is mixed with hope and disappointment. I keep hoping. You had mentioned that Miss Anne is alive and living in Brighton. I have painted her in my mind as a villain. That is probably not all together just. I trust that she is well and that you, Mr Finch-Hatton and the children are all keeping well.

Your cousin

Elizabeth

'Good of you to write sympathetically, for we must save all our emotion for looking forward to your mother's letter and hopefully her arrival.'

'My mother bought her own manumission, she's a free woman, she should be able to travel. I'm trying to deal with my rage and feelings of injustice. I don't forgive the deed but I want to forgive the persons.'

'You're admirable.' John embraced Elizabeth.

My daughter

I just finish off the laundry — only my own few dresses — if you was here I would be washing your clothes and hanging them out on the line to catch the sun and the morning breeze. The girls do their own washing.

She was at the washtub in Pensacola. It was such an early memory. She sees still the sun-whitened stones, the soapy washed clothes laid out to bleach in the hot sun under the stretched lines of rope for hanging out sheets like sails in the wind that slap her in the face. Her mother's black arms reach up, her black hands secure clothes to the line. She hums a hymn for comfort. She is constantly at her side, close as the wet clothes, which cling to her skin, wet with the perspiration down her face and arms, her odour of labour since dawn at the tub with the scrubbing board, the blue soap kneaded into the clothes. Constantly bent over, her breasts held to breaking from her wet blouse, the front of her dress soaked, clinging to her legs: she gathers her skirt, to wring out the dirty water as she capsizes the tub to drain out over her splashed legs, swamped feet. *And what you doing here child in my way this morning this Monday morning — come let me finish this work. I get no rest. The things I have to do sweet child. And you is clinging to me so. Come now.*

Her mother's words and her own memory of the past came together. She continued reading, feeding herself:

I thinking I must write to you my daughter and see if I can't reach you this time after so long. I keep wondering what the matter is with these letters and I take my time one morning to speak to the gentleman who looking after the post and conveying messages to the packet when it come to harbour. He saying I doing everything correct and he not sure why they not getting through if that is the problem because I can't believe you will go so silent on me. There was that one letter. But I suppose as I tell myself one day to comfort myself is like writing what some young mistress like I used to have might write a kind of journal they does call it of what going on. To write to you is to feel you reading what I say. If only I could read what you say in return. But where the letters where they reach? For I sure you write them. I write as I say like a journal but I don't even have it to read what I say last time because I send it on its way.

She had got that first letter. She wrote down the margins filling every fettered space. She remembered that the pelican pecked at its own breast to feed its young with its blood. The pelican, yes, that swooped in with its piety. A mother sought to feed her daughter with the poetry of her words. *I running my own abolition movement here you know. So much talk of that with them big men in the parliament and still nothing happen.*

She is running her own abolition movement, Elizabeth thought. I wish I could join her. How pleased she would be to hear of the work her daughter was doing with Mr Bridges.

Charles had survived the return to school and the ferrying of the boys by Mr Bridges was working well. He had stayed on last evening for supper to discuss with Elizabeth what he wanted her to do concerning a pamphlet the Society was publishing to spread their work more extensively in the north of the country. He valued Elizabeth's sensitivity in the wording and the choice of a title, *From the Sommersett Case to the Zong Trial: what have we learned? Mr Arthur Bridges in Consultation with Mrs Elizabeth d'Aviniere.*

Her mother's later letters inspired Elizabeth to stop being obsessed with her own rage and grief and to focus on what had to be done for others. Her obsession with the past at Caen Wood had also faded. She was in the present and feeling better. Mr Bridges was more than delighted to stay for supper and to learn what her mother had been doing in Pensacola with runaways.

Lydia was at home having recently returned from being with her mother in The Rookery. The old woman had rallied. Lydia was also feeling better and getting on with her usual chores. Elizabeth was glad for her return. Life did not seem normal without Lydia.

'It's the post, Ma'am.'

'Oh, what do you think? Florida? Where?'

'Brighton, Ma'am.'

'Brighton?' Elizabeth broke the seal.

Dear Elizabeth

I address you by your baptismal name which Beth informs me is what you use now. I must agree with her that it is quite strange to think of you as anyone else but Dido. Nevertheless, Elizabeth it shall be. I thought I might have heard from you on the death of my cousin, Lady Marjory. But it has been some years and Beth tells me that you had not been informed. My cousin did always take your part, but it was I who had to run the house and make sure that the wishes of my uncle and aunt were adhered to, keeping the closest watch on expenditure and recording it strictly in my ledger. That is what I endeavoured to do at all times, carrying out their wishes. Beth informs me of what she calls your sense of injustice, and uses the word, outrage, at the plan for your mother's and your own letters. It was for your own good and a clear signal that your mother should stop writing. She never did. Letters were being received till I left Caen Wood. You have that as proof of her love. I understand that you have now located your mother. That seems almost miraculous if I may risk exaggeration. I have no idea what such a relationship can possibly mean now. Beth tells me that your health is poor at times. I remember it well having to order expensive remedies from the apothecary your master insisted you should have. I am an old woman now and do not wish to be worried by the past. The family tried to do their best for you, given our uncle's decision to keep you in the family as it were. Other decisions might have been more expedient but that is as it was. I wish you and your family the best in your present circumstances.

Anne Murray

'Good Lord! You should read this Lydia. I'm reading such wonderful letters from my mother that I am shocked by the harshness of these words. I wonder why she wrote. Do you think this is some kind of an apology?'

Lydia read the letter slowly, gasping at intervals. 'She was always a one, Ma'am. I'm not surprised. That's Miss Anne, always by the rules, not like her cousin Miss Marjory who would stop and chat and give a hand in the pantry if she was passing through, always interested in the young girls. Miss Anne was always hiring and firing.'

'What should I do? What can I say to her?'

'Leave it for a while. You may think of the right thing to say, in the circumstances as she puts it.'

'Lydia, what a world they've made for us. I wonder what her more expedient plan might've been. You know my Master was exceptional, though narrow.'

'You were lucky, Ma'am. And I hope your luck brings you news soon from your mother.'

'I hope so, Lydia. I must keep well. I'm moved by her letters and learn so much.'

Sweetest child for so I must always think of you.

I tell the girls about you my daughter in England and that your father is a lord and that you are cared for — but I ask are you loved? I ask that again. Are you loved? Today I did something I said I would never do. I buy a little boy. His owner had to make some money. He had lost a lot of money with his crop going bad and he dressed up this little boy and brought him down by the market and he put him on the scales the same he selling his hogs and he want to sell him by the pound. The little boy well dress up by his owner wife with beseeching eyes to attract a master — one buyer watching the boy all the time with lascivious eyes so I make up my mind though I say on principle I never do such a thing. I buy the child and bring him home and right away I think how to get him manumitted so that I am not some slave owner here in my house by the wharf waiting for you my sweetest daughter. What you go think of me that I do such a thing like that. Is to save him. Is to save you your father let you stay a slave for the uncle of his for your mother that is me to leave you in their hands. I hope by now you have the right papers. I adopt this boy. He is my son. Now his name is Tobias. In the Christian people book they say there is a Tobias who make friends with an angel who drives away demons. I think that is a good name for him. I am his angel and I drive away them cruel men preying upon the child. I call him Toby. He is your brother and I hope one day you meet sweet daughter flesh of my flesh skin of my skin yellow woman — is so they would call you here. What they call you there?

Elizabeth had had a half-brother and sister from her father. She did not know them. The only time she had seen them was at Lady Betty's funeral. They never came looking for her. Now she had another, adopted, whom she hoped she could meet. How was this going to happen?

Billy, back from school and playing in the garden, looked up to see his mother laughing out loud for no reason he could see. Poor child, she thought. She waved to him and then he returned to his obsession, building enclosures with little stones, forts and battlements, assured that his mother was herself and that she had not lost her mind.

22

Sweetest baby I ever had

What troubles I now have dear daughter. When the day done and I weary and sit by the window looking into the harbour thinking of you I get my paper out and I write to you. I tear a page off the nail. I write across I write down with all the things I have to say. If I lucky I find a captain who will post this in London town. I very weary this day. All morning I am caught up with the terrible tale of the older woman who must separate from her husband. They both slaves of a Mr Edwards...

Elizabeth interrupted the reading of her mother's letter to speak to Mr Bridges who had just arrived back from school with the boys.

'Boys, boys, keep your voices down, I must talk with Mr Bridges. Homework, games in the garden?' Billy wanted to perform a speech from Julius Caesar. Charles was happy to get down to his geometry.

'Billy, can we wait with your performance? What about visiting Mrs Halifax? Straight there, nowhere else, and then straight back. Her nephew is staying from Nottingham and wants to play. Listen, you know how anxious I am, even just down this street...'

'I know, Mama.'

'Mrs d'Aviniere? You were saying?'

'I want to show you this. Maybe it's a letter you might use. I need to think about it and speak to Mr d'Aviniere. Here's a story in my mother's inimitable style...'

All morning I am caught up with the terrible tale of the older woman who must separate from her husband. They both slaves of a Mr Edwards and he insist that he must sell one of them and separate the two — the husband to go far away up rivers to a plantation which brings horror into the heart for what we know go on there on plantations under the sun and the whip. I cannot afford to buy the husband. I persuade Mr Edwards to sell me the older woman. I buying slaves now. He open her mouth to inspect her teeth to think to put up the price. I sit there and watch the scoundrel, even old Mr Edwards let himself become. He needs the money so he agree. The husband was too expensive for my pocket if I am to keep going — his wife cheaper — must be her teeth. Imagine that. She is a gentlewoman who looks to me and towards her husband already out the door joining some coffle to go north guarded by men with whips and some grotesque in mask of iron and rusty bits on their tongues protruding from their mouths. Is not to terrify you child I tell you this. Is your mother everyday life, even if on an evening the sunset so beautiful that you must believe and hope for a better world. Even if the waves so gentle on the shore paint by the dying sun bring peace and comfort in colour. And she the gentlewoman and myself spend the evening like this one writing letters. Only thing she does get letters back from that dear husband who learn himself to write hide away. She tell me the story of him under a dim lantern every night to learn to read and write to free his mind and body to write his wife. How the letters passing between them is a secret trail. She cries when his letters come but they do come. He who gone to live somewhere in Louisiana writing her letters — such letters of love and concern that it is a most tender moment to see her. Her name is Sarah or so she want me to call her. She and I go together to the wharf to find stray girls throw away after a voyage of misuse with some sailor or captain or her own negroes as they call them these men like I know a boy so far back. My memory is only of a child like me in a village among women pounding yam and men returning from a hunt so I wonder what they teach those boys now men to do to girls like I was. It can only be the terrible passage of abuse where the stronger learn to abuse the weaker one. She beginning to talk about the ship she come on which has enlivened my memory to those things I never tell you daughter in London. Now why I should come to tell you this tale child, only that as you there in London and hear talk in the fine castle you living in you will know that trees bear fruit here you would never want to pick.

'Mrs d'Aviniere what atrocious things are going on...'

'Mr Bridges, I want you to look at this one also. The vivid account is most distressing but so informative in its detail.'

This man he get warn. Sam John is his name. He get warn by his master not to lose the implements he give him for ploughing and he swear he wont. Only one morning he wake to find them all gone stolen from the barn break open. He so frighten to tell his master. So instead he sling a rope upon a branch of a willow tree seen his master do it many times. He know how to tie a rope for a man to hang not too far from the brim of water by a stream where the branches hanging low upon the flow. He can reach so he hang himself the way others do. So many does get hang by masters. Poor child to get this sad tale. They let him drop in the stream and go down to meet the big river to the sea. Sam John too terrified to say he lose a plough. But he revive. Must be the water. They lift him out again. Is not some bad behavior. Sam John say, master please — the master already with the rope around the poor man neck to hoist him up to hang him again himself so his toes don't touch the waters brim. He feel out done by Sam John try take he own life. He making sure his toes don't touch the silver stream. Sweet child what things I telling you to terrify your enlightened mind. We keep asking we self how to bury slavery in the ground and give we people freedom.

'Mrs d'Aviniere, I've heard terrible accounts, but this at first hand in a letter to you, a daughter, is so immediate, so real, not in any way tampered with for publication. So raw...'

'This maybe one of those letters you want to publish...'

'Definitely.'

'My mother's mind runs away with her. Her meanings are clear to me though they do tumble one upon the other. She has outdone herself with work and worry about her daughter whom she enlightens.'

'Indeed.'

'Mr Bridges, you must help me with my fragments, the story that I've been writing. I need your help. My fragments and my mother's letters you must help with the book.'

'You must give me what you've written and I will also look at the letters, these that you have suggested and the others. What an honour.'

'Thank you, my boys, my husband...?' She could not help her tears.

Elizabeth entered into her own questions. What would she have done with such stories when she was younger? She could imagine Lady Betty wondering how to pass such a letter on. Would she have understood it, a bulletin from the front in some war, from places of torture? What did she do with these stories? Did she tell them to her husband? She would not have wanted to give Beth nightmares. How did they sound being read in her dressing room, folded, each small parcel hidden away? Did she open them again, whisper them in conversation to her sister, Mary? That she kept them, that they were saved from the fire in 1780. Not that by that time she was going to change her mind and let Dido read her mother's mind. Did she, Lady Betty, give the word odious to her husband upon reading such tales, taking the time with patience to keep reading her mother's hand?

Then her mother arrived, walking up from the garden. She emerged from a long distance, from the sea, the smoke of battle through stories of islands and stories of separation. Her mother in her skirts trailing in the mud...

'Madam, are you feeling well? You went away from me there. We must think of moving many more people other than ourselves...'

'We must, Mr Bridges. Thanks for your concern.'

Elizabeth wanted to let her mother know that here in London she was working like her, for freedom. She wanted to tell her of the pamphlet they were planning.

'Let's hope that can happen soon,' Mr Bridges concluded. 'Maria Belle's name must be there on the cover. And your own story, Madam, that too must be published...'

'Mr Bridges, your projects are running away with you. Your ideas... There is though a project I would like you to consider apart from our work. My boys. You must assist my husband after my death with their futures, their professions. Do assure me of this.'

Mr Bridges looked surprised at first that Elizabeth should talk in this way, but he understood. She needed his reassurance. 'I'm honoured to be of assistance to Mr d'Aviniere. I knew his foster father at the Meeting House and I am acquainted with his sister. Yes, indeed, I will advise about the boys. They are bright and the world is changing. Charles is already showing an interest and an aptitude for printing and publishing. There is time for Billy to choose his direction. The world is expanding, hopefully it will be a free world.'

'Mr Bridges. You're a man of vision. Thank you, Mr Bridges.'

Elizabeth could not bring herself to reply to Miss Anne. Then she relented with a note:

Dear Miss Anne

Thank you for writing. You are correct. My mother's continuing to write all those years without a reply from me is indeed proof of her love. I'm grateful to have the letters now, to have that proof. My hope is to have her here soon with me, to heal the separation that should never have been.

Elizabeth d'Aviniere

Elizabeth's recent good health took a turn for the worse. The continual waiting for news of her mother had begun to tell on her. She had been up all the last night coughing. Dr Featherstone had prescribed complete rest but she would be allowed to come downstairs. She insisted that she and Mr Bridges must be allowed to complete their work.

Lydia would run the house.

Billy was thriving at school and Charles was not complaining. Her husband was getting home earlier so that he would have time with his sons. They would have to look after the garden, now overgrown with the warm, wet weather, Seamus having little time now from his apprenticeship in Peckham.

Loveliest

This morning the loveliest yellow girl I find sitting on my stoop. She sleep there all night. Some other girl down by the wharf tell her to come by my house if she want freedom. Like I am some major abolitionist in the country. How will your mother survive but I must do my best for this girl. She is call Glory she tell me with a smile — imagine with a smile. She will be abused sooner than most for the yellow skin girls are wanted so wretchedly not that the black girls are overlooked. I think of you my yellow daughter. They fetch good prices from those abusive masters who make them their belle. I will keep her here illegally for as long as I can hide her. She escape from some brute who will be needing to have her not just to work some everyday labour but to satisfy the illness of his mind and the lechery of his body. I not list his abuses for your gentle mind my child. I think that we need a doctor to heal minds before we see any liberty in this world. What a way it is for a mother to write a daughter to say I loves her beyond imagining. But these are matters that fill my mind day in day out. I must get money to buy her. For Glory I must save. For what might she do with that child she carrying. We must save each one and forgiveness for the mothers who throw away their children, rather than have them in bondage.

Elizabeth went silent, speaking to herself: A yellow girl? Glory? The girl Captain Richardson had met? I'm a yellow girl. I've had Hal's hands all over my body for his use, before I knew to speak it out, to spit it out and to be saved by the tender hands and feelings of my husband, John. But still I know even today the ghost of those acts are still on the footsteps of the stairs, knocking at the door of my comfort, are still standing at the side of my bed to fool me that I have not escaped entirely that time when I did not understand what was happening to me. I had had to take some joy in some of what felt like pleasure in order not to be vanquished forever. It was a risky strategy that frightened me. Could I have been his slave? I imagine my mother's girls under tannia leaves and hidden in bamboo patches. It frightens me now when I think upon those dark moments caught in a passage way, on a path through the woods, in the enclosure of a hedge where the branches have made a small room for two to take part in dark secrets that leave shame smeared all over me and I am too scared to take the stairs to the bathhouse for fear that he who stalks me will be standing there waiting, even that close to the steward's room. I must hide in a shadow. There was so little protection, I do not know now how I scrambled through to take flight and save my body, or indeed, my soul, as some call that other part of ourselves.

Elizabeth looked out on her garden.

Look at that child of mine, she thought, that small boy. What would he make of the state of his mother's mind? How will he be formed? I look ahead to what will become of him, what world lies ahead at this time of wars abroad. A soldier? Away in Empire's lands, deserts plentiful and dark forests that drip with rain all day, islands in an arc, an archipelago?

'Billy.' He looked up from his game where he had been pulling up weeds for his mother. He waved.

'Your brother Charles will be home soon.' Elizabeth did not think he had heard her. He was lost in his own obsessions, forts and soldiers, slaying tyrants. Weeding had been abandoned.

Child
   This time of year is mosquitoes. Between them and the sand blown by the wind there is much to deal with keeping house here in Pensacola. And now there is talk of a war coming. War is never far away. This land has been bounty of war passing hands between the Spanish and the British and they say the Spanish want this place the French want a piece of it too. They want this whole stretch of land that they say get take from them so the old Spanish lady on the corner speak.

It was a wonder that Captain Richardson had found her mother. In another letter she had said, *This land is vast they say more than any can imagine from this here south to that far north breadth of east to west, extravagant and enormous. America.*

There was this letter, which Elizabeth had not read before and she put it aside to show Mr Bridges. It had escaped her till now. It had not looked like the others, written down and across the pages filling the margins as she did lines fitted in vertical and horizontal. There was that recognisable method in her writing but as well utterly fragmented and not as easy to read, the writing as if a rook had stepped in ink and hopped and smeared the white page as they did upon a winter's day upon a snow-driven field at Caen Wood.
   Elizabeth read slowly to decipher the calligraphy.

Dearest child
   Is Glory   the girl who living with me   she tell me the story of her name
   I lie down next to the child to listen   all night I listening
   I try to understand the way the journey write itself in her mind
   Each night she dream it
   How you get such a name   I ask the dear child
   She say a woman on the ship call her so
   She tell me that story upon the ship
   She whisper like someone else who whispering to her

That woman lips who tell her a tale upon the ship
She have to be near the woman lips
as she try in that fettered place to sleep
in that stench to wake   wake to when the woman so slowly pass piss
down she leg   so she feel such a friendly warmth
in that already stifling room
the knock of waves beneath the floor boards
the hot shit follow   the stench to stay with her
till they take them to the air above
to wash them down with the brine

She tell Glory that she will soon be leaving before the morn
before the sunrise   before the force feed
before the coals upon her lips   before the chain gall her ankles
no skin   no flesh   only bone
You must go where I can't go   I come too far   I come far enough
You will make it   child   the woman say   call her Glory
Then she pass over   her head upon Glory lap
All broken were Glorys words

Elizabeth was forced to re-read slowly, and to decipher, to catch the story of Glory and the old woman upon the ship.

This was Glory who Captain Richardson had met.

It seemed weeks now that Elizabeth had had her old strength. She had been laid so low, the lowest ever. Her husband told her that he thought he had lost her. Both he and the boys told her this. 'We thought you had died, Mama,' though he tried hard to guard the children from the worse of the coughing, the evidence on the linens and the visits from the doctor.

Lydia helped to clear up the mess, and made several visits to the apothecary. How did Lydia carry on, so long in service? She had to believe that Mr d'Aviniere would make her settlement firm, if it ever came to that point that he must attend to her prospects, arrange for her future after the death of his wife.

Charles of course was most aware and was at times demanding. Elizabeth found it easiest to talk about how nature taught these matters of the last things. She used what she had learned from her Master's Cicero: *There must, however, of necessity be some end, as is the case of berries on the trees and the fruits of the earth.* She spoke of nothing directly, protecting his young mind and heart. Though she knew that her boys understood a great many things, having parents like herself and their father.

There was a lesson about a vixen with her cubs abandoned without reason, and recently a friend of theirs down the street had had their dog die and it caused much sadness in that household, and together Charles and Billy had helped bury it at the end of the garden under a weeping willow. They talked of these things without talking directly about her leaving.

The boys with their father went to put flowers on Johnny's small grave. Elizabeth was ill that day and stayed at home with Lydia.

Was that Lydia back? She must have slipped away and then woken now when it was quite dark. Was it Mr d'Aviniere just back? 'Mr Bridges? Is anyone there?' Elizabeth asked in a whisper and then continued reading, the letters scattered over the floor. Eventually, she packed the letters away in their linen-lined box. There were a number that could be published. She would discuss them with Mr Bridges and ask her mother's permission.

Days and weeks had passed. Elizabeth woke with a start. She thought it was her mother calling. It was a dream, not altogether clear. But she remembered a window looking onto the sea and some fine lace curtains moved by the breeze.

Such a warm July and the roses were so thick on each bush that the scent was intoxicating. Lydia had picked some before they were overblown and arranged them in a bowl and rested it on the table next to her.

Both boys were seldom out of her sight now during the break from Mr Bridges' lessons.

'Come, come and let me read to you...'

In the evening she and her husband sat at the open French windows. The air was warm and the light seemed to go on and on and they sat and watched the swifts circling. They talked of the money that Miss Marjory had left to her and was to be used for the boys. Education was all that was necessary for their passage through life, with that they could fight for their own and the freedom of others.

'Remember how they called me a black bird in the street just beyond Holborn...'

'Rest, my darling.'

'The boys. What will become of them? I fear for Charles in particular with his black skin. I don't think anything will restrain Billy. He's got such confidence. I want you to stay together as a family.'

'We will, dear. Should you be worrying yourself?'

'And you, my sweet. You will have to take another wife, won't you?'

'Lizzie, how am I to imagine this? You know I can't.'

'A tincture of laudanum will do no harm.'

Her husband administered the dose.

The blackbirds were singing into the darkness. 'So sweet, they pretend that they're nightingales.'

Such an early memory arose out of a story from her mother, of a coast with black rocks washed with white water, breaking beneath a gleaming white castle built upon the rocks; white castles along the coast, a name, an echo, Elmina. There was white water and then of boats all narrow and pointed like canoes and putting out, and her mother looking over her shoulder, a young girl named Abenna,

Tuesday. Then she disappeared into the dark till she reached the end of a tunnel and the blinding light and the roar of the sea, way ahead, and the slaver waiting out in the bay, moored and waiting for the voyage.

Weeks had gone by and still there was no news from Captain Richardson. Elizabeth had nearly given up hope. Her work with Mr Bridges had kept her going. She was alone and there was a knock at the front. It took her sometime before she could reach the door. She used a stick now. She called out in the hall that she was coming but her voice was so low. She was anxious to open the door. 'Wait, wait,' she called. She opened it and it was the post and she had to return to get the money that she had been keeping for this purpose in the bowl on the small gate-table. She stood with the front door still ajar, the warm draught filling the house and a carriage passing in the street. She stood and listened, holding a letter in her hand not daring to look too closely, or to open it. She glimpsed the stamps and seal upon the letter, Pensacola, and the name of a ship she did not recognise, *Orion*. Above all she recognised how the letter was folded, how sealed and stamped. It was one of those little parcels.

Elizabeth sat and settled herself with the letter on her lap and looked out into the garden of roses and savoured everything she saw. Sounds were loud and distinct, the wasps and bees, the robin at the edge of the path, the thrush with a worm, and high in the blue, the swifts, and nearby on a branch, a blackbird was singing with a full throat. She began to unfold and to press the paper out on her lap. She now had spectacles, which were resting on the table where her books were kept next to her chair. She put them on and read the familiar opening that she had learned from the other letters in the box:

My Dearest Daughter
  I can hardly stand up without falling down when Glory give me your letter. What a puzzle. What a dirty trick. What a deception laid upon us.

But I must be wise like you woman of forty-three years mother of two boys
— already buried one small child and a husband so tender by your side.
As many people here say now Praise the Lord. I don't know about that but
I giving praise to who ever want to take it loud and clear. I call I call to the
women and they right out in the yard. Look I tell you I tell you I have a
daughter in London England and one day I must hear from her. I must.
Look here what she write. Look where she asking if I still here. What has
happened in the world to bring this about. What am I to say. Where am I
to start to fill the years since I stop writing but not ever not ever forget you
or think ill of you. I know there has to be some reason. Not this that you
tell me. But as you say no rancour. No rancour but like you I must bundle
that rage and put it down. All I desire now is to see you is to come to you
and tell you everything where I sit with you and fold my grand children
into me. I must find a way to come to you — how in this world. I have
ways. I must come to you and you must hold on. I bring you potions for
that cough. I know it since you young. I know they will help. Yes I strong.
Well why going into the ailments when it is all the strength I need to make
a passage on some ship to reach London. I watch the Orion there in the
harbour. It must be going back and then come back again and by then I
will have a passage to come to you. But I know people who will help. I am
coming. I am coming to you my child. You hold on hold on. You mother
say so. I go by the ocean with the women who live with me and we throw
flowers on the water and cry — A re A re Yemanja! Olomowewe. We thank
her mother Yemanja, goddess of the ocean for bringing your letter so safely
on the sea and ask her take this one for you. You hold on — hold on. Only
thing child I don't want to hear you talk of master again. No word like
master must pass your lips. You are a free woman always was — never
slave of any man though man enslave you. Done with that.

Your mother

Elizabeth wept herself to sleep.

Her mother's letter was on the floor when she awoke. She had read
and reread it many times. She did not know how much time had

passed. The room was full of the scent of roses. She heard herself whispering, *Hold on, hold on*. She seemed to keep saying that phrase over and over, *hold on*. She kept telling herself this for days, for weeks, till time passed. She had no idea how much time had lapsed.

Her children's voices were loud and clear, Charles and Billy calling their mother, 'Mama, Mama, hold on.'

Lydia was calling, 'Ma'am, hold on.'

John was at her side, whispering his love into her ear, 'Sweet, my darling.'

Elizabeth kept on saying to herself, 'Hold on, hold on, hold on.'

Then she heard her mother calling, *Is me Lizzie, your mother, your mother, child.*

'Mammy? Is you? Is really you?'

She saw her mother sitting with her grandsons folded into her. They were all smiling, her sons and her mother, her husband and Lydia.

Is me, your mother, hold on still longer and then rest, she told her, reaching for her hand.

The room was full of the fragrance of roses. Then Elizabeth swore she heard a peal of bells as clean as any air of freedom was clean, like that rinsed out cleanness after a shower of rain, coming from across the hills and the rivers across the land, across the marshes and the meadows The voices were crying, the bells were ringing, freedom, with each toll.

It was some months later that Mr Bridges came to the house in Ranelagh Street with the outcome of the work that he and Elizabeth had been working on before her death. This was work she had entrusted to him, the making of a book compiled of fragments of her story put together with the letters to and from her mother. Charles had assisted his tutor back at his printery, where Seamus was also now working. They were all labouring for the cause of abolition. Mr Bridges offered John d'Aviniere his wife's book, where he stood with the ever curious Billy. Seamus and Charles came into the house with a stack of the volumes carrying the title:

The Story of Elizabeth d'Aviniere

&

Her Mother, Maria Belle
Concerning the story of Abolition

&

Freedom from Capture

'What a grand book,' Lydia said, coming into the room and opening the pages of one of the volumes. 'Let me go now and spread the word down the street, call Mrs R and Mrs Halifax to come and see what a birth this is, so long in the making.'

Historical Note

Dido Elizabeth Belle was born in 1761. In 1765 she came to England with her father John Lindsay, a naval officer, and her mother, the African-born Maria Belle, who was legally Lindsay's slave as was their daughter. Dido was taken to live with Lindsay's uncle and aunt, Lord and Lady Mansfield, at Kenwood House, in north London, where she spent nearly 30 years. Dido's freedom was confirmed by Mansfield, the Lord Chief Justice, in 1783. Ten years later Mansfield died and in that same year Dido married John d'Aviniere. They had three sons and lived at Ranelagh Street in the Pimlico district of London. Elizabeth died in London in July 1804.

Maria Belle bought her freedom when she returned to Florida in 1774. John Lindsay died in 1788.

The accounts of the Mansfield judgments as used in the novel are based on historical fact but serve the story of this fiction.

ABOUT THE AUTHOR

Lawrence Scott is a prize-winning novelist and short-story writer from Trinidad & Tobago. *Witchbroom*, his first novel (1992), was shortlisted for a Commonwealth Writers' prize (1993) Best First Book, and was read as a BBC Book At Bedtime (1994). He was awarded a lifetime literary award in 2012 by the National Library of Trinidad & Tobago for his significant contribution to the literature of Trinidad & Tobago. His second collection of short stories, *Leaving by Plane Swimming back Underwater* was published in 2015 and, in the same year, was longlisted for both the Edgehill Short Story Prize and the Frank O'Connor Short Story award. His most recent novel *Light Falling on Bamboo* (2012) received an honourable mention from Casa de las Americas prize, Cuba, 2014; longlisted for the international IMPAC Dublin literary award, 2014; received a special mention from the Grand Prix Littéraire de l'Association des Ecrivains de la Caraïbe from the Congrès des Ecrivains de la Caraïbe, Guadeloupe, 2013; shortlisted for the OCM Bocas prize fiction category and longlisted for the overall OCM Bocas prize (2013). His second novel *Aelred's Sin* (1998) was awarded a Commonwealth Writers' prize, Best Book in Canada and the Caribbean, and was longlisted for the Booker prize, the Whitbread prize and for the international IMPAC Dublin literary award (1999). His first short-story collection *Ballad for the New World* (1994) included the Tom-Gallon Trust prize-winning short story, *The House of Funerals*. His novel *Night Calypso* (2004) was also shortlisted for a Commonwealth Writers' Prize, Best Book award, and longlisted for the international IMPAC Dublin literary award, 2005, and translated into French as *Calypso de Nuit* (2005). It was a one Book one Community choice in 2006 by the National Library of Trinidad & Tobago. He is the editor of *Golconda: Our Voices Our Lives*, an anthology of oral histories and other stories and poems from the sugar-belt in Trinidad (UTT Press, 2009). Over the years, he has combined teaching with writing. He lives in London and Port of Spain and can be found at www.lawrencescott.co.uk.